SOLDIER OF FORTUNE 4

OPERATION NICARAGUA

SOLDIER OF FORTUNE 4

OPERATION NICARAGUA

Chris Pullen

First published in Great Britain 1994
22 Books, Invicta House, Sir Thomas Longley Road,
Rochester, Kent

Copyright © 1994 by 22 Books

The moral right of the author has been asserted

A CIP catalogue record for this book is available from the
British Library

ISBN 1 898125 27 9

10 9 8 7 6 5 4 3 2 1

Typeset by Hewer Text Composition Services, Edinburgh
Printed in Great Britain by Cox and Wyman Limited, Reading

Prelude

Max Steiner had lost face and the operation was compromised. Soldiers in real armies who no longer trust or respect their officers generally continue to function more or less as they should: they have been conditioned not subtly but well, like Pavlov's dogs. And if conditioning fails then fear of the penalties for insubordination, let alone mutiny, keep them in line. Mercenaries acknowledge no such sanctions.

The problem was that Steiner, like most of his troop, was not jungle-trained. His father had been an SS *Hauptstürmführer* who had gone down the 'Vatican line' to Argentina in 1946 and Steiner himself had been brought up to lead urban death squads – in Argentina, Chile and El Salvador. Most of his men had been in the same line of business, though four of them had served with El Pastor, the Nicaraguan Contra who had operated until the previous year out of Costa Rica. Steiner had tried to put them through a couple of weeks of jungle training near the Pacific coast of Costa Rica and to impress them had gone off on his own for twenty-four hours – proving to them it could be done. And he had returned without his pack, without his father's SS dagger, and, most criminal of all, without his Heckler & Koch MP5. No. The loss of the sub-machine-gun was not the most serious failure: the lack of any explanation was worse.

So at the Playboy Club, on the outskirts of San José, the capital of Costa Rica, orders had been disobeyed.

Two nights of debauchery, Sunday and Monday, had been encouraged and paid for. From noon on Tuesday through to two a.m. on Wednesday, the men were to eat well and rest. But they had not. They had continued to carouse and Steiner's attempts to discipline them had failed when two Cuban exiles had chased each other and a naked mestiza whore all over the complex and finally into the Playboy Grill, where they attempted to knife each other and the girl too.

And there the second blow to Steiner's authority was struck. Both men returned to the floor the troop occupied, one admittedly bloodied by the beating Steiner had given him, with the same story. The black woman who had been singing salsa with the three-piece combo had thumped him in the face, toppling him into a trolley of trifles, gâteaus, and overripe tropical fruits.

The only cohesion the troop now had was the certainty that they would not be paid the second instalment of their hire if the mission failed. Since the first instalment had been handsome enough this was not all that much of an inducement. Soldiers of fortune, all else being equal, are as likely to take the money and run as the rest of us.

At two in the morning a hired Ticabus took them to a private hangar in the freight area of San José's airport. On the coach they changed into DPM fatigues, some ending up with clothing too large, others too small. Inside the hangar the small arms were issued: twenty Armalites. Heavier weaponry, M60E1 machine-guns, RPG7 rocket-launchers, Chinese 60mm mortars, two of each, and two uninflated inflatables had already been loaded on to the unmarked Boeing CH-46 helicopter that stood on the brightly moonlit tarmac.

Following standard drill, they fitted magazines into their rifles, made sure there was nothing up the spout, and put on safety-catches. Nevertheless one gun went off.

The report echoed in the cavernous space, and the bullet whined like a very angry hornet, ringing and clanging off concrete and metal for perhaps three seconds during which eight of the twenty men flattened themselves on the ground. Steiner cursed them, and with Coetzee, his white South African 'NCO', lashed out with Malacca canes at the three Hondurans, one of whom he thought might have been responsible, and all of whom he knew to be too cowardly to retaliate.

They then filed untidily into the Chinook, whose two large rotors were already revolving to the low-rev chug-chug of its engines. Its history was not untypical. When it was forced down in Kampuchea in 1972, hill tribesmen beheaded the US crew and passed it on to a Pol Pot cadre. They in turn shipped it across the gulf to Thailand, where they sold it to a small-time arms dealer for peanuts. Several tons of peanuts. He sold it on (making a very large profit) to a Filipino firm that specialized in leasing out, on a no-questions-asked basis, anything that could fly.

The pilot was ex-Royal Australian Air Force and knew what he was about. He would have liked a navigator but the one contracted for had lost his way at Heathrow and missed his connection. Under an almost full moon he took the chopper up to a thousand feet and settled with some relief to following the ribbon of the Inter-American Highway north, keeping it some three kilometres to his right. That way there was no chance of bumping into the cordillera and volcanoes that lay to the east.

After an hour the broad expanse of Lake Nicaragua, a huge polished silver tray, appeared in front and to the right. The next twenty minutes were a touch more difficult. He took a right through two hundred and eighty degrees, almost a U-turn, settling on a south-east by south bearing that put the lake on his left and the cordillera and the last of the three volcanoes on his right, and kept him in Costa Rican airspace. The rainforest below was for a time unbroken, virgin.

Behind him the Anglo-Saxons among the mercenaries sang, the noise just audible through the pandemonium of the engines and rotors. The 'Horst Wessel Lied' was shouted down, and 'God Bless America' or 'God Save the Queen' and 'Land of Hope and Glory', all with scatological words, followed. The fourteen Ladinos passed a couple of rum bottles between them. They did this in an entirely calculated way, knowing Steiner could see them but not so obviously that he would have to act to stop them.

A much smaller patch of water, Laguna Ceño Negro – Black Scowl Lake – marked the last change of course. The Chinook swung north again, lost height, crossed the border into Nicaraguan airspace just west of Los Chilos, the largest border town, and sped on, the turbulence from its rotors shaking the tops of the tallest almendro trees. Five minutes later they crossed the San Juan river. They were now over fields, and a small village slipped behind them on the left. Two minutes later the moonlit complex of the agricultural research station that was their target floated into view through the forward Perspex blister.

Two white, single-storeyed buildings formed a right angle. Three smaller controlled-environment units placed in echelon stepped away from the end of one of the main buildings, so that the whole compound formed an irregular, squared-off U-shape. The Chinook swung over it, only fifteen metres from the ground. The pilot positioned it so it was pointing away from the buildings, thus presenting as small a target as possible, and brought it gently to cleared ground, four hundred metres from the nearest building and roughly opposite the centre of the U.

Led by Steiner on one side and Coetzee on the other,

all but five of the men tumbled to the earth, fanned out and blazed away at the buildings. The five still on board hefted out one mortar, one grenade-launcher, one M60E1. The clattering motors crescendoed, dust and palm leaves swirled around them, and the Chinook lifted, tilted, and roared away over the fields towards the river.

There the last five, led by ex-Marine Grabowski, occupied an island in the middle linked by a bridge to the north bank. Along with the rest of their equipment they also dropped the inflatables. The island had to be held, otherwise the river could trap the main force inside Nicaragua. No way would the Aussie bring back the chopper for them: a second visit would be no surprise and a mortar or even a ground-to-air missile could well be waiting for him. And in any case, ferrying them out was not the only part he had to play in the operation.

On the ground things at first went more or less according to plan. One of the rocket-launchers failed but the mortar did not. Within minutes the buildings were blown apart and burning well. The controlled-environment units – made of whitewashed glass with a computer system that raised or lowered each pane according to temperature and humidity – exploded in a particularly satisfying way.

There was no opposition – there was no one there. The scientists and technicians who worked in the compound slept in the village two kilometres away, towards the river and lake. The two twelve-year-old boys who had been on watch were already on their way back to it as fast as their legs could carry them before the helicopter had even touched down.

The first casualty was one of the Nicaraguan Contras. He stumbled drunkenly into friendly fire – M60 tracer – and was shredded. After that things got worse, and not least because there had been no actual fighting at all. After two weeks of quite severe training, two and a half days of debauchery, and two hours of nasty suspense in the hold of the Chinook, this brisk, noisy firework display was an anticlimax. There wasn't even anything to loot or rape. Dazed by the noise they had made, bewildered by the lack of any real action, the men wandered aimlessly, shooting at shadows, passing the last of the rum from mouth to mouth. They ignored the attempts of Steiner and Coetzee to get them to form up and march for the bridge.

With three kilometres to the river, and twice as far again to the border, and less than two hours till daybreak, the situation was deteriorating. Steiner therefore shot one of the drunks with his Walther P38. The 9mm parabellum bullet took the top off the man's head; living debris spattered the men behind him while he was still on his feet, and brought them somewhat to their senses.

Coetzee led, Steiner came last, promising to shoot stragglers. They followed farm tracks up over a low rise through a grid of maize and rice fields, and then down towards the river. There was no way they could get lost, even though a thick blanket of mist was rising, luminous and pearly in the moonlight. It was, however, possible to end up upstream of the bridge. Grabowski was expecting them to appear downstream.

Meanwhile a small group of villagers and agricultural technicians who had seen three years' work destroyed were moving into the downstream area. They were led by an ex-Sandinista guerrilla and they had two Kalashnikovs that worked. They did not know that Grabowski with four men, the second M60E1 and a mortar, held the island.

The ex-guerrilla saw Coetzee and his men coming towards them, their heads and shoulders floating comically above the mist, and opened fire. Since the mercenaries were in line facing them, only Coetzee was hurt, and not seriously.

The rest, including Steiner in the rear, crashed to their bellies beneath the surface of the swirling mist.

Grabowski had seen the line of men approaching through the mist, heard the gunfire from the other side. He believed he had seen a section of Nicaraguan border guards, possibly professional soldiers, fired on by the returning mercenaries. He therefore promptly and accurately laid down a carpet of tracer and mortar shells while his spare man raked the area with his Armalite. Thus the whole troop returning from the research station was killed or maimed by friendly fire except Steiner himself, who, when the firing started, had contrived to get even further into the rear than he had been.

When half his ammunition had been used Grabowski ordered a cease-fire. Steiner emerged and identified himself. He came down the line of fallen men and shot the four who were still more or less alive, including Coetzee, who died cursing him. It was important that none should fall into Nicaraguan hands: apart from anything else they would testify to the monumental cock-up the whole operation had become and Steiner's credibility as an *Einsatzkommandoführer* would be destroyed. The villagers, impressed by their fire-power, ruthlessness and sheer lunacy, melted away into the mist.

The six survivors paddled one of the inflatables the two hundred metres across the wide river, abandoned it, and walked over six kilometres down jungle tracks and back into Ticoland – Costa Rica. As dawn broke they heard, amid the cacophony of waking birds and the shrieks of monkeys, the percussive rumble of a DHC Beaver heading north. Its pilot, the Australian who had flown the Chinook, continued to enhance his reputation for cautious competence. Coming in low over the fields round the station, the Beaver shed a thin, sickly orange mist that streamed from a vent just in front of the tail unit. It spread out and left a swathe across the plantations. Then the plane climbed, banked, the gold sun glinting on its wings, and back he came on a different bearing. But just as again the plane began to spew out its poison, the pilot saw ahead of him, tiny between stands of maize, the half-crouched figure of a peasant with what he knew all too well could only be the tube of a Stinger rocket-launcher on his shoulder.

He cut the poisonous flow, opened the throttle as wide as it would go, hauled back the control column, and put the plane into a climbing spin. The tell-tale plume of white exhaust spiralled past – a very near miss. Straightening out, and for a second or so very close to stalling at just under five hundred metres, he headed south in a long, low dive, aiming to get below the visual horizon as quickly as possible. Six hectares remained unsprayed.

Later that morning Francisco Franco, the Mexican link-man between Steiner and the people who employed them, dapper in a dove-grey suit with a pink silk tie and pink silk lining to his jacket, sat drinking coffee on the veranda of a tiny clapboard hotel in Los Chilos. Behind him a small boy pushed dust off the boards with a broom.

Steiner appeared at the end of the dirt street. His face was grimy, his DPM fatigues torn, with blotches of caked yellow mud covering most of the disruptive camouflage pattern. His holstered pistol smacked against his thigh. Franco watched his progress with disapproval. To walk about so obviously armed might be all right in Guatemala or El Salvador. In Ticoland it could provoke arrest, or at any rate a polite enquiry from the local police.

Steiner had a lot on his mind. He kicked a chicken that did not move quickly enough, and set chairs clattering on his way to Franco's table. He slapped both hands down on it hard. The coffee jumped, splashed. Franco's eyes flashed and he dabbed at the stain on his knee with a tissue taken from the chrome dispenser on the table.

'We were betrayed,' Steiner shouted. 'Betrayed.'

He raised his hands to slap the table again. Franco pushed back his chair.

'Bushwhacked. Oh yes. You can tell your boss the job was done. Perfectly. No problem. According to job specification.'

The scar on his cheek showed hectic beneath the dirt as Steiner strove to screw yet more sarcasm into his voice. Then he pulled a chair beneath him, slumped into it, and stared across at the Mexican, eyes wide, filled with horror.

'Fourteen men lost. Fourteen good men. Heroes. Christ!' He shook his head like a caged beast. 'Jesus! The mother-fuckers were waiting for us. Shot us up almost as soon as we landed. My men fought like heroes, like mad dogs. And we won. Drove the bastards off and then got on with the job. Fourteen men. Christ! I need a drink.'

Franco snapped his fingers at the small boy.

'*Un cuarto de ron. Flor de Caña. ¡Súbito!*'

'The laws against alcoholism, señor. No liquor before twelve noon . . .'

Franco grabbed the small boy's ear and twisted. The voice rose to a high squeal. He hissed in the boy's free ear: 'Get it.'

'You got it.'

And when he came back he brought ice and slices of lime as well as the small bottle of white rum.

Steiner drank. Franco passed thin fingers across sleak, black hair. 'Are you sure? Are you sure they knew you were coming?'

Steiner wiped his mouth on the back of his hand. 'Sure of it. We walked straight into it. A trap.'

Franco registered that this time they had walked into

a trap that previously they had been dropped in, but said nothing.

Steiner went on. 'You tell the boss. He needs to check his security. I'll do it for him. I make dumb men talk. Women too. You tell him.'

'I will.' Franco stood and shelled a hundred-colones note on to the table. 'But the job was done?'

'Perfectly.'

'I'll tell him that too.'

1

But of course the job had been done less than perfectly. Which was why, five years later, a senior executive of Associated Foods International flew into Heathrow.

Maud Adler was a big woman in every sense of the word: lean, tall, dark, tough and brutally ambitious. Which was why, at fifty-five, she had reached a position only one step below vice-presidency in one of the world's three biggest food conglomerates. She booked into the Grosvenor Hotel, Park Lane, a stone's throw from the US Embassy: not that she for one moment thought of throwing stones at it. After a short period of nervousness she and her kind had found they could do business with the Clinton administration as readily as with his predecessors.

She lane-swam in the hotel pool for half an hour before an American-style breakfast in her room; then she dressed in a severe but very expensive dark-brown cashmere trouser suit and took a cab through the cold rain to an address off Baker Street. She found herself on the pavement outside a three-storey house built in the reign of William IV, double-fronted, painted white with a red door. The polished brass door knocker represented not the traditional lion's head with a ring in its mouth, but the head of a savage dog, possibly a wolf. The brass plate above the brass bell-pull was engraved with two words: 'Wolf Hound'.

In prompt answer to her ring an elderly man, thin with

very short white hair, wearing a black sweater with black shoulder patches above black trousers and heavy shoes so highly polished that the black shone like silver, showed her into a reception room.

'The Colonel's respects, madame. He'll be with you in a moment.' The accent was Scottish – that much she knew. She did not know it was Glasgow working-class Protestant.

The reception area was spotless and orderly. Current copies of *The Field*, *Country Life*, the *Financial Times* and *Design for Safe Living* sat four-square on the mahogany table. Contemporary prints of Peninsular War infantrymen hung in neat gold frames in the alcoves. The room was warm: it was heated by a small coal fire in an Adam grate of polished steel and black iron. Maud Adler was amazed to see it was a real fire. The small chandelier's drops had the slightly grey look that reproduction crystal cannot match. She was impressed.

'Come up to my den, Miss Adler, and we'll have a chat.'

She was even more impressed with Colonel Finchley-Camden. He was tall, tanned, had silver hair, wore a green jersey with brown shoulder patches over a check shirt, and cavalry twills. He spoke in the slow, easy, confident drawl that only Eton, Sandhurst, and ten centuries at the top can bestow. She judged him to be a very fit, well-preserved sixty-plus.

His 'den', in the first-floor front, was less formal than the downstairs room, and looked like a wealthy bachelor's sitting-room. The armchairs were dark leather, the carpet was from somewhere east of Samarkand, and there were silver trophies, polished but used to hold pencils, pipes and so on. A Sheraton wall table carried drinks in decanters and fresh coffee in a Cona flask. A silver-framed photograph offered the only hint that this all belonged to a married man – a pale, blonde lady surrounded by black flat-haired retrievers and children dressed in Laura Ashley smocks peered coldly and myopically into the lens. Unless it was an old photograph she was considerably younger than her husband. The large desk, three telephones, fax and answering machine, a grey filing cabinet and an Apple Mac LCIII showed that it was also a place of work. He waved Adler into one of the armchairs.

'Coffee?'

'Please. Black, no sugar.'

Finchley-Camden poured black liquid into tiny bone china cups and moved in behind the desk.

'Because I am a security consultant . . .' There was a hint of something – evil was too strong a word – not quite pleasant in the smile. '. . . I am naturally a touch paranoid about security. Why did you come to us?'

'You were highly recommended. Prima Fuerza in Madrid particularly suggested you could help us.'

She was referring to a right-wing, some said fascist, organization of businessmen, politicians and military, both Spanish and Latin American. Wolf Hound had done business with them in the past.

'Fine, fine. But surely someone nearer your own patch would have done as well . . .'

'Not necessarily, Colonel.' She leant over the arm of the chair, placed her already empty cup on an occasional table. Adler's movements were not exactly graceful, but they were confident and economical. 'We are very concerned about our profile with regard to this project. We want to keep this angle of the operation as far from home as possible. There's another factor. We want the best.'

He waited.

'My predecessor organized an operation designed to achieve the same ends as the project we are hoping you

13

will undertake. That was just over five years ago, using more or less local resources.'

'Against the same target.'

'Yes.'

Finchley-Camden leant back and put his fingertips together beneath his chin. Perhaps now one would say the smile was a touch evil.

'A cock-up?'

'Not entirely. The work we wanted done was partially carried out. We should not have waited five years had it not been. But they sustained fourteen casualties, and all the result of friendly fire.'

'Oh, dear me.'

'So you see, this time we do have to have the best. Or at any rate the second best.'

'I don't quite follow you.'

'Well. The SAS are the best. But they are not available to us.'

'I think you'll find we come pretty close. There are after all more men in the UK who have served with the SAS than are actually serving with them now.' He leant forward again. 'I think you had better tell me all about it.'

It took her nearly an hour. At the end he had only one question.

'How will you pay?'

Adler frowned, but the answer was brisk, prepared.

'One-off payment from a Swiss bank account by EFT to an account of your choice. It is important that only one global payment is made. It should cover your fee, those of the people you employ, and all expenses. I guess you'll need a week or so to cost it?'

'Not necessarily. We have carried out this sort of operation in the past, and more than once not a thousand miles from where we're talking about. But if the payment is to be a down-payment in advance, with no supplementaries, then you will expect me to build in cover for unforeseen contingencies, unexpected moves in the arms market for instance, that sort of thing.'

'Of course.'

'That's fine, then. Miss Adler . . .'

Finchley-Camden touched a desk button, rose, and held out his hand. 'Wolf Hound is happy to do business with you.'

'My pleasure, Colonel . . .'

'Ah. Duncan.' The elderly Scot was already in the doorway. 'Miss Adler is leaving now. Would you be so good as to call a cab for her?'

He thought for a moment after she had gone, then flipped up a number in his personal directory, a number which would take him directly into the private office of the chairman of one of London's most prestigious merchant banks.

'Archie? Finchley-Camden here. I have a query you might be able to help with. Associated Foods International have a quite considerable job for me to do, which they will pay for out of a Swiss-based slush fund. A one-off payment. Now they want me to cost it, but I don't think that's really the way . . .'

'You want me to guess the ceiling they'll go to?' The voice was gravelly, with a slight Birmingham accent underlying the demotic City vowels most businessmen adopt to conceal their generally seriously wealthy origins and appear the self-made man. 'They really are deep in doo-doo, are they? I mean they wouldn't come to you if they weren't, would they?'

'That's the way I see it.'

'And it's a big operation?'

'At least twenty men, taking out a defended position on the other side of the world.'

15

'That is big. And they must be aware it's going to cost. I'll get their current profiles up on screen, run a couple of programmes through them. Give me fifteen minutes. I'll get back to you.'

Finchley-Camden tapped out another number – this one he knew by heart – and as the call signal purred, checked his watch. Eleven fifty-seven. Damn, he had thought it was later.

'Sam? Finchley-Camden here.'

'Dickie? What can I do for you? Bauxite's still below par, you know? I could get you a very sound future in bauxite.' This time the voice was smooth yet husky, Wimbledon gentrifying Golders Green, but always the hint of Whitechapel two generations back.

'Come on, Sam. I'll never forget how you got me into tin ten years ago. And left me to extricate myself. No, I wanted Nick actually, but I suppose he's on the floor. I thought it was later than it is. Just ask him to give me a bell as soon as he's free?'

'Of course, Dickie. No problem.'

Sam Dorf, fat, shiny, in a pearl-grey double-breasted suit with a tie his granddaughter had bought him in Cecil Gee for his sixtieth, leant back in his big office armchair, glanced at the sunburst clock on the wall that faced him and waited until the minute hand clicked on to the hour hand. Instantly a bell rang, short and sharp. Dorf hoisted himself to his feet and padded out on to the circular gallery. He looked down through curved glass into the bullpit below.

Dealing was slow for the first three minutes during which Dorf kept his eyes fixed on Nick Parker. Lean, early thirties, not tall, but dark with a quiff of black hair lolling over his right eyebrow, Parker prowled the edges, made a quick deal here and there, buying and selling,

nothing of importance, but ears pricked to catch a rise
on the floor of a tenth of a point, or maybe a drop of
two. Dorf noted the upturned corners of a smile that
had charm as well as venom, and the dark, beady eyes
suddenly alert like those of a cat ready to pounce, and
he knew Parker was waiting, waiting to do just that. The
hand clicked on. One minute. Thirty seconds. And then
there it was – a sign he'd picked up from a tall woman
in a charcoal suit, low-cut blouse, with a cordless at her
ear in the third row of the benches, and he was straight
in, first to one dealer then another, scribbling fast, pages
torn off and exchanged, at least four of them in twenty
seconds, and BRRRRRRRRR, the bell again brought it
all to a halt.

Had he been buying or selling? Clearly both. Selling to
begin with, discreetly using his reputation to depress the
market those couple of points, then storming in with a
big order to buy.

Dorf met him as he came off the floor. Nick Parker was
on a high, eyes bright, a sheen of sweat on his forehead.
Possibly it was chemical, though the excitement of very
fast successful trading could have been enough on its own.
He handed his pad and the leaves he'd exchanged with
other dealers to one of Dorf's clerks, wiped his palms on
a handkerchief and grinned, the way a thirteen-year-old
does when he's just beaten the high-jump record at his
prep-school sports day.

'Sam. Hi. One of the Sabahs. Quarter of a million. But
he wouldn't buy, not unless I could get it down a couple
of points. And I did.'

'Nick. One day they'll gang up and cut you up.'

He meant the other dealers.

'So you always say, Sam. But I always keep one or two
in my pocket to let me know when the Ides of March are
upon me. What's up?'

'Dickie wants you to ring him. I think he's got something for you.'

'Damn. I thought you were going to buy me lunch after my little coup back there.'

'No way can I afford the sort of lunches you like.'

He allowed the younger man to open the door to his office, and waved him to the telephones.

'If it means you take a holiday – a month, whatever – that's fine by me. Unpaid, of course.'

'Sam, how could you? You know how you'll miss my smiling face.' He picked up the phone, began to punch in the numbers, then paused. His eyes took on a sort of dreamy, anticipatory, yet tormented look: the way a junkie who's been off it for half a year might look if an ounce of pure came his way at a reasonable price. Then that grin again.

'But you know, I really could do with a "holiday".'

Finchley-Camden was once again in touch with Archie, the merchant banker. In his ear the Brummie voice laid it on thick.

'It's all a question of liquidity,' he said. 'Even the big guys, even the Yanks, don't like to leave too much serious cash just lying around doing nothing. And they won't want to realize assets to meet your filthy demands. Still, I think you can go up to a million. Sterling.'

'I don't want to push them too far. You know, haggling, getting into a Dutch auction, playing silly buggers like that.'

'Of course not. But since they probably are in serious shit, and considering the quality product you deliver, and the difficulties of getting it anywhere else, I don't think they'll consider a straight million to be OTT.'

Just as Archie hung up, the other phone rang. It was all Finchley-Camden could do to keep the grin that was splitting his face from ear to ear out of his voice.

'Nick? Yeah. Right. Something ... qui-i-i-te big has cropped up. And I'd consider it a favour if you, Goodall and Bennett could see your way to popping down to Wrykin Heath this weekend. Let's say you arrive by Friday teatime, and the others Saturday middayish? Yes? Fine.'

But as he put the phone down it was the thought of the straight million that made the grin on his face stick. He must surely be able to hold on to at least four hundred grand. And that was precisely what he owed the Lloyd's syndicate he belonged to. The tide of seriously deep shit that had threatened to drown him might at last and at the last moment be on the ebb.

2

'Listen, will you? I was not abused by our dad, or any other shite I can remember. Not what you call sexually. Right?'

'But your sister says . . .'

'Fuck me fuckin' sister, all right? Now and then he'd take his belt to us, but that's not abuse. Not what they'd call abuse in Wallsend, eh?' Tim Goodall allowed himself a harsh laugh at his own wit.

'But, Tim, many people do think hitting small children with heavy belts is a form of abuse.'

'I wasn't so small,' he said, recalcitrant, refractory.

'Tim, all violence is abuse.'

Big, heavy, hair once red but now fading a bit and thinning a lot, freckles on his fair skin, Tim Goodall looked sideways at the woman in the Parker Knoll chair angled at forty-five degrees to his. She was not wearing the white coat he had expected, but the sort of tweed suit he connected with vicars' wives – not that he had seen many of them despite his forty-three years. Presumably she was educated, possibly she had some common sense, though precious little sign of that commodity had been shown so far.

'Fuckin' load of abuse about, then.'

The psychotherapist recrossed her legs and sighed.

'It must seem like that to you.'

'But it don't to you?'

On the attack now, he allowed his accent to build, put it on a bit more than he normally did.

'Listen, hinny. There might not be much violence or abuse in your life, but read the papers. Serial killers in Gloucester, serial killers all over Bosnia. But there's more to it than that. You've got me life story on your knee. Read it.'

'I have.'

'Well then.'

He sat back and waited for the next dollop of nonsense. The plain bare room was warm with its orange curtains, yellow walls, thick carpet, table and two chairs. There were worse ways of spending a wet, windy morning on Tyneside.

For her part the therapist fingered the brown manila folder on her knee and recalled some of its contents. Surface worker at the pit at sixteen, underground with his dad at eighteen, pit closed just before his twentieth birthday — the first big round of closures under the Callaghan government back in the mid-seventies. Army — the Duke of Newcastle's Own Rifles — with three tours in the Special Services. Without being sure she supposed that meant the SAS. Then at thirty-eight his regiment had been merged with three others to form the Royal Buff Caps and Company Sergeant-Major Goodall was back on Tyneside looking for a job. He blew his severance pay buying a share in a Grimsby trawler that could not compete with the new super-trawlers. His Army pension and the fact that his wife was in paid training to be a nurse excluded them from income support, but left them, quite simply, poor.

She wondered if, in some way, the frustrated boredom of a once very active man had contributed to the tragedy that had brought him here.

Not long after he joined the Army he had married a Wallsend lass he'd been going steady with for a bit and they had had two sons: Jack and Bob, after the

Charltons. And that was where the trouble had started. Tim Goodall had put the eldest, sixteen, in hospital with cracked ribs and severe contusions to the head and face. Not only his son but his son's best friend too. In court the police surgeon had said it was one of the nastiest cases of parental assault he had ever seen. Sentence suspended pending psychiatric reports.

'You got on all right with your father?'

'Still do.'

'Wor Dad' was dying of diabetes, obesity, and emphysema, caused by coal dust, in a sheltered council flat. Tim went to see him at least twice a week and sometimes took him out for a run in his clapped-out Capri.

'So perhaps it was doubly horrible for you when he beat you. A sort of betrayal.'

Tim shifted his hard heavy bulk in the low, too soft chair.

'Maybe. But I always know according to his lights he had good reason.'

'What I'm getting at, what I'd like you to consider, is the possibility that the beating you gave young Jack was a sort of revenge for the beatings your dad gave you.'

This was so stupid it took Tim a moment or two to think it through.

'Listen, will you? If I wanted to get even with me dad, like, it'd be his head I'd pull off – not wor Jack's.'

The therapist sighed, looked at her watch, and put the manila folder on the table.

'Time's up, Tim. Same time next week, all right?'

He stood up, looking down at her, and felt the wave of bewilderment crash over him as so often it had ever since this business had started.

'What I can't understand,' he said, 'is why no one can accept I had every good reason to do it, and for those good reasons I done what I done.'

Maybe, thought the therapist, looking up at him with worried thoughtful eyes, but you're not telling us what they are, are you?

Ten minutes later, in a waterproofed-cotton jacket with the collar pulled up, but not the hood, he strode away from the Wallsend Medical Centre, and across the dog-turd-covered green. He liked the feel of the cold rain sweeping across the crowded hills, filled with terrace after terrace of drab, damp council housing, liked the sting of it on his thick neck and cheeks. It felt cleansing, and cleansing was what he felt he needed after these sessions with the therapist. She always seemed to want to find some nasty dirty little secret between him and his father, or between him and his son. And there wasn't one, no matter what his mad sister might say. He felt quite a lump in his throat and had to bite his lip, because if there was something in his life he really treasured, that meant more to him than anything else, it was the good times he'd had with his father, and then with his son. On the terraces at Roker Park. Fishing for mackerel with the other lads off Whitby Bay. A bit of hare-coursing up on the moors. That sort of thing. And that was why he had had to do it. Why it had been right to do it.

He'd come to the place now. A road junction, narrow pavements in front of low walls, a bit of privet, and a concrete lamppost that still leant at an angle of seventy-five degrees. And yes, people were still leaving sad little bunches of flowers, chrysanthemums this time, the paper they were wrapped in already sodden.

It was here that the Porsche Jack and his friend had hot-wired over in Jesmond finally went out of control, mounted the pavement and crushed a pram against the wall. Although the whole estate, including the baby's mother, knew who had been in the car, and even eventually the scufters too, the boys were still free.

No way would they be able to pin it on the lads without witnesses or a confession, and no way would they get either. But the feeling had been there, not just personal, but sort of communal, that something should be done. So Tim had done it. And the scufters knew why – hence the pressure. If he broke now, blew it, they'd get Jack on a murder charge, even though he hadn't been the one driving.

If he had been, it would never have happened. Wor Jack can drive, Tim thought, with a touch of pride, even though he's a month yet off seventeen.

Five minutes later he turned through the tiny wrought-iron gate, walked the five yards to his front door and let himself in. The steamed-up windows and the cabbage smell he hardly noticed.

'Tim? Letter for you.' Mary, his wife, was in the tiny hall on her way out, with her shoulder bag and a plastic raincoat over the blue of her trainee nurse's uniform. 'Special delivery too. See you, love.'

She pecked his cheek and was gone. She didn't like what he'd done to her Jack, and she knew it would be a year or two before she got over it. If ever.

He found the envelope on the kitchen table. It was postmarked London SW3. That had to mean it was from Nick Parker. Brass bands played in his ear, bright tulips blossomed in his mind's eye. Ex-Company Sergeant-Major Timothy Goodall felt better, a lot better, even before he'd opened it.

Neil Bennett, Gordon to everyone but his mother, who was dead, and his wife, who had started an affair with a Royal Buff Caps bandsman while he, Gordon, was trying to keep warm on Mount Kent, lived now on his own in a tiny flat in Bognor Regis, his home town. The flat was part of the first floor of a mid-Victorian building that still had a bit of late-Georgian about it. It overlooked the prom and the sea. The other remarkable feature about it was the kitchen, which was superbly equipped with every modern cooking device you could think of apart from a microwave. Gordon abhorred them.

His friends reckoned he was mad, but if the subject of microwaves came up he didn't argue the toss. The thing was he had been very happy with his wife and thought she was happy with him. They had decided he'd jack in the Army when the Falklands were over, and with a bit of money her father had left her open a small but classy restaurant on the sea front – in the premises still occupied by a rock and gift shop beneath the flat he was now in. They'd specialize in seafood and fresh fish, but do the classic steak dishes as well and make a point of cooking the sweets, soufflés and suchlike, to order, as well as the main dishes.

He'd always been a good cook; he was determined to become the best, dreamed of Michelin awarding him a fork, or even two. Now, on his own, he cooked; while Tim Goodall was trying not to scream at his psychotherapist, Gordon was cooking. Tall, thin, dark, saturnine even, with strands of black hair pulled across his domed forehead and dark eyes set in grey, skull-like sockets above thin lips, he moved about his kitchen with easy, lithe confidence.

Jim Partridge, who had been at the Westloats Lane Secondary Modern with him thirty years earlier and still worked the small boat his father had left him ten years later, had come in on the tide with a two and a half pound live lobster. Gordon had already poached it for ten minutes in a *court bouillon* of water, salt, freshly ground black pepper, bay leaf and thyme and left it to cool. Now, working over a shallow bowl set there to catch the juices, he broke off and cracked the claws, and extracted the coral. Then he cut the body shell in half, removed and discarded the intestinal cord, and levered out the white meat. He cut this into tidy cubes and sautéed them in butter for a moment or two, finishing off this stage by flaming them in cognac.

Then he made a sauce. He put the lobster in a preheated serving dish, spooned rice round it, and poured on the sauce.

He took three forkfuls of the mixture and drank half a glass of wine. Then he took it all back into the kitchen and emptied the dish into the rubbish bin.

He was putting away the cognac when the phone rang.

'Bennett here.' Not the Regis Oyster Bar and Restaurant, and 'I'm sorry but we're fully booked this lunchtime'.

'Gordon? Nick Parker. Finchley-Camden wants you over at Wrykin Heath, Saturday, midday. Can you make it?'

'Will it be worth the trip?'

'Yes, Gordon. Well worth it.'

'All right, then. I'll be there.'

'Gordon? What was on today's menu?'

'Lobster Newburg.'

'Great. I'm pretty sure there'll be a hell of a lot of seafood where we're going. See you then. Day after tomorrow.'

'See you.'

Fucking lucky I didn't ditch the rest of the wine, he said to himself, and settled into a basket chair to finish the bottle as the tide went out and the gulls came in. As he did so, he relished the thought of having something real to do again.

Finchley-Camden, with Parker beside him, paused on the brow of a low escarpment covered with brown autumnal heather, and took in the view: one of the best in the area, and one he felt he owned. Heath tumbled into woodland and meadows, water gleamed on the ox-bowing Avon as it meandered the last five miles into Christchurch. The coastal towns from Hengistbury Head to Poole, with the Purbecks blue in the distance beyond, were far enough away not to be an eyesore.

In the foreground, a bare quarter of a mile away was the house, Wrykin Heath: a row of six former farm cottages knocked into one long building. A guelder rose with clusters of shiny red berries like currants hung across a stile which was the way through to roughly cut lawns and shaggy, autumnal flowerbeds. Hazy sunlight rolled back a frosty mist and the sharp smell of a bonfire cut across the fainting fragrance of a hedge of dead and dying sweet peas. The house was not exactly his – it belonged more to the bank than to him. But Operation Nicaragua should make it possible for him to keep it.

The two men, both in Barbours and flat tweed caps, broke their guns and extracted the cartridges. Finchley-Camden's was a Purdey 'best', with stock and furniture nearly a hundred years old, though the mechanism had been replaced. Parker's was a newish 'over-under' Beretta, just a touch flash in the Colonel's judgement. Then they began the descent towards the stile, using a zigzagging track of fine white sand carved through the heather by rain draining off the high plateau. Benjie, one of Finchley-Camden's retrievers, lolloped behind them and behind the dog came Duncan, panting in tweeds and leather gaiters, humping the bag of a brace of partridges, two rabbits, and a snipe.

A Lear jet came in low overhead, dropping towards Bournemouth International, the regular run from the City of London Airport, and then a small bird of prey broke out of a solitary pine in front of them. For a moment they watched its neat, sharp-winged flight skimming the gorse, swooping occasionally like a swallow. It arced back towards them, climbed to a pitch above ground below them so the bird itself was not that far above them, and hovered.

'Kestrel,' said Parker. 'Lovely little chap.'

'Red-footed falcon, actually.'

'Oh, really?'

'The mail, that is the breast, is slate-coloured, the pounces red. He should be back in Egypt by now. As you saw, he feeds primarily on insects. Oops, there he goes. Ah, I think that's them. Round the front. They must have arrived together.'

'Do you think we can persuade Bennett to knock us up a game pie?'

'We can but try. But I think he'll say it all needs to hang for a week.'

'No problems getting down here, then, Goodall,' said Finchley-Camden heartily.

'No, sir. No problems.'

'Good chap.'

He'd done it almost in one. Hardly had he stuck his thumb out on the A1 bypass close to Blaydon than he'd been picked up by a refrigerated beef lorry from Aberdeen heading for Paris via Southampton. The only problem had been the stopover in the Nottingham overnight lorry park. Naturally the trucker had taken the bunk compartment above the cab, leaving Goodall to do the best he could across the seats. For much of the night the driver had been having it away with a motorway service station whore who clearly believed that a lot of oohing and aahing at appropriate moments heightened the customer's pleasure. By dawn he was wondering whether it would all show up on the tachometer.

'Bennett?' said Finchley-Camden.

'No problem. Just a quick dash up the M27 and then on to the A31.'

'Touch more beef for you?'

'Thank you, sir.'

Duncan had laid out a cold buffet of nearly raw roast beef and smoked salmon accompanied by Ringwood Fortyniner drawn from a keg.

'When you're ready Nick will take you to the billiard room and let you in on the whole show. I've already briefed him as well as I can, so I shall be keeping a low profile. Possibly even a horizontal one. Duncan will get you anything you want. Then if you'd like to stop over the night that's fine by me – the sprouts are at school and the boss is with her ailing mother in Scotland. Perhaps, if there's time in hand, Bennett might like to knock us up a game pie?'

'Not unless the game's been properly hung, sir.'

'Ah. Quite. Well, I'm sure Duncan has something in hand.'

Ailing mother, my arse, Nick Parker said to himself. If the gossip in the United Services Club has it right, F.-C.'s wife has taken her toyboy to Montego Bay and is not likely to be back before the Christmas hols.

*   *   *

The maps and photographs which had been spread across the covered, full-size table were lit by the long-tasselled overhead light. Tobacco smoke gathered in swirling banks above them: Goodall's German Senior Service – a friend with the NATO rump still on the Rhine sent them to him; Bennett's miniature Hamlets; Parker's Dunhills. And for drink they had the Colonel's brandy.

'Right, then. This is the target,' Parker said, edging out a double-plate black and white glossy photograph so that none of the other papers was covering it. It was grainy, but with good definition. 'This building, two-storey as you see, has a laboratory, storerooms, and offices where data is stored in fireproof safes. Client wants it taken right out, razed to the ground and everything in it destroyed. Ten-out-of-ten demo job. Ditto these three green houses – controlled-environment units they're called. That should be less of a problem since they're mostly glass. And finally there are nine hectares of agriculture here to the south of the buildings, divided as you see into nine square plots. Client wants them torched, properly torched. There you are. That's the job description. Straightforward? You'd think so.'

He ground out the Dunhill in the hard palm of a dried black human hand, a souvenir of Borneo, which served as an ashtray, and sipped his VSOP Courvoisier.

'Problem number one: the whole thing is in Nicaragua close to the Costa Rican border, and in case you've forgotten the geography you were taught at school, they're two of the funny bits between Mexico and Colombia, just where America gets wasp-waisted. Next problem . . .'

'These two buildings here, ruins they look like, what're they?' Goodall's heavy finger prodded down.

'They are, in a sense, part of the problem. Five years ago some local hicks were hired to have a go and by and large they cocked up. The result is the site is now protected by ex-Sandinistas.'

'What are they, then?'

'Well, it's a long story.' Parker straightened, pressing his back against the mantelpiece. There was no fire: the central heating was more than adequate. 'I'll keep it as brief as I can. They were called Sandinistas after a guy called Sandino who saw the Yanks off in the thirties, but then got himself assassinated by a pro-Yank President. Through the seventies and the early eighties they were a guerrilla movement devoted to kicking out the Somoza family, who ruled the place as if they owned it. I suppose in many senses they actually did own it – like the Sabahs own Kuwait.'

'These weren't the guys who invented vegetable samosas, were they?'

'Not so far as I know, Gordon.'

'If they were they deserved to be seen off.'

'Nothing wrong with a samosa,' Goodall put in. 'Our chippie turns in a good samosa. Makes a change from bangers in batter, like.'

'Anyway, by the mid-eighties they'd won, had an election and won that,' Parker went on. 'But the Yanks didn't like it, gave them all sorts of aggro, including supporting a group of Nicaraguans called Contras, and promoting a civil war. In 1989 there was another election: a lady called Victoria Chamorro won at the head of a centrist coalition . . .'

'What's centrist?' asked Goodall.

'Neither left nor right. And she left a lot of Sandinista guerrillas out in the cold with nothing to do, and it's fifty of them you'll have to cope with.'

A long silence fell over the room. They all knew why but it was Bennett who coughed, stubbed out his tiny cigar, and helped himself to another brandy before saying it.

'We'll need two troops. More.'

You don't need to have been at Sandhurst to know that the ratio of attackers to defenders holding a fortified position, all other things being equal, has been set at five to one since war began – if the attackers are going to win, that is.

'Yes. Well, for reasons I won't go into now, and believe me they are to do with more than money – there's plenty of that about – we're talking a couple of sections, twenty men or, Hereford-style, five patrols.'

'I'm off home,' said Goodall, who had been fiddling with a cue but now put it back in the rack, and walked purposefully to the door. He stopped, though, turned and grinned. 'Now tell us the good news.'

'Well, there are several aspects which favour us.' Parker pushed the black forelock off his forehead, and the corners of his mouth lifted. His arms came down from the mantelpiece and he ticked them off on his fingers, one by one. 'These Sandinistas are experienced in jungle guerrilla warfare, and I don't need to tell you about that. But essentially it's offensive. Hit and run, take out a small military post, a post office, blow up a filling station, that sort of thing, and then pick off anyone who dares follow you back to your jungle hide. It's the sort of fighting we like best as well: room for individual initiative, lots of movement. Basically they're hunters. And just as you do – don't deny it – they make bad defenders. They won't like sitting around on their arses for months, and they won't take to routine garrison discipline.' His hand reached forward for the brandy balloon left on the table in front of him.

'Two, they are no longer part of the official army and the only equipment they have is what they have been able to hold on to, or fetch out of jungle caches left over from the war. Basically we believe they've got a Kalashnikov each and maybe five hundred rounds, plus some other small arms, maybe a mortar or two, that's about it. Thirdly, they're barracked two kilometres away in the village, and only fifteen or twenty are on site at any one time . . .'

'Ah. Now it begins to look sensible.'

'I thought you'd come round to seeing it my way. Right. First the run-up. Client wants it all over and done with in two months from now. What I propose is this. I'll take Tim out there and we'll suss it out together at first hand. Meanwhile Gordon will act as recruiting sergeant and round up twenty good lads. Which brings me to the second bit of good news and the answer to the question you have so politely not asked. Though I'm sure it's on the tip of your tongues.'

'Dead right, man. How much?' asked Goodall.

'Fifteen grand each for you. Five up front, ten when it's over, and that includes, worst case, next of kin. Five for the troopers, two up, three to come.'

The men's reaction was predictable, but they managed to confine it to swiftly exchanged grins.

'Well, I told you there was a lot of money about. We aim to have the lads out there, in Ticoland, Costa Rica that is, with the equipment, by 15 October. Two weeks' intensive training and briefing, and we go in on 5 November, fireworks night.'

'Mr Parker.'

The Tynesider was looking suddenly thoughtful, even worried: there was a haunted look in his eyes, as he scratched his cheek and chin.

'Tim?'

'There'll be no question of me coming back between the recce and the training, will there? Once I'm out there I stay there until it's all over, like?'

'Of course.' Parker thought about it for a moment, but judged it better not to ask what lay behind Goodall's question, not yet anyway. 'The money may be good, but swanning unnecessarily to and fro across the Atlantic is definitely not on.'

He moved back to the table and pushed the photographs and maps about again.

'What we have to do now is make up an optimum shopping list, and then a worst-case one. And let me make it clear from the start, we're coming in over land, so no choppers, no jumps, and everything has to be carried.'

'How far?'

'Ten kilometres of jungle tracks in friendly territory, then five through cultivated land which, if by any horrible happenstance they know we're coming, could be hostile. There's a river, so we'll need Gemini inflatables or Rigid Raiders. As I said, the money's there, and if possible I want us to be kitted out to full battle order, Sabre squadron specifications. Maybe not the very latest gear, but certainly up to what you chaps would have expected five years ago.'

'You can get all that?'

'Hopefully, yes. If the money's there you can generally get anything you want. But that's why I want two lists – one optimum, one the absolutely basic without which we don't do it.'

Bennett pulled a small notebook from the top pocket of his shirt, and a pencil, which he licked.

'Two GPMGs, one thousand rounds each.'

'Two 81mm mortars.'

'Two?'

'In case one fucks up in training.'

'White-phosphorus bombs?'

'What for?'

'Get those crops burning nicely.'

'I thought we might go for the M202 portable flame weapons.'

'There's a case, isn't there, if there is so much dosh sloshing about, for asking for both, and we can try them out, see which works best . . .'

In the early evening, when he knew Goodall was having a shower, Parker found his way into the kitchen, where Bennett was knocking up Steak Diane with Duncan's grudging assistance. He had a special request for Bennett.

After they had eaten a rather stilted, best-behaviour meal with Finchley-Camden at the head of the table, Bennett suggested he take Goodall in his Cavalier down to Ringwood for a pint or two. Goodall was happy to accept. They parked in the Furlong Inn car park, put their heads inside the pub and decided it was too crowded and noisy, filled with weekend yuppies and their girlfriends tanking up before beginning their assault on the town's three curry houses.

A back alley took them to Market Square, where they found a very pleasant snug at the back of the Star – a small bar with comfortable chairs and a real log fire.

'Brown for you, then?' Bennett asked from the counter.

'You're joking. They brew it special for south of Watford Gap, leave more sugar in. Like fucking barley sugar. I'll take the local brew.'

They sat and drank for a time, talked about nothing very much, which in a way gave the game away. Bennett knew he had family, two sons, so why wasn't he asking after them?

'So what's this about not wanting to come back once you're out there?'

'I reckon you fucking know.'

'I suppose I do. But Mr Parker don't.'

'And he's got you to find out. Doesn't he read the papers?'

'Perhaps not the right ones. Anyway I don't know the details.'

'I'm out on police bail. I have to check in Mondays and Thursdays and if I don't they lock me up until the court reconvenes for sentencing. Early in the New Year.'

'Why'd you do it?'

Tim told him the whole story. He ended up: 'If young Parker don't know about it now, I don't see why he should, all right? My shout.'

He got up. 'What's it called?'

'Old Thumper.'

'Stupid name, but it's not bad. Five or six and it could be journey into space time.'

He put the drinks down on the little table between them.

'Those aerial photographs. They were CIA satellite – I clocked the codes printed along the bottom.'

'I thought they might be.'

'And these Sandinistas. I don't know anything about it, but in my book they were the good guys.'

He held Bennett's cold, grey eyes for a moment, but they flinched away. A log fell and sparks rose.

'Maybe. But ours not to reason why.'

'No. Anyway, not while there's fifteen grand to tell us not to.'

4

A man thin like Jesus Christ on the Cross, but the difference was he'd dirtied his loincloth, was hauled across the compound. The men manhandling him were wearing sandy-coloured DPM fatigues beneath small black turbans. Pakistanis perhaps? Afghans? Matt Dobson couldn't be sure. JC looked white, though not Euro-white. His heavy stubble made it difficult to be sure and his face was so screwed up in one long unrelenting scream that it was hard to say whether the apparently Oriental cast of his eyelids was genuine or simply facial distortion.

The men in black turbans did indeed more or less crucify him. They stood him up against a post with a cross-bar, fastened a strap around his waist and the upright and two straps to secure his spread wrists, pulling the buckles tight against the cross-bar, and then walked briskly away. Left to himself, JC's body slumped, the tendons and muscles on his very thin arms standing out as they took the weight of his emaciated body, though his head still came up in a scream that would not stop.

Then a third soldier stepped forward with a Browning High Power handgun which Dobson recognized was a 9mm FN BDA 9. He removed the empty magazine and handed the gun to one of his companions. Meanwhile he held up a single round. Instead of the usual smooth-cased projectile, this one looked like three tiny traffic cones stacked on top of each other. He slipped it into the magazine, took back the handgun, slotted in the magazine, and pulled back and then released the slide mechanism. He moved briskly forward to a line on the ground marked, in white paint, '50m', went into a professional half crouch with both arms forward and elbows slightly bent, and fired.

Unfortunately JC was still twisting and turning – had in fact got on to his toes – just as the projectile hit him. Consequently it crashed into the lower-right part of his ribcage and it took him a minute or two to die. As he did so a voice boomed out.

'As you see, gentlemen, the wound is nearly ten centimetres in diameter and there is no exit wound.' The voice was mellifluous though precise, with the pure English vowels one associates with the Indian subcontinent. 'In other words the projectile has dumped all its energy in the body, adding hydrostatic shock to the other damage inflicted. There is also no danger of shoot-through. Although death is not always instantaneous, head and body wounds are always fatal, and limb wounds almost always so since they will result in immediate and enormous loss of blood as well as fatal trauma.

'The cartridge will fit all standard 9mm small arms and is a credit to our arms industry albeit it is still in its infancy. One of you noted that it looks remarkably like the *Société des Munitions* THV round. Well, it does. And no, we do not have a licence to manufacture. And yes, we do produce and sell it at a fifth of the cost of a French-produced Très Haute Vélocité round. Need I say more?'

JC died, and the lights came on.

'Oh yes, and by the by: the poor fellow was a convicted anal rapist suffering from AIDS.'

I doubt it, thought Matt Dobson. They'd hardly let HIV-positive blood spill about the place like that if he was. More likely a rebellious hill tribesman. He turned to his neighbour, a Japanese who looked rougher round the edges than most Japanese businessmen do. Military perhaps? No, I've got it, the Filth.

'Well,' Dobson said, 'I've seen some snuff movies in my time, but . . . well!'

The Japanese maintained his traditional inscrutability.

Dobson looked around the low room with its drab acoustic panels, at the big fan slowly revolving in the centre of the ceiling, at the seven or eight other men sitting there. A murmur of conversation slowly rose, but no one stood up. Were they, like him, waiting for their erections to subside?

As the credits rolled up on the large video screen a messenger boy in brown singlet over brown trousers, with the hotel's logo embroidered on his left breast, floated across the carpet towards him.

'Sahib in reception asked me to give you this.'

Matt Dobson glanced at the visiting card. '*Colonel R. H. Finchley-Camden*,' it read, and then, on the next line, '*Wolf Hound*'. Jesus H. Christ, thought Dobson, he must be desperate.

'Sahib will be in the roof bar and hopes you will have lunch with him.'

Dobson stood, did up the middle button of his silk and mohair jacket, dark-slate with a misty-blue pinstripe, and then thought, no, I won't hurry, I'll make the bugger wait. And he joined a small group that had gathered round the presenter, a dark chap in the sort of uniform British staff officers wore thirty years ago. He even wore shorts and had a swagger stick. They were discussing the possibility of discounts on orders of more than half a million rounds.

Up on the terrace Finchley-Camden was happy to have twenty minutes or so sitting in a high-cushioned cane chair, with a Scotch and water, long and strong, at his elbow. From this height the smells and squalor of the city spread out below him could be ignored, while the panorama of high rises among the gilded domes and minarets of mosques and temples was splendid. It was just a shame that with the rainy season imminent the chain of peaks, the foothills of the roof of the world, which usually filled the northern horizon, were obliterated behind equally spectacular if more ephemeral palaces of cumulus and anvil cloud. And apart from being grateful for enough time to enjoy the view and his drink, he needed space to both recover from what amounted to nearly fifteen hours' continuous travel and finally psych himself up for the meeting ahead.

He had never met Matt Dobson although they had done some business in the past through intermediaries, and he was slightly in awe of his reputation. It was unusual for a Finchley-Camden to be in awe of anyone, but then Dobson was an unusual person.

Connected to some of the most powerful people in the land by family ties and favours given and received in the past, and above all through knowing some of the innermost secrets of Cabinet and Whitehall, Dobson apparently roamed the world at will, buying and selling second-hand weaponry. He had a reputation for being willing to handle anything, no matter how small or large the deal was; nevertheless, part of Finchley-Camden's potential embarrassment lay in the modest size of the order he was presenting. But then, he told himself, not for the first time, he was willing and, thanks to AFI's Swiss-based slush fund, able to pay well over the odds.

He was just about down to the ice cubes at the bottom of the glass when he saw Dobson coming across the terrace towards him. The arms dealer was in his late thirties, with thick, dark hair and small, dark eyes in a face that was just beginning to take on the podginess of a surfeit of good living. His suit was, by Finchley-Camden's standards, too obviously very expensive, the colours in his tie glowed just a shade too luxuriantly, and his shoes were not the sort a gentleman wears. After all, thought Finchley-Camden, despite the fact that his mother rose to be among the highest in the land, the man remains the grandson of a fishmonger. And it shows.

Dobson swung a document case on to the cane-topped table. Its red cordovan leather and gold fittings went with the rest of his appearance. Briefly he shook hands – no grip – and sank into the chair beside Finchley-Camden. He did not need to raise a finger: the bar-wallah was already at his elbow.

'Large G and T for me . . . are the bottles cold?'

'Very cold, sir. Refrigerated twenty-four hours.'

'Lime, no ice. And another of whatever the Colonel's drinking. I tend not to touch the ice, Colonel – they too often fill the trays from the tap even though they say they use bottled Himalayan spring water. What can I do for you?'

Finchley-Camden unfolded a sheet of embossed writing paper from his inside pocket.

'It's not a lot, really. But I need it in Costa Rica by 15 October.'

Dobson snapped on black-framed, tinted bifocal Ray-Bans, opened his case and took out an electronic notebook with integral calculator. He tapped away for a few moments, gestured a cheers when his drink arrived, and finally put the computer away and took off his sunglasses.

'I take it it all has to be absolutely kosher. No "made in Hong Kong" labels in the lining, that sort of thing.'

His speech was clipped, fast, Kensington-cockney.

'Absolutely not,' replied Finchley-Camden.

'No problem with the jungle DPMs, bergens, boots and so on, all the soft kit. I can arrange for them to fall off the back of a lorry between the warehouse and Hereford. The Brownings, I can get them too' – momentarily Dobson's lips creased at the memory of the sales video he had just seen – 'and if you like I can get you THV-type rounds for them, not kosher I grant you, but they work. But from there on upwards you're in shit.'

Finchley-Camden winced, drank (was there enough whisky to neutralize the possibility of cholera in the ice?) and waited.

'If you'd given me nine months I could have got it all using the double shimmy, and at a reasonable price.'

He waited for Finchley-Camden to ask what a 'double shimmy' was, and when he didn't, told him anyway.

'Double shimmy: client not flavour of the month with HMG comes to me and I go to a chum in Oman, Dubai, Malaysia, wherever. Chum, Minister for Arms Procurement, whatever, places a legitimate ex-factory order, whiter than white end-user certificate all in order, HMG happy to keep the workers in Coventry, York or wherever toiling away, no questions asked. Then nine months later my chum sells on to me, below the counter, and I to the client who came to me in the first place. Last month I shifted sixty Saracens to an Uzbek warlord using that route, but, you see, he placed his order in January. But this lot . . . six weeks.' He sucked in his lips with a hiss, and shook his head.

This character really is a huckster, Finchley-Camden thought, any feeling of embarrassment now forgotten, and pushed his lean, brown fingers through his silver hair. But if I wait he'll make me an offer. Though I suspect it will be one I ought to refuse.

'M16A2 assault rifles are just not on. Indeed Armalites of any sort are in very short supply. Bosnia, you see? I could get you twenty used SLRs, no problem.'

The rifles were semi-automatic, two kilos heavier, longer, and larger-calibre, making them less suitable for the short-range work they expected the operation would involve.

'But it's the heavy stuff: the mortars and the gimpies,' Dobson said, using the SAS argot for a General Purpose

Machine-Gun. 'That's where your real problems lie.'

'I thought the L96A1s might be difficult.'

'The Accuracy International sniping rifles? Got a chum out in the Gulf — no names, no pack-drill — thought he could use them as hunting rifles for mountain lion. But the plug got pulled on that when some conservationist leaked what he was up to, so I reckon he'll be quite happy to offload them. But the mortars and the gimpies . . .' Again the pursed lips, the hiss, the shaking head. 'Of course it depends how high you're able to go.'

Finchley-Camden held his tongue and forced as blank an expression on to his face as he could manage, mainly by taking an intense interest in a fly that appeared on Dobson's document case, attracted perhaps by the smell of leather warmed by the sun.

Dobson lurched forward, close enough for Finchley-Camden to smell the freshener on his breath, still over-riding the gin.

'I could round up most of this stuff from guys who have it but are not likely to need it over the next couple of months. What we could do is arrange a leasing set-up, covered by a deposit in escrow to the value they set on the items in case whatever you're up to springs a leak.'

'You mean I hire the stuff, and if I return it in good order then all I pay is the rental? But if anything gets lost or damaged then the sum needed to replace it is taken out of escrow?'

'That's it. Except that it's not the replacement value you cough up, but the value my chums set on them.'

Nevertheless, Finchley-Camden thought, this could work out a lot cheaper than I expected. He had been prepared to go as high as two hundred, a fifth of what AFI had made available, but it looked now as if he might be able to get what he wanted for tens rather than hundreds of thousands.

He drank his Scotch, looked round at the sun flashing

off gold domes set against the deep purple of distant storm clouds, and felt a sudden surge of warm euphoria – every pound unspent was a pound that stayed in his pocket, or rather winged its way to that blasted Lloyd's syndicate.

'I think we can sort something out on those lines. Lunch?'

'Tiffin, or whatever they call it in these parts? Why not?'

Dobson's smile was like sunlight on an assassin's knife.

After a series of intercontinental phone calls had been made throughout the long, hot, sultry afternoon, the hiring and transportation costs worked out at just over £90,000, which was more than Finchley-Camden had expected, plus a non-returnable twenty-four grand for ammunition of all sorts, four types of mortar bomb, tracer, and so on. Worse still, the sum to be deposited with a firm of London solicitors whose reputation for handling escrow accounts had remained unblemished for a century, was £250,000, which he reckoned was about a hundred thousand more than the market value.

Nick Parker had better not fuck up on this one, was the phrase Finchley-Camden's jet-lagged mind repeated again and again, mantra-like, as the Air India jumbo carried him home.

Travelling in the opposite direction, Dobson felt smug self-satisfaction. He'd net around £25,000 in commissions, which wasn't bad for an unscheduled afternoon's work. Moreover, it shouldn't be too difficult to find out just what Wolf Hound was planning in Costa Rica, and if he could it should be possible to arrange for a fair whack of that two-fifty grand to come out of escrow, not the way it went in, but his way . . . Pity he hadn't made it a round three ton – the money was obviously there.

5

Gordon Bennett rang the four secretaries of Regimental Associations whom he knew personally. They came up with a hatful of names and addresses. Then he threw three drip-dry shirts, three pairs of pants and three pairs of socks into a holdall, together with a spare Guernsey sweater, a pair of jeans and his shaving kit. Finally he checked that his road atlas of Britain was in the glove compartment of his Cavalier.

'And so we say farewell to Mickey Mouse Land,' he murmured aloud to himself as he passed the LEC factory and the sign that said Bognor Regis was twinned with Saint-Maur-des-Fossés slipped away in his right-hand wing mirror.

In Lambeth, in a bedroom hidden away in a warren of red-brick medium-rises with a maze of entries, staircases, lifts and open corridors, Winston Smith was being humped by Rosemary Fitz, a sixteen-year-old chick bunking off from her double period in GCSE Home Economics – the unit entitled Mothercraft.

She was gorgeous. Overall small and compact, her breasts were so firm they hardly wobbled at all as she rose and fell on his glistening shaft. Only the nipples, the colour of the flesh of plums against skin almost as purply dark as their skin, swayed a little above Winston's open and gasping mouth. Her tight but broad arse seemed to hug the length of his prick like wet insulating tape round a live cable.

Five minutes earlier, when she first saw it and then held

it, she had said: 'Shit, man, you'll never get that inside a bumbo as small as mine.'

And he had replied: 'Look, I'll lie on my back, and you sit on top of me, and you slip him in as gentle as you like.'

There had been an ooh and an aah and then for a couple of minutes, though it seemed like eternity, she'd half-knelt, half-sat there quite still and he'd gone into his usual routine of saying his seventeen times table to stave off possible disappointment for both of them. Tentatively at first, and then with more conviction, she had begun to move herself up and down on it, and now the oohs and aahs were coming back but with quite a different timbre.

'Oh boy, oh shit, what a lovely little mover you are,' he cried. 'Two hundred and fifty-five,' he said to himself, 'two hundred and thirty-nine.' But it was no use, his big black hands reached up and gripped her upper arms, her hands came down inside them and pushed rhythmically on his chest, almost as if she were attempting cardiac resuscitation, then they both exploded and she rolled down on him, twisting and writhing and moaning, and he could feel the spasms inside her like he'd never felt them before and then his prick flopped out between them.

'Honey,' he said, once his breath was back enough for speech, 'that was the best ever. The best I ever had.'

Between gasps she managed: 'You say that to all the girls.'

He did too, but he tried to make a joke of it.

'How you do know that?'

'Me mam told me,' and she giggled but cut the giggle off as if with cheese-wire. 'Christ, did you hear that?'

He had, his ears as alert as they had been in the Brunei jungle three years before.

'The front door latch?'

She nodded, eyes wide and white with panic, and clutched the bedspread around her.

'It's me bros, it has to be. Mam's out at work. They'll kill you.'

As the door handle began to turn, Winston whipped the back of the one wooden chair in her room beneath it, grabbed his white leather tanga briefs and stepped into them, then span round for his shirt, but as he did so the chair began to break to violent thuds and shouts from outside.

'Rosie, you fucking whore, we know you got that stud Winston in there, and he's gonna be two stones lighter by the time we finished with him . . .'

The chair splintered and the two brothers, one a light-heavyweight with serious ambitions, the other his sparring partner, tumbled in as Winston tumbled out. Through the window.

He did it right. The block was designed on an alternating plan, with bedroom and bathroom windows looking straight out into open air, above and below open walk-ways, where the front doors and living-room windows of the intermediate floor were. With his fingers on the sill of Rosie's window, Winston was able to swing his long legs into the space above the wall of the floor below. It wasn't easy and he gave his back a nasty scrape on the top of the wall, but it was better than falling four floors on to concrete.

He loped off down the passageway to the lifts and staircases. When he got to them he stopped and listened. No sound. Then a shout from the far end. Down? No, that was what they'd expect. So . . . up.

For punchies they turned out not to be entirely out to lunch. One waited round the first angle, while the other pounded down the walkway to cut him off. Winston turned, leapt back down the stairs and met the second with a roundhouse kick that felt as if it had broken his ankle and should have taken the boxer's head off. He saw it coming, and took it on his huge shoulder, but even so it threw him back into a half crouch. Winston hurdled him like he was Daley Thompson, and now he was clear. Only trouble was, he was still in his birthday suit apart from the minimal tanga, and they were right behind him.

He made it to the ground floor, shot through the entry like a bullet, and there, cruising round the quadrangle at a walking pace, obviously looking for a reasonably safe place to park, was a Cavalier. Winston tumbled into the back and growled: 'Drive, man, drive like shit!' Then: 'Fucking Christ, Sergeant Bennett. What the fuck are you doing here!'

'Looking for you, sonny. What else?'

Bennett looked in the rear-view mirror, saw two very large, very muscular black men coming out of the entrance to the flats, in hot pursuit. He put a little pressure on the throttle.

'You could have handled them.'

'Course I could, Mr Bennett. But you can see, like they're serious. I'd have had to kill them to stop them from killing me. Or' – he remembered the threat to leave him two stones lighter – 'ripping me bollocks off.'

They turned into Kennington Park Road.

'Let me guess why they were after you. You were bonking their sister?'

'How'd you know?'

Gordon Bennett shot a distasteful glance down at Winston's legs.

'You're leaking.'

'Their kid sister. Mr Bennett, take a right for the Elephant and we'll find a place you can buy me some cool grunge.'

'Gordon Bennett! What a lovely surprise.'

'Gina! You're looking as wonderful as ever.'

They exchanged warm hugs. Bennett was tall, but in her bare feet Gina was just about on a level.

'Shit, I've left paint on your jumper.'

It was true. Gina Brown, sixty if she was a day, was wearing a long man's shirt over sweater and jeans, the shirt she wore when she was working.

'Never mind.' She pulled him in off the drab East End street, post-war terraces on the other side, original late-Victorian on this: dockers' two-up two-downs, but no dockers now.

'Come on through.'

The tiny house had been gutted and rebuilt by Geoff, her boyfriend of nearly ten years, ex-soldier, ex-sculptor, part-time builder, part-time soldier of fortune, some fifteen years younger than her. The ground floor was one room now, a studio for Gina, filled with huge canvases stacked against the walls, and the one she was working on facing the back wall, which was all glass.

'Come on up.'

He followed her up the stairs, admiring her bouncy dark-red hair (OK, dyed, but did that matter?) and her still-lean figure.

'I know you really came to see Geoff. But before I tell you where he is, you can sit down with me and have a chat and a noggin.'

And they did that, drank tea and neat gin in the tiny back kitchen, overlooking the poky yard filled with dismantled scaffolding.

Finally Bennett had to say: 'So where is he? Where is Geoff?'

'Fucking Bosnia,' she replied, and her big, brown eyes suddenly filled. 'Go on, Gordon, bugger off. Geoff's never there when you want him. Story of my life as well as yours.'

* * *

Jack Glew cradled the huge bloom of a classy dahlia in his big fist. Its hundreds of spear-shaped petals were deep purple with a white outer rim. For a year he had nurtured the plant, just for this moment. And so it was with very mixed feelings that he stooped with his Wilkinson secateurs in his right hand, feeling for the correct point on the stem with his left. He severed the stem and then placed it carefully in his wheelbarrow along with the ten others he was entering for the Gedling Dahlia Silver Cup the next day. He straightened and looked out over the allotments.

'Bugger,' he muttered.

Picking his way through the grid of tiny plots, each with its padlocked shed, came a familiar figure from the past, lean, stooped, slightly sinister.

'Gordon. Gordon Bennett.'

They shook hands and Jack Glew listened to Bennett's spiel. And at the end he asked: 'And who's the skipper? Not that mad bastard Nick Parker?'

'Well, yes. But it'll be a push-over.'

'Maybe. Maybe not. But that Parker's a loony. And frankly, Gordon, I don't need that kind of money any more. Half a million on the Pools, yes. A pony down at the betting shop, yes. But what would I do with five grand? Nothing worth risking me life for.'

He turned and stooped to lift the handles of the barrow. As he straightened, he saw Bennett was already off, off into the chill gloaming. He felt a moment of regret, but reckoned he'd done the right thing: he was too old at nearly fifty to be gallivanting.

But Bennett had other ideas. The daft bastard, he said to himself, will stay here until the frosts get bad enough to turn those bloody flowers into handfuls of wet straw. Unless something else gets to them first. He knew a couple of hard cases over in Calverton who'd do almost anything for a fiver . . .

6

Back in his den off Baker Street, Finchley-Camden was waiting for a progress report from Bennett. He tapped away on his desk calculator, jotted figures on a pad, and the more he did so, the less he liked the way they were shaping up.

Weapons: anything between ninety grand and, worst case, three-forty. You've got to calculate on the basis that the worst can happen. Wages: one at twenty, two at fifteen, up to twenty at five – that's another hundred and fifty. Twenty-three return air tickets to Costa Rica, say forty grand. Accommodation, food and so on for nearly three weeks, say eight. You've got to allow at least a hundred for the unforeseen. Damn! He blinked at the LCD, cleared it, ran it again, and again the bleak black figures stared back at him: six sixty-two. And, if he was going to keep all this – he looked round at the trophies, the prints, the fine carpet and the rest – then he had to shave the costs by at least that sixty-two thousand. The problem was – and it was one he was not fully aware of – the four hundred grand he owed his syndicate had become a symbolic, obsessive figure, and this contract with AFI his way of meeting it. It had become a sort of grudge thing with fate that he should make the four hundred grand he needed on this deal, and not a penny less. A penny more, if he could, but not a penny less.

The green phone rang.

'Bennett here.'

Bennett. He'd be billing Wolf Hound for expenses, as would Parker and Goodall, who were already swanning around San José. Two more batches of bills he had not included in his calculations.

'Gordon. Where are you?'

'Liverpool, off Scotland Road. Colonel, do you think Mr Parker will mind if we take the Strachan twins on board?'

'Dear Lord, that's scraping the barrel, isn't it? I thought they were still in jug.'

'Just out, and looking for work. Fact is, sir, I'm having a bit of trouble getting together the five patrols you asked for. Bosnia's proved attractive, at least to the nutters . . .'

'Whom we can well do without.'

'. . . and there's been a couple who shied off once they knew Captain Parker was OC on the ground.'

'That seems a bit unfair.'

'Maybe. Anyway, what about the Strachans?'

'Needs must when the devil drives.' Euphoria had begun to swell in Finchley-Camden's chest. He tried to keep it out of his voice, which he made as serious, even as solemn, as he could. 'Gordon, you know the briefing as well as any of us and you have the experience. If it comes right down to it, what is the minimum number for the job? The bottom line.'

There was a long silence.

'Can I come back to you on that one? Give me half an hour to think it through.'

Bennett left the phone box, oddly unvandalized, and got back into his car. The rain sheeted down, slipping rather than running down the windscreen, which began almost instantly to mist up. He turned on the fan, reckoning that the battery could take it after the run up the M1 and then across the Pennines on the M62.

Outside, the hinterland of council estates and back-to-back terraces loomed grimly, but already, in his mind's eye, he was far away, huddled in a sangar improvised out of loose rock on the broad back of Mount Kent. 'Every time we run into an Argy patrol, they leg it . . . We ran into one the other night, though. Took two, wounded two, killed three,' he said to himself. On another night he had been point man, and rounding a bluff, they'd come face to face at thirty yards. He squeezed off a double tap which took out the Argy point man, but not before the number two had been able to lob a grenade. It fell short but left him with a shrapnel scar in his upper arm that still niggled a little in cold weather. And that was that: the rest had scarpered, tumbling, slithering, sliding down vicious scree rather than face it out.

Weren't they all the same, Latin Americans? Wouldn't these Sandinistas turn out to be much the same? OK, they did well in their own country, fighting a regular army – but a regular army of their own kind, poorly equipped, poorly trained.

Kalashnikovs. Once the best in the world. The Yanks in Nam threw away their M16s, which tended to jam, if they could pick up an AK47. But that was a long time ago. No gun is reliable after twenty-five years of fairly heavy use. And no weapon that old can match the technical advances that have been made since.

He shifted in his seat, slipped out a thin packet of Hamlet cigarillos, peeled the cellophane from one, snared a Swan Vesta on his nicotine-stained thumbnail, and remembered with photographic exactitude the maps and satellite pictures they had studied at Wrykin Heath. If they had an 81mm mortar, the latest update, a standard British adapted FN machine-gun, and a couple of good snipers with L96A1s, and if they had surprise on their side and knew the exact dispositions of the garrison, then they ought to be able to put down enough fire-power with twelve or fifteen men to neutralize the garrison before the enemy could get together any serious opposition.

He could see it. Pre-dawn light, three four-man patrols closing in on three sides. Then a well-planned carpet bombardment, the mortar in the rear chucking in 'mixed-fruit pudding' capable of firing the crops and the green-houses with white-phosporus bombs as well as conventional high explosive, stun and flash grenades to create maximum confusion, tracer from the gimpy scything into anything that moved. Five minutes of that, then the final assault should be no more than a mopping-up operation. If you're still alive and all you've got is a twenty-five-year-old AK, you don't hang around in the face of a firestorm like that, no one would, and certainly no spic, not spics like the young Argies he'd chased off Mount Kent.

He let himself out of the car, chucked the Hamlet butt into the gutter, and back in the telephone box fumbled out a twenty-pence piece.

'Colonel, if you've got together all the hardware we asked for, then I reckon fifteen will do it. But fifteen minimum. And to tell the truth, I think that's about as many as I'll be able to lay my hands on.'

Back at Wolf Hound, Finchley-Camden went back to his calculator. Twenty-five thousand saved on pay. Savings on fares and board. And above all five sets of weaponry, including probably one mortar and one machine-gun, which could all stay unpacked and safe in the warehouse in Puerto Limón, leaving at least eighty grand of the two-fifty in escrow safe as houses. It all added up to a substantial saving, enough to bring his worst-case profit margin well above that magic four hundred.

But would Nick Parker wear it? Yes. A, because he could now offer him a substantial rise, and, B, because

Nick loved a challenge – clearly something that men who had served under him still bore in mind.

Meanwhile, back on Merseyside, Bennett let out the clutch and turned into the road that would take him to the Strachan twins. Hard cases, seriously hard and thick as a stack of thick planks, they had been caught leaving powerful handguns lying around where their mates on the outside, rogues all, could pick them up. Under cover on fucking Moss Side at that. Court martial, dishonourable discharge, eighteen months in the slammer, and they'd been back a couple of times since. At least they'd throw a scare into any spics they tangled with . . .

And when he'd sorted out the Strachans, got them in tow, then there was a Chinese down in gentrified Docklands that Egon Ronay had very nice things to say about. The promise of sea-bass with fresh ginger and finely chopped spring onions, maybe some dim-sum dumplings for starters, the ones with king prawns in, brought a smile to his thin lips. Gordon Bennett had been saving himself for this and had eaten nothing at all but Bath Olivers and Cox's apples since leaving Bognor two days before.

7

Parker and Goodall left Miami at eight in the morning, arriving in Juan Santamaria airport at five in the evening on an LACSA 737. This final leg had taken in a lunchtime stop at Belize City, and a change of planes at San Salvador. By touch-down in Costa Rica they had been in each other's company for virtually twenty-four hours, and it had not been easy. In the transatlantic jumbo Goodall felt he would have been happier in what Parker called 'steerage', and what everyone else called 'economy' or 'tourist', along with his own sort, but Parker had insisted that since Wolf Hound was paying they might as well do it right and travel in comfort.

Goodall was not sure he had worked out just where the added comfort came from. Business or Club Class, whatever it was, seemed to mean a wider aisle but no more leg-room, free drinks which, since Wolf Hound was paying, would have been free anyway, and more frequent and bothersome visits from the air hostesses. The menu had said 'steak provençale', which turned out to be a lump of overcooked meat in a herby tomato sauce. He'd have been happier with the ham salad he was used to on charter flights to the Spanish Costas. And chocolate mints with the coffee had struck him as decidedly nancy . . .

To begin with, Parker had tried to chat, but by the time the west coast of Ireland was disappearing behind them he rumbled the Tynesider was not the chatting sort. He felt, correctly, that this was not because Goodall was essentially antisocial, but more due to his deep suspicion of toffs who attempted to be patronizing. So for the next eighteen hours or so, including a too short stopover in Miami, they had hardly said a word to each other apart from what was necessary to sort out practical problems: 'Excuse me, need a leak' or 'I think my spoon's under your feet.'

Belize City broke the ice. They had both done tours of duty there, though not at the same time, had tales to swap about the strange town of hot, damp buildings roofed with rusty corrugated iron, the bars and the whores, and anecdotes concerning the stupidity and general peasant-like quality of the Special Boat Squadron men and Green Berets who shared the training facilities with them.

The conversation had ended with Goodall asserting that he'd never open a tin of Heinz baked beans again without thinking of a night he'd spent with a young girl – 'A darkie, of course, and I swear she was only sixteen' – in the Fort George Hotel.

'Baked beans? Why?' Parker suspected a fart joke was on the way.

'The entire crop of Belize beans goes to Heinz. Did you not know that?'

By the time the descent to Juan Santamaria began they were sufficiently at ease with each other to point out and exclaim at the volcano they passed, and remark on the almost prairie-like quality of the high central *meseta*, after the lowland jungle. In short, they were prepared to be in each other's company but outside the job in hand communication would not go beyond what came naturally from their surroundings – there would be no more attempts at false camaraderie.

A taxi, a Chevvy ten years old but in good nick, took them the seventeen kilometres into downtown San José and a swiftly falling dusk. Their first impressions were favourable, at least once the four-lane blacktop had crossed the shanty-town girdle that circled the city. San José itself turned out to be made up of mostly twentieth-century blocks laid out on a grid system with well-kept streets, some tree-lined. Plenty of people about, the traffic heavy but moving, bars, restaurants, and *sodas* – small fast-food bars – doing good business as office workers made their way home. On the pavement outside the Hotel Fortuna they again remarked to each other that the air was cooler than they had expected and that perhaps this was not so surprising since San José is as high as Snowdon.

They separated on the first floor, where they had adjoining rooms.

'Um . . . look, tomorrow I have to see some chaps about all this, you know? We could meet here in the evening, say nine o'clock, by when I'll know where we're at and where we're going. So, day off for you, old bean.' Parker thrust a fistful of funny money into Goodall's palm. 'Compliments of Wolf Hound. Have, um, a nice day.'

And by and large he did. First thing in the morning, after a breakfast of hot bread rolls and coffee like he'd never tasted before, he picked up a couple of leaflets from a rack in the hotel foyer. They were in English as well as Spanish: 'Spend a day in San José' and 'This Week in San José'.

With their help he explored the wide boulevards, found the jade museum and the gold museum, both of which were fascinating, especially the jade museum, with its artefacts back-lit so the semiprecious stone glowed as if with an inner fire. In the shops of both he bought jewellery, jade earrings, and a gold brooch, whose designs were based on artefacts he had seen in the museums. Even though they were real jade and real gold they were surprisingly cheap and he hoped they would help him and Mary to rebuild the bridges between them. He would have liked to buy something for Jack and Bob, something really nice, especially for Jack, as he'd always done when 'wor lads' were still young enough to be really excited by a Malaysian knife sheathed in leather or a shrunken head from Borneo.

Still, coming out into the bright sunshine and walking through a park filled with tropical flowers and even humming birds, he felt a great wave of euphoria, almost joy: this was *the* life, not just thousands of miles from Tyneside and the deep shit he was in there, but a different planet.

'Mr Parker, Señor Franco will see you now. Come with me, please.'

To the ends of the earth if you like, Parker thought. He climbed the gentle black stairs behind her, holding on to the curving chrome rail, past huge photographs of black cattle grazing on savannah with forest-clad mountains in the background, but all he saw was an arse held like two bright tomatoes in a scarlet miniskirt above black tights that went on for miles and miles, and dark hair tumbling down the cool white silk of her blouse. Even her perfume made his head swim. And her name, according to the sign on her receptionist's desk, was Afrodita O'Donnell González. Afrodita – Aphrodite – the Greek Goddess of Love.

Francisco Franco was another matter, conforming at first glance to every prejudiced Anglo-Saxon's expectation of a spic spiv. Black hair slicked back in corrugated waves, sallow, pock-marked skin, dark eyes that never smiled, a mean mouth that never stopped and a handshake too close and held too long, so that when he finally let go you wanted to check he hadn't lifted your wallet with his free hand. White shirt, gold cuff-links that looked as if they might have been looted from an Inca tomb, pink silk tie that matched the lining of the dove-grey jacket that was hung across the back of his big, black-leather executive chair. He dismissed the girl with a wave of his hand, which Parker thought was a pity. He would have preferred to kiss her goodbye.

'Coffee, Mr Parker?'

'Please.' Surely that might mean Afrodita's return? But no, there was a flask on a side-table, with white porcelain cups. But the coffee was as good, even better perhaps than the hotel's: always say yes to a coffee in Costa Rica.

Franco then made the usual noises about the journey out, the standard of the hotel . . .

'Not the best, I know, but I have been instructed that your profile should always be low.'

'It's fine. Comfortable, reasonably quiet. Got everything we need . . .' Except Afrodita.

'*Muy bien*. Well, let's get on to the . . . brass tacks.'

The brass tacks turned out to be a serious snag. It had been presumed from the outset, that is from Maud Adler's visit to Wolf Hound, that the task force's cover would be as a team of hi-tech tree-fellers and that their equipment would be brought into Costa Rica in a container documented as holding state-of-the-art logging gear. Bullburger's operation in Costa Rica consisted of clear-felling rainforest, putting in peasants to slash and burn and then giving them tenant farmers' rights to grow maize on the peripheries of the forest while they kept the main swathe clear until, in a couple of years, it had become savannah. Then in came the beef cattle, which in turn ended up, from the Rio Grande to Tierra del Fuego, between seeded baps as . . . *Bullburguesas, las burguesas con cojones* – the burgers with balls.

'But what head office forgot,' Franco went on, making appropriate gestures to the big framed map of Costa Rica on the wall behind him, 'is that our beef operation takes place entirely on the drier Pacific side of the cordillera, of the mountains.' – he pronounced it 'mount-ines' – 'whereas your target lies just over the border in the centre north. There the land is flat, wet, and the jungle far more difficult to clear-fell, and we have no cattle stations at all; nor is it likely that we ever will.'

None of this was entirely accurate. In fact a large amount of the area Franco was talking about had been clear-felled and converted into cattle pasture, but the concession had gone to an even larger producer of beefburgers than Bullburger. Bullburger (Costa Rica) S. A. were a Johnny-come-lately in Costa Rica and had had to be content with the poorer land to the west.

'So?' Parker said as he leant back in the big armchair Franco had offered him, cheek on his palm, ankle over his knee. Franco, he thought, this is your problem, not mine.

'So. We think you will go in as researchers, botanists, ecologists, that sort of thing. A special team from . . . from some British university. Specially funded by Bullburger S. A. It could be quite good PR, you know?'

'Quite honestly, I don't think any form of publicity is too good an idea.'

'No? Perhaps not. But the important thing is we must get government permission for you to be in the forest not too far from your target, with the training facilities you have asked for. Do you know of a university or research foundation we could say you were funded by? Perhaps some EU organization?'

'Lord, no. I'm really not up in that sort of thing at all. Anyway, isn't all that rather more your problem than mine?'

White teeth flashed across the desk at him.

'Of . . . course . . . it is! I just wondered if you had any ideas about it.'

'Well, no, I haven't. And you haven't got an awful lot of time to do anything about it. There's another aspect. What we liked about the clear-felling scenario was it provided a really good reason for bringing in containers. I doubt botanists and so on carry much hardware.'

'Ah, Mr Parker, that is where you make a mistake.' Franco leant forward, rummaged at papers on his desk, and pushed across a copy of *National Geographic* already folded back at the page he wanted. 'La Selva,' he went on, 'about a hundred kilometres south and east of where you will be. A research station where they studied the forest canopy with a system of pulleys and ropes, and pre-built platforms, even cabins, in the tops of the trees. We can say your people need the same sort of equipment.'

Parker hardly gave the magazine a glance.

'As I said, it's your problem not mine. Good Lord, what's that?'

The room had suddenly got darker, lightning flickered, distant thunder boomed, and rain, as if a tap had been turned on, sheeted down into the street outside.

'The rainy season.' Franco shrugged. 'Every afternoon it's the same. But less each day now. It will all be over by the end of October.'

Parker turned back to the Mexican.

'So what's on tomorrow?'

'You go up to the place we have found for you. So you can make the reconnaissance you asked for. A taxi will be at the Fortuna for you at nine o'clock. Meanwhile I will look into these problems we have been discussing.'

The rain caught Goodall as he sauntered up the Calle Central admiring the flower and fruit stalls. It didn't seem to bother the Ticos – he knew by now that that is what Costa Ricans like to call themselves – most of whom ignored it, though a few plastic macs came out and a few umbrellas went up. Conscious that he had only one change of outer clothing, he looked around for shelter and spotted the terrace of the Grand Hotel Costa Rica. It looked ritzy, but that sort of thing didn't bother him: he trotted up steps and found a sheltered table on the open veranda.

He was followed, very closely, by a black woman, with a daughter of five or six, nothing like as black as herself. The waiter was at his elbow almost before he'd straightened his denim jacket. He ordered a coffee, which came with biscuits like macaroons in the shape of a cat's tongue, while the black woman, explaining briskly to the waiter in fluent Spanish that they were not together, ordered *té con limón* for herself and an ice-cream for her daughter, Zena.

He grinned shyly at them. They were both very good-looking: the mother in a severe, fit, almost handsome way, the child with the lean, fresh beauty of a girl still a long way from the problems of puberty. Then, slightly embarrassed at his apparent inability to speak Spanish, which was what he presumed they spoke, he sat back to watch the poor, in from the shanty towns, selling pineapple slices and bananas or touting to clean men's suddenly soiled shoes. The Mercs, the Caddies, the Plymouths, Toyotas, and the VW Golfs, except they were called Caribes here and were built in Mexico, shunted up and down San José's main thoroughfare in time to the changing lights. And then there was a VW Beetle, also new, and also made in Mexico. And suddenly he knew: that was what Jack would come out of hospital to see and own, a VW Beetle. That was why he was here, here in Costa Rica, nearly halfway across the world: it was so he could buy the son he had so nearly murdered a VW Beetle for his seventeenth birthday.

'The only Central American state where they obey the

lights.' Her accent was . . . well, there was American in it, but basically Brixton. 'You from Newcastle? I thought so. Even ordering a coffee in phrase-book Spanish you can hear it.'

They exchanged pleasantries while Zena dug into the huge ice-cream but, Goodall reflected later, her mother was as reticent as he about what she was doing in San José. Resident, tourist, on business? Neither of them – the black girl from Brixton, the ex-SAS man from Wallsend – gave anything away.

'This Week in San José' told Goodall there was a football match that evening, a cup tie: Puerto Limón against San José Atlético, and after a shower and a quick meal in a restaurant close to the Fortuna he decided it would be a better way of passing the time than watching Gala TV in his room.

The modern stadium at the end of Paseo Colón was about three-quarters full. Most of the Puerto Limón team were black, like many of their supporters. They had come up from the Caribbean by bus – the railway their ancestors had built a century ago was destroyed in the 1991 earthquake.

Goodall, who enjoyed football when played well – that is, with cynical exploitation of the rules – sided privately against them. He was not, he believed, racially prejudiced. During his army career he had worked with Gurkhas and Fijians, and had fought and learnt to respect as worthy foes – that is, as serious threats to his own physical well-being – Indonesians and Arabs as well as Argies and Micks. Nevertheless he did feel all these breeds had their place in the order of things, and it was below his. He recognized superiors, but very few: the one or two officers from middle- or upper-class backgrounds who were also good soldiers. Nick Parker was, by reputation, one such.

Goodall would know if the reputation was deserved once they came under fire, but until then he would reserve judgement.

Meanwhile, on the dark terrace, with all eyes fixed on the brilliantly floodlit Astroturf surrounded by advertisements for Mustang jeans, Sinco Cola, Bullburguesas – *burguesas con cojones*, with everyone absorbed in the shifting pattern of play as each side probed the other's skills, Goodall studied the pattern of tropical flowers on the shirt in front of him, the way the black skin on the neck bulged over the collar, the pimples and tight, black curls just visible beneath the narrow brim of the pork-pie hat and picked his spot – the exact pressure point where sudden traumatic force applied with both thumbs would result in immediate unconsciousness and probable death. He estimated his chances of slipping away through the crowd before anyone took in what had happened.

Then one of the Limón players brought down the Atlético striker as he swooped on the ball just outside the penalty box, and pandemonium broke out: car horns, bells, chants, flares, drums – the ideal moment, but half of Goodall's mind was now on the game and he waited to see how the free kick would turn out. His attention was also caught by a vicious jab in the solar plexus delivered by the elbow of an Atlético mid-field player who had got on to the end of the Limón wall. It was skilful, and filled the defender with bile, resentment, a sense of injustice.

Goodall relaxed, aware that the game would not be without interest. The man in front of him shuddered a little and said to his neighbour: 'I just felt footsteps on my grave.'

Could Goodall have done it – brought off a mindless killing just to reassure himself that his old skills remained fine-honed? Yes, certainly he *could* have done it. But *would* he have done it? Maybe. You don't have to be psychopathic to be a trained killer, which was what Goodall was. But it helps. He grinned to himself as the ball curved gracefully into the top corner of the net, the thought crossing his mind that the therapist back at the Wallsend Medical Centre didn't know the half of it – in fact knew piss-all.

8

Geoff Erickson was no psychopath, but he was obsessed, obsessed with Gina Brown and her work, which were, in his mind, one and the same thing. She'd picked his name out of Yellow Pages the day she got the idea of converting the entire downstairs of her tiny east London house into one big studio, fifteen years before. She had been forty-five then and he thirty-two and within forty minutes of his setting foot in the house she had him in bed with her. He'd stayed with her ever since.

Geoff was an oddball. He had got into the Royal College of Art at the age of eighteen to train as a sculptor on the strength of a portfolio of drawings and ten plaster-of-Paris maquettes. Four years later he lost confidence in himself and joined the Army instead. He reached the rank of sergeant and, having transferred to the SAS, did two tours before a viral infection caught while training Aussies in the Papuan jungle nearly killed him and led to his early discharge. Back to his native heath – the Isle of Dogs – and life as a jobbing builder with an old Ford Transit, a set of tools, and a sublime confidence that no job was so big that it couldn't be bodged. Gina's was one of the first he had taken on.

There had not been a lot of sex in his life up to then, and he had had no idea that it could be . . . well, like that. Overwhelming gratitude plus a huge and genuine admiration for her painting – mostly semi-abstract and deriving from natural objects and expressing the powerful life-force that, it seemed to him, surged through her – left him with one burning ambition: to see her recognized, fêted, adored and rewarded as one of the great painters of the twentieth century.

It was an uphill task. Gina was extravagant, painted big, and no gallery would take her on – she was too old already, too much an artist of the sixties. She hardly ever sold a painting, and the canvases already filled a lock-up Geoff had hired underneath railway arches off Mile End Road, and what he made as a builder simply was not enough. So, whenever the opportunity arose, usually in the shape of Gordon Bennett, he returned to soldiering – but, as he put it, as a soldier of fortune trying to make a fortune. When Gina tried to dissuade him he'd always say: 'It's a dirty job, but someone's got to do it.'

Now he swayed to the swing of the Tube train that was carrying him right across London, from Acton Town – where he'd left the eastbound Piccadilly Line from Heathrow – to the heart of the East End.

Not tall, but solidly built, with big bones supporting lean muscle, he had long, straw-coloured hair tied back in a pony-tail, very blue eyes and thickish lips. His complexion was fair but outdoor ruddy beneath a stubble that never seemed to vary much in length. He wore a navy-blue donkey jacket above jeans and the only luggage he had after five weeks in Bosnia was a cheap holdall. In spite of the monotony of an hour on the Tube, the dullness of the few people in the off-peak train, he was glad to be back, and even gladder as the stretches in the open air became more frequent when the line broke away from the City. Aldgate East, Whitechapel – his efforts would be crowned once he had Gina in the Whitechapel Gallery for a couple of months – Stepney Green, and on to Mile End Road. Rain, of course, but at least it wasn't the mean, penetrating snow that had begun to fall above Sarajevo.

He'd travelled a lot one way and another, and had no real taste for it. Left to himself, he'd stay on his own patch, which was a whole world to him and had more foreigners, it seemed to him, mostly Bengalis and Irish, than many places he'd been to abroad. Why go East when a walk north of Commercial Road took you into a bazaar as exotic as anything in Calcutta and without the poverty and dirt?

A pint of Bass in the Horn of Plenty to prove to himself he really was home and a quick call to Gina, although she was only ten minutes' walk away, to give her time to kick out the lovers who moved in while he was away. It was a joke, but he always felt there might be a grain of something there – he felt he hardly deserved to have her all to himself.

'Gina. It's me. I'm back. At the Horn. OK, I'll wait. See you in ten minutes, then. Why? The Serbs could pay but wouldn't. The Muslims would pay but couldn't.'

And he'd seen things the Serbs had done that were worse than anything he'd come across in all his soldiering years and after. Nothing he could do about it, but he didn't have to be part of it, did he? He took a long pull at his beer, relished the clean cool taste, and wondered if he might not have a whisky chaser.

And when Gina came in, looking like a million dollars, as she always did, to Geoff anyway, in spite of her sixty years and the streak of cerulean-blue paint on her cheek, the first thing she said after kissing him warmly and ordering a pint of draught Guinness was:

'Gordon Bennett's been looking for you. Three weeks in Costa Rica, five grand, you lucky sod. And Gordon's cooking on top of it.'

'Gordon Bleu,' said Geoff, relishing an old joke.

*　　*　　*

Gordon Bennett was in a sangar on a Welsh mountainside in icy, driving rain, peering through a Minimodulux lens attached to a Canon SLR camera. Although the dusk was still gathering and the rock-face he was watching was just about visible through the curtaining rain, he would not have been able to work out what was happening without the night-vision attachment.

'They're good,' he said.

'They're bloody good.'

Two lads, eighteen or nineteen years old, and he could see they were solidly built beneath their bright-orange weatherproof anoraks and trousers, abseiled carefully on to a ledge about a metre and a half wide and thirty metres below the crest. The drop below was a further sixty metres to steep scree. On the ledge lay a long bundle simulating someone disabled in a climbing accident.

'But not as good as you,' Bennett added, with regret in his voice.

The big man by his side, heavily bearded with black hair like an upside-down busby, and like him clothed in weatherproofs, grunted in reply.

'Belt up, Bennett. I'm not doing it. Forget it.' The accent was the soft lilt of mid Wales.

'It'll be a laugh, Gareth. A holiday, a themed holiday in one of the world's beauty spots. There are birds there, the feathered sort, like you've never seen . . .'

'Fuck off, Bennett. I know what birds there are in Costa Rica. But I've done Papua and Borneo, and that'll do me for a lifetime.'

'Pacific beaches, seafood, the best rum in the world . . .'

'The seafood's more in your line, isn't it? Now this could be interesting.'

The two lads were now safely on the ledge and were weighing up the options: whether to lower the bundle to the scree below, which would leave them with very awkward terrain in near darkness, or to hoist it up to the ridge, which left a longer but fairly easy walk over grassland and heath.

'Why not, Gareth?'

'Too much to lose. This job, basically. They'd take it away from me if it ever came out I was bunking off to join a mob like yours. And I like this job. A lot.'

Gareth was the director of a tough rehabilitation centre for young offenders.

'They're going for the drop. Good lads. But they'll need the rope that got them there so we'll have to see whether they belayed it properly at the top. They're good lads, Bennett. Take them. They go free this Friday. Be waiting for them at the gates. I'll recommend you. Five grand is just what they need to set them up honestly.'

'But they're not fucking soldiers, Gareth. I need soldiers.'

'They're hard, you know? Manslaughter, they got off with, but although it was a fight, they picked it and knew how it would end.'

'Tell.'

'Three years ago, when they were only sixteen, they took on a crack-dealing mob on their estate. Killed two, the third won't walk again. With iron piping. Now that was neat, neatly done . . .' He meant what they were doing now; not the killings they had planned and committed three years before.

The bundle had begun its slow descent, and one of the lads was abseiling with it, alongside it, carefully ensuring that the 'head' did not bump against the rock-face, while his mate fed the line out from above.

'And they looked after themselves since in some pretty nasty places. Feltham Remand, Strangeways. Just passing through before they came here. Hospitalized a couple of guys when a gang tried to rape them. Give them a support role. They won't let you down.'

'Maybe, maybe. Brothers, are they?'

'Cousins. Bill Ainger and Colin Wintle. Only a couple of months between them. Friday, nine o'clock, the main gate. Be there.'

'Shit, Gareth, I've had enough of this . . . I'll be there, if it's not raining.'

He handed the Minimodulux to a spotty youth on his other side, another of his old friend's 'clients', climbed over the low rocks that formed the sangar, and let himself into one of the three Land Rovers parked behind. There, as the windows steamed up, he reflected that the way things were going they'd be bloody lucky if they had any bodies spare to form a support group and at that moment his mobile phoned burbled.

He fetched it out of the deep pocket of the Barbour Gareth had lent him, and snapped down the tiny mouthpiece.

'Bennett here.'

'Gordon? Jack Glew. Gordon, I've changed my mind. That is, if you still want me.'

'I want you, Jack. But why the change of heart?'

'Some fucking bugger, some fucking bugger . . .' – Jesus, thought Bennett, he's damn-near crying – 'scythed me dahlias and torched me shed, and I'm just so pissed off about it I might kill someone if I stay here . . .'

'Hotel Biarritz, Earls Court, Monday, seven pip emma. Dress for a hot climate. See you.'

That, reflected Bennett, was money well spent. It had cost him a pony, but that's inflation for you. He tapped numbers off on his fingers: yes, with Glew and the two lads he'd pick up on Friday that made fifteen. Enough? Parker thought so. No doubt Finchley-Camden did too, but Parker liked a challenge, a wild fire-fight, surprise and sudden death – not the boring compilation of a safe campaign, ends achieved with minimum or no loss; and F.-C.? No two ways about it, all he was interested in was the loot and the fewer he contracted for the job the more would be left over for him.

Fifteen against fifty rifles? Kalashnikovs in the hands of battle-tried guerrillas? He gave a little shudder as a drop of cold condensation fell from the Land Rover roof between his collar and his neck. Maybe he'd catch flu. Maybe he'd just load the poor buggers on to flights from Heathrow to Miami, and stay at home. Maybe.

9

A taxi was at the door of the Fortuna promptly at nine. Parker clearly expected Goodall to sit in the back with him, but Goodall always preferred to ride in the front. It wasn't a class thing, though he did feel that undermining the master servant relationship between driver and passenger which was implied when you sat in the back was a good thing, but mainly he sat in the front because you get a better view.

This vehicle was older than the one which had brought them from Juan Santamaria airport. The windscreen was curved and split, the upholstery cracked, and the steering-wheel-mounted gear-stick had a Perspex blob on the end out of which a tiny black skull grinned – that is, when the driver, huge and fat, wearing a flat leather hat and with a cigar clamped in his right hand or between his teeth, wasn't wrenching it with his huge paw.

Resplendent in blue and with a sunburst halo, a Virgin, mounted on a short silvered pillar, had been placed above the dashboard and obscured the driver's view of a fair-sized sector of the road in front, but, Goodall reflected, no doubt she's keeping a look out for us even if she is facing the wrong way.

The cabby took them up on to the Paseo Colón and then west along San José's main street. The posh shops gave way to ones less smart, and soon the trees lining the avenue petered out. They crossed a short suburban residential area and then on the outskirts things picked up: first the stadium where he had watched the football the night before, then the Playboy Complex, finally substantial villas set in their own grounds. Beyond these was a small airfield, Tobías Bolaños, where the rich kept their Lear jets and less expensive light planes could be chartered to anywhere in Costa Rica for US$120 an hour.

Franco met them in the foyer of the administrative building and for a moment Parker's heart stood still. Gooodall's did a handstand. Rising from a low-slung seat next to Franco's was a vision, Afrodita O'Donnell González herself. She had changed. Her clothes and hair, that is. Her hair, raven's wings with reddish-gold highlights, was tied back in a scarlet silk scarf. Her olive-dark face had a shiny, unmade-up (apart from bright-orange lipstick) early-morning freshness. She was wearing a scarlet blouse tied above her navel, exposing an inch or so of soft but lean flesh above black designer jeans cropped three or four inches below her knees. Her slippers were gold. Today her perfume was outdoorish, less musky than the day before but just as heady.

'. . . consequently, I have asked Señorita O'Donnell to accompany you as interpreter and also to act as my agent in the event of any dispute. You haven't been listening, have you?'

'No,' Parker admitted. 'Not really.'

Franco sighed.

'There is a large ranch sixteen kilometres from Los Chilos owned by a rich *yanqui*. He has agreed that you should use the old *finca*, the ranch house, as your headquarters: of course we are paying him a huge rental for this facility, you understand? Now, he does not want to be involved, so negotiations and day-to-day requirements will all be handled by his staff, none of whom speak English. So, Deeta will go along with you to act as interpreter and general liaison officer . . .'

'Deeta?'

'Afrodita O'Donnell González. She likes to be addressed as Deeta. By her friends.'

Parker turned to the young woman.

'I am to call you Deeta?' he asked.

'It is easier. My full name is somewhat a mouthful.'

'Then that must mean we're going to be friends.'

He hoped the grin on his face was nearer a smile than a lecherous leer.

'Perhaps,' she shrugged.

Parker pulled himself together and followed Franco, who was already moving to the door marked '*Salidas*', departures.

'And what is our cover to be?'

'As I suggested yesterday, rainforest researchers. Thomas Ford's land has some rainforest still uncleared . . . There is no current licence for felling so there is no question of your being lumberjacks.'

Nevertheless, like lumberjacks, it looks as if we are going to be OK, Parker thought, conscious of Deeta's presence on his left and just behind.

Out on the short, lush grass, beneath a sun suddenly hot, with the airport buildings behind clad in bougainvillaea and some flower that let off a sweet scent of frangipani, and less than twenty kilometres away the craggy, forest-clad slopes and the jagged peaks of Volcán Barva and Volcán Poás towering above them, and this tall, slim goddess beside him – Goodall again felt the buzz of it all. He checked his watch: Thursday again already. They'd be looking for him by now, questioning Mary and the neighbours. Would he ever go back? A pang, a stab even, of longing. Perhaps he'd find a way of staying out here. But if he did, then he'd miss them. Mary and the boys. Any road, he'd see Jack got his Beetle. A shadow fell in front of his feet and he only just ducked beneath the wing strut of a single-engined, bull-nosed DHC Beaver, painted white.

'Stupid limey bastard.'

Goodall swung angrily, but was met with a wide, cheerful smile beaming out of a lean, tanned face beneath short, yellow hair. The speaker wore a beige linen safari suit, and was clearly an Aussie. Certainly the face was not as young as the rest of the figure suggested and Goodall guessed: yes, here's another guy who can't cope with civvy life and clings on to a lousy job because it still uses some of the know-how he learnt flying Harriers and Tornadoes for the RAAF.

'Doug Harvey. Fly me.' He looked at their holdalls. 'No need to open the baggage compartment for those. Stack them behind the seats.'

He led them up the three steps and into the cabin, all but Franco, who turned briskly on his heel and walked back to the terminal with his dove-grey jacket flapping slightly in the warm breeze. A moment of awkwardness: how should they arrange themselves? Who would sit next to Deeta with only a tiny gangway between them? In the event she sat behind but on the other side from Harvey. Parker and Goodall took the two seats behind but with Parker on the opposite side to her, which meant he could see her profile and lean across to chat. Damn it all, he had figured, rank must carry some privileges.

Harvey unclipped an RT unit from the console in front of him, settling headphones over his ears and a tiny mike on a stalk in front of his mouth. He flipped a switch and his voice came to them, slightly amplified.

'We'll be flying at two thousand metres, so pressure and temperature should not be a problem. A mean speed of one-fifty knots should get us there in about an hour. The weather is good and though cloud may begin to build towards the end of the run, we should make it well ahead of the afternoon storms. Coffee and drinks behind you, also a chemical lavvy, which I hope you won't have to use since I have to empty it myself. No smoking. At all. Ever.'

He changed a couple of switches and was cleared for take-off, then pressed the starter button to set the propeller rotating. As they trundled out on to the grass runway Goodall felt a moment of panic. Had he ever flown in such a small plane before? Yes, once, out of Newcastle Airport on a one-hour trip for Jack's tenth birthday. And he had been sick.

The views he had through his window, bigger than on most airliners, soon took his mind off such trivial worries. Once they were clear of the conurbation of San José, Heredia and Alajuela, linked by a network of roads and shanty towns, the long line of the cordillera, ravined and forested, punctuated by the volcanoes, rose to the right. Over to the left a gulf of deep-blue water filled the space between white sand beaches and a peninsula beyond. It was only a backwater but it was the Pacific, all the same. Goodall had never seen it from the eastern rim before. But almost immediately they turned north, leaving the volcanoes behind, crossing the cordillera at its widest and lowest point and just for a moment it was possible to see, according to Harvey, the Pacific and the Atlantic at the same time – but the Pacific was already behind and the Atlantic, a hundred and sixty kilometres to the east, was swallowed in haze.

From now on they followed a road north over an undulating plain. Villages and hamlets clustered near it, fed by minor tracks. There were fields divided into square plots. It wasn't clear what they were growing – sugar cane and bananas perhaps, but more likely maize – and they were raising pigs and chickens too. Then there were larger expanses of pasture with black cattle, tiny like ants, and occasionally stands of secondary forest where the trees had been allowed to grow back. Over to the right, more and more frequently, expanses of virgin forest. Cloud shadow drifted across in uneven shapes, turning emerald and yellow into purple and indigo. Goodall thought of Borneo and Papua, but this was different, flatter, nothing like as mountainous. Would Jack Glew be on board? He hoped so. The silly sod was a bit stupid about rainforest flora and suchlike, but Jack was reliable, no question.

Parker shifted on his buttocks, pushed the forelock off his forehead, leant forward and flashed his quick grin across the tiny gangway. Deeta pretended she hadn't seen it, then relented. The space was too small to do otherwise.

'Coffee? Drink?'

She recrossed her legs, took the thumbnail she'd been nibbling from her mouth, and offered him a totally artificial smile.

'No. Thanks.'

'Coffee, Tim? Beer? G and T?'

'If it's cold I'll have a beer.'

Parker, put in the place of servant to the servants, cursed beneath his breath, took the cap off an Aguilar and ripped back the top of a premixed gin and tonic. Half an hour later the short descent began.

10

The wide circle the Beaver took over the hacienda revealed most of it to them before they touched down. Basically it was a bowl of savannah carved out of rainforest that had covered a low hill. The bottom boundary was a gently meandering stream with stands of maize on the far side which ran for five kilometres roughly north and south. There was a bridge with more fields and a tiny shanty hamlet on the far side, clustering round the north end, and secondary forest – that is, new trees growing where old trees had been cut down twenty years earlier – to the south. The grassland, richly green at the end of the rainy season with tall, bluish, rye-like grass, stretched up to the hill's ridge almost five kilometres from the river at its furthest part. A couple of hundred black cattle, steers for the most part, grazed without enthusiasm: they were quite happy to give eating a rest for long enough to check out the small plane buzzing above them.

There were two groups of buildings. Roughly in the middle, with a corral of crude fencing, stables and related buildings close to it, was a Spanish-style *finca* with white walls and red tiles, rather rambling as though chunks had been stuck on to the original building as afterthoughts over a century or so. And on top of the gentle slope, just below the ridge, and with virgin forest behind it, there was a modern building, long and low, split-level with terraces and a lot of glass that flashed at them in the late morning sunlight. Quite a pad, Parker thought, don't mind if that's where we basha while we're here, especially if Deeta is within easy grasp. However, the more professional side of his brain suddenly became preoccupied with the fact that there was nothing much in the way of an airstrip that he could see.

There was, though, out there in the savannah, a trickle of blue smoke lifting from a fire fed by a peasant in T-shirt and baseball cap worn askew, which might possibly have been arranged to give Doug Harvey an indication of wind direction. A nearby swathe maybe two hundred metres long and three metres wide, cut out of the long grass, was presumably where he was meant to land. The fact that the peasant took off his hat and waved it at them seemed conclusive.

'Crash position, eh, Tim?' said Parker.

But they both leaned into the tiny gangway to get a better view of how Harvey handled the situation: possibly also competing to be the first to come to Deeta's aid should the plane turn over, lose a wheel, or stick its nose in the ground.

Again Goodall felt the buzz, and this time with an added jigger of adrenalin, especially when, at about six metres off the ground and with fifteen metres to go, Harvey throttled back to what should have been stalling speed. But the plane sank more gently than that, the tail held up as Harvey knew it would, and what was now almost a glide also held until the wheels touched, bumped, rose again, rumbled, bumped, slewed a bit, the tail sank and the Beaver finally came to rest.

'Friends all, that is what I call flying,' said Harvey. 'You don't get the fun of that putting a Harrier on the deck.'

'Nice one,' Parker remarked, again flicking the lock of hair off a forehead now slightly damp. 'But will you be able to get her in the air again?'

'Bloody hope so. Great STOL ability this old crate has.'

The Australian glanced at his watch. 'Got a couple of elderly Yanks meeting me at San José at six pip emma, expecting me to taxi them down to Puntarenas for the cocktail hour, so pardon me if I ask you to shift your rosy cheeks . . .'

Not even on *Neighbours*, Goodall thought, do Ozzies talk like that.

And sure enough, as soon as they'd got their bags out, as well as their arses, Harvey asked them to help him slew the plane round so that it was facing the other way. Deeta lent a hand lifting the tail unit with Parker, and as she stooped beside him he saw for a second, through the gap in her scarlet blouse, naked breasts, firm and brown-nippled. He also saw her pectorals flex and realized that she was fit – not just fashionably fit or healthily fit, but seriously fit. Probably she could have done the job on her own. But then, he thought, so could I.

Harvey thanked them, shook hands briefly, then thrust a card into Parker's hand before climbing back into the plane.

'There you are, sport. Any time you need wings, phone that number.'

The Beaver trundled for a moment, the engine roared, almost screamed, Harvey held her on the wheel brakes, let them go, and the plane shot forward and lifted to clear the tall grass at the end of the apology for a runway with less than a metre to spare below the fixed undercarriage. He left behind him a rapidly dispersing cloud of orange dust, swirling grass, and the smell of not completely combusted high-octane fuel. He came back above them, wiggled his wing-tips, and roared away.

'Well,' said Parker, 'there's a guy who knows what he's doing. Now what? I mean like where's the welcome?'

'We have to use the old *finca*,' Deeta said.

'Not the jolly place at the top of the hill?'

'No.'

'OK, then. Lead the way.'

Which was silly since the way was obvious enough: three hundred metres or so of tall grass lay between them and the red tiles that showed above it. But at least that way he was following her, following those trim buttocks in the tight jeans, those shapely calves, and, oh, them golden slippers. Behind Parker came Goodall. And Goodall was thinking, and said so, that it was disgusting the way his CO was behaving like a mongrel dog tracking a fancy bitch on heat.

Meanwhile, large and very nasty-looking flies gave up buzzing the steers and homed in on them instead. The stench of cattle, not unpleasant in itself, unless in concentrations as thick as these, thickened around them, and the sun suddenly seemed very hot, even though it was now intermittent through gathering storm clouds. Thunder rumbled, and a spot or two of heavy rain splashed on Goodall's shoulder – like a Tyneside scufter was feeling his collar – but the proper rain held off for at least another two hours.

There were corrals round the *finca*, and three more farmworkers leant on them chewing grass stalks with more interest than the steers managed; then what was obviously a clapboard bunk cum cookhouse with a stove-pipe chimney. Next, quite grand stabling with bits of wrought iron here and there and some tired tropical begonias in a flower-bed in the middle and a stable clock with flaking gold leaf on black on the tiny tower, which gave the whole thing rather a Home Counties look. Six of the boxes were in use – three with quite useful-looking but small palominos, three with glossy, robust mules – and there were a couple of small grey donkeys tethered in a shady corner next to a small blue Ford tractor. It all looked a touch sleepy, but used, working.

Not so the ranch house itself. They rounded a corner out of the stable yard and came on to the part-terrace, part-veranda that looked down the slope towards the stream. All the windows were shuttered and the shutters bolted on the inside. Paint was flaking, the paving was cracked, and the wrought iron that supported the canopy over the veranda part was rusty. In the centre, flanking steps that led up to a double door of silvery timber, were two ornamental terracotta urns filled with the dead stalks of pelargoniums, reaching like brown, skeletal arms begging for water. Deeta lifted one of them with apparent ease.

'There should be a key there.'

There was. Goodall picked it up and with only a slight grunt of relief Deeta replaced the urn. Parker held out his hand for the key, but bugger that, Goodall thought, and opened the doors himself. The key was rusty but the lock had been freshly oiled, perhaps in anticipation of their arrival. If that was the case it was the only preparation that had been made.

They moved through the ten or so rooms, mostly large, throwing open shutters. The windows were not glazed and probably never had been. Dust rose round their feet. There was no furniture, not a stick, no pictures or ornaments. The only signs of life were the geckoes which hung around the shutters waiting for unsuspecting flies to alight on the sun-warmed wood, and the remains of a nest with dead chicks in a fireplace that filled half one wall of the largest room.

Sawn pipes and wrenched fittings showed where basins, a bath or two, and toilets had been, but the only tap that had been left stuck out of a wall in what might have been a kitchen; it was, of course, dry. Goodall flicked a couple of brass switches set in old porcelain fittings by the doorways, and again, nothing.

They came back to the main door.

'Well, sod this for a lark,' Parker growled. He turned to Deeta. 'You'd better get up to the other place and tell the landlord, Ford, whatever his name is, we want something to sleep on, food, main services reconnected – in short, the whole place made habitable.'

Her eyes narrowed, a frown ploughing a swift furrow between them.

'Señor Ford is American. You don't need me to interpret. You tell him if you like. But he will be very angry if you do. The chief condition of our tenancy, apart from the very high rent, is that none of us go any nearer than where we are to his house, and that we never see let alone speak to him.'

Outside, the whining grumble of a lightweight jeep, apparently coming down the hill, reached their ears.

'Sod that,' Parker repeated, even more angry now. 'I don't know the full details of the bargain your lot struck with him, but I imagine they included provision of the minimum in the way of civilized living . . .' He strode through the door.

Two men sat in the back of the jeep, their feet hanging over the lowered tailgate. They wore combat fatigues, red bandannas, and looked, to Goodall's eye, just the way Latin American bad guys should look. The impression was confirmed by the way one of them spat in the dust before both pulled back the bolts on their old but almost certainly very serviceable Garand M1s: eight-shot automatics; the first automatic rifles ever put into regular service.

11

Matt Dobson liked his job, moving the engines of death about a troubled globe. It was, he often reflected, the perfect market – for the entrepreneur, that is, the thrusting middleman, for whereas providing a customer with a commodity usually satisfies a need, which means that that corner of the market is at least temporarily satisfied and closed, selling arms creates a need. You buy arms to defend yourself against an aggressor, or possibly to deter him. You buy arms because you yourself aspire to be an aggressor. Often you buy arms for no other reason than to create an impression, demonstrate to those around you that you have more clout, more standing in the world than your neighbours. But no matter what the reason, these or any other, you create a need: your neighbour, your rival, your enemy is going to want to buy arms simply because you have.

The result is that the richest nations equip and re-equip themselves with ever more sophisticated hardware and software, thus making redundant all the old-hat stuff. So there is always plenty lying around waiting to be sold on to satisfy, for a very short time, the insatiable appetites of the rich but not richest, and so on, right down the pecking order of nations. And below them and beyond the pale there are the freedom fighters, the terrorists, the criminals. Not that Dobson ever sold or bought on their behalf but he was aware of their existence and how they kept the whole business moving.

Private armies like Finchley-Camden's were about as low as he went.

Of course, a front has to be put up, a system of hypocritical codes, standards, guidelines, laws even, to control the constant rush of weaponry to and fro across seas and frontiers, and institutions from the United Nations down do everything they can to suggest that all this evil trade is being conducted or at any rate monitored in the best possible way in this best of all possible worlds. But a trade declared illicit, or even merely unsavoury, will immediately spawn the unscrupulous, the shady, even the downright wicked, who, for huge profits, will supply what is needed where it is needed: in arms just as with drugs. The difference is that while, say, Iran or Indonesia will be very beastly indeed to anyone caught trafficking drugs, they welcome the arms dealer into the divans and inner sanctums of the mightiest in the land.

All of which gave Dobson great satisfaction, and was on the way to making him a very rich man indeed. But there was another, darker side to the whole business – at least as far as he was concerned.

His mother had looked to be not only the next leader of the Tories, but the saviour of a party which had nothing to lose since after nineteen years in government it had lost almost everything it had. And then along came Mrs Dobson: a fat, large lady, with a Yorkshire accent she would have died rather than lose, though in fact she had lost it once, after just one year at Cambridge University, and had had to have elocution lessons to get it back. In the late eighties she was a junior minister at the DTI. By the mid nineties she was Chancellor of the Exchequer after the podgy incumbent of that post had risen to be PM. And he had turned out to be as weak as his predecessor, so she was in line to succeed him as soon as he lost the imminent election. It was 1975 all over again. Another Thatcher loomed. Nothing for it but for the nobs in the party to organize catastrophe, nemesis. An Official Inquiry had cast only the vaguest aspersions on her conduct when at the DTI nearly ten years before, but they had been enough for the PM, anxious not to feel her dagger in his back, to demand Mrs Dodson's resignation from the Chancellorship.

It was, she said, and of course her son agreed with her, a plot put up by the Aristos, the Old Guard, the Good and the Great, to make sure that a glory or fiasco (depending where you stood) like the Thatcher Years should not occur again.

Which meant that Matt Dobson bore a grudge: a big, heavy grudge against anyone who belonged to that seemingly unshiftable gang of upper-class shits who have had our country in thrall ever since their ancestors, the landlords of Britain, got seriously wealthy from their West Indian sugar estates, worked by slaves, in the eighteenth century. And Colonel Dickie Finchley-Camden was one of them. F.-C. was related to the duke of this, the earl of that, of course, and at least one of the Chiefs of Staff. Screwing him as well as making a few hundred thousand would give Dobson all the rich satisfaction that his ancestors had had poaching salmon in the Yorkshire Dales a century or more before. And of course he was much aided in this by his beloved mother, a single parent when he had been born, though that was something only the Murdoch papers knew about and had sat on until it was too late to be useful. Albeit ousted, she had still accumulated a lot of dirt, a lot of connections, and had many favours to call in, all of which helped him a lot. It took him a mere fortnight to get together the items on Finchley-Camden's shopping list – that is, to arrange their leasing and their disposal in sealed containers around the eastern rim of the Atlantic, in the bonded warehouses of three 'free' ports:

Gibraltar, Tangiers and Las Palmas. What he needed now was to get them to Puerto Limón, on the Caribbean coast of Costa Rica – the port of destination designated by Finchley-Camden. But he also needed someone who would be prepared to make a small effort to find out where they were to be moved on to after that. He knew just the man: Henry Wallace, a semi-retired ship-broker. He'd fix the enshipment but with a sweetener might be able to find out who the Puerto Limón agent was acting for. Dobson called him and offered lunch.

'Have to be Thursday, old boy. Wednesday and Thursday are my only days in any more, and I'm booked Wednesday,' said Wallace.

Dobson remembered that Wallace didn't really need to work at all – at the top of the City dung-heap that deals with shipping, he only really needed to broke a couple of giant tankers a year to make a very decent living indeed. But he still came in – to keep in touch, and, on Wednesdays, to visit a four-storey boarding house in Spitalfields where very young girls and boys acted out scenes from the *Kama Sutra*, and, if the money was right, invited audience participation.

So it was on a Thursday that Dobson took a taxi down Lombard Street, through sheeting rain, past ranks of thrusting, whirling black umbrellas, paid off the cab, deaf to the cabby's abuse about the size of his tip, and threaded his way through a brief warren of alleys and yards to Simpson's. Not his favourite lunching place at the best of times, it seemed more awful than usual: the vinegary smells of old beer and old wine, grilled meat, baked onions, were even further soured with that of heavily soaked serge; the crowd, red-faced and raucous, even more dense than usual, storm-driven into a log-jam four deep behind the bars. The loud, braying voices of the City's Brat Pack could be dismissed but not shut out.

It was not the chauvinism of the banter, nor its banality, that got to Dobson. It was the infantile element. He felt he wanted to bang their heads together, show these silly pups that there was a real world out there. It was a relief when Wallace appeared at the far end of the tiny bar.

Once tall, now stooped as if the weight of wool on his back was too much, like chain-mail on an ancient horse-soldier, his eyes hidden by drooping eyelids and his nose pitted like a strawberry, Wallace waved at him in the vexed way lollipop ladies use at school crossings. Dobson briefly gripped a leaden white hand, getting rid of it as soon as he could. They pushed their way through the bars to the dark-brown narrow tables and benches in the dining area.

'Stick to what they do best, shall we? Loin chops. Braised onions. Bubble and squeak. House red.' The waitress, Irish-cockney, was brisk and jolly, there before they had even sat down, treating Wallace like an old but favoured cocker spaniel. 'Count the City lunches on one hand I've had anywhere else. Cheap, you see. Quality too. And old. That's good. I like old things. See those racks?' He pointed up to ancient cradles of wood above their heads. 'They're for top-hats.'

They folded their coats on to the racks and squeezed on to the narrow benches at the end of an already overburdened table. They got down to business at once.

'Got just the job for you,' said Wallace. 'GC coaster out of Gib, calling at Tangiers, will take those two containers – cubes, aren't they? – on to Las Palmas. Then all three on a smart new fast reefer with spare deck-room, actual first port of call Puerto Limón. Be there by 23 October. Couldn't be better.'

Dobson recalled that 'GC' was a general cargo boat, probably in this case not much more than a coaster trundling between the Canaries, North Africa and Spain.

A 'reefer' meant refrigerated — from deep-frozen to chilled for fruit. It was likely to be half or more empty going into the Caribbean, would come out with coffee kept chilled to keep the flavour, slowly ripening bananas and pineapples, beef, fish, shellfish and so on.

'All routine so far, except that I don't for one moment believe the manifests saying gear for forest research, but that's your business not mine, eh?' Wallace tapped the side of his strawberry nose with a wedge-shaped finger, then sawed away at the big brown onion on his plate. 'So why the free lunch?'

'They're booked to a Puerto Limón agent. I want to know who he's acting for.'

'Bloody hard to find out for sure without going there. But if you'll come round to the office with me when we're finished here I think I might be able to come up with a pretty sound pointer . . .'

Pleased that the lunch really was just about free for once, Wallace made a meal of it: apple pie with clotted cream, overripe port-fed Stilton, and two more bottles of house red — which had turned out to be a sound Rioja. The restaurant was virtually empty by the time they left, and the rain had stopped.

Wallace's office was no more than three minutes' walk away but within that distance he contrived to slip three times on the wet pavements, and Dobson had to grab his shoulders and steady him. He discovered that the old ship-broker was even heavier than he looked. Puffing and wheezing, he pushed Dobson through the door of a ground-floor office, just the three rooms but large and spacious, on the ground floor of Plantation House. There was only one secretary, a middle-aged and unattractive woman who strove to keep up appearances by doing her nails in front of a large screen. Market shifts across the world scrolled down in front of her.

'Anything doing, Doris?'

'No, dear. Been very quiet these last three weeks. Chunnel's dropped a packet but not enough yet.'

Wallace went to his desk, pushed about in the in-tray and came up with a sheaf of fax paper. He folded out bifocals and perched them precariously across the huge swollen nose as his cracked thumbnail tracked down a list.

'Here we are, then. Puerto Limón. Dock C, Wharf Six. That's where your three containers get offloaded. Now let me see . . .'

He stumbled over to a bookcase filled with big volumes bound in black leatherette.

'I ought to keep these updated, but I do so little now it doesn't seem worth the expense . . . and anyway you'd be surprised how rarely things change.'

It took him some time to find the right volume, but at last he looked up and over the spectacles.

'Here we are. If things ain't altered in three years, and I doubt they have, that wharf is reserved entirely for the operations of Associated Foods International. Now I wonder why a bloody great firm like AFI should want to import the sort of thing you trade in into Costa Rica. Don't make a lot of sense really, do it? Unless they're planning a coup.'

'Thanks, Henry.' And Dobson went, suddenly bored and angry with the bumbling stupidity of the British upper classes who had brought low his mother, and Mrs Thatcher before her. And the whole bloody country come to that.

12

'I'll take the one on the left, sir, if you'll take the one on the right,' said Goodall.

'Why not?' answered Parker.

Deeta shifted from one foot to the other, and put her deep-orange thumbnail between her teeth again.

They couldn't shoot, and knew they couldn't shoot. Goodhall and Parker knew they knew they couldn't shoot. Only as a last resort. At the worst they would use the Garands as clubs, given the chance. They were just bullies, bullies whose status was conferred on them by the rifles, by their fancy dress, by the jeep. And certainly not by training: Costa Rica is one of the very few countries in the world with no standing army at all, and even the Rural Guard are famed for shooting off their toes on the rare occasions they feel a need to draw their tiny pistols.

So as Goodall began his lightning strike his man's instinctive reply was not to level the rifle and pull the trigger, but to raise it vertically, both in defence and to strike out with it. Goodall's first kick smashed the knuckles clenched round the stock, his second, coming in a karate-style roundhouse, smashed into the man's side in the gap between his pelvic girdle and his ribcage. The rifle flailed in the air and thumped the head of his companion. Goodall caught his loose right arm and with the sort of flap you give a heavy mat to get the dust out dislocated it at the shoulder. In this sort of fight Goodall never, ever used his fists: bruised knuckles could be a liability later, a sprained wrist an immediate danger.

Parker, retaining habits learnt at a savage public school and then Sandhurst, did use his fists, as well as his boots, but SAS training had put a gloss on the Marquess of Queensberry's rules – he went for the soft parts, particularly the jugular in his victim's neck, and then as his victim's diaphragm relaxed with the first blow, he hit him very hard just above his navel. Then he clenched fists to deliver a raking double uppercut through chin, lips and nose. It was at this point that the other man's rifle butt made contact.

While Goodall tidied two pairs of legs into the back of the jeep and fastened the tailgate behind them, Parker picked up the rifles and carried them on to the veranda. He carefully uncocked the first, and pulled back the bolt, expecting it to eject the round the cocking action had fed into the breech. Nothing. He turned the gun over. The Garand magazine holds only eight rounds and fits flush with the furniture in front of the trigger. There was a black, empty slit where it should have been.

'Oh dear, oh dear,' he said, and then louder so that Goodall could hear him above the whimpers of the one with the dislocated shoulder, 'the guns weren't armed. Empty as a bottle of Jameson's on 18 March.'

Goodall laughed, stretched his clenched fists above his head against the bruise-coloured sky. His grin stretched from ear to ear.

Parker turned back to Deeta.

'Where were they coming from, then?'

'It's illegal in Costa Rica to carry weapons off private property. So they must have come from up there.' She tossed her hair in the direction of the modern *finca* on the hill above them.

'Yes. I reckoned so. Come on, trooper, You can drive

me up there. Time to pay a call on Nob Hill.' He turned back to Deeta. 'You needn't come. Since you were told not to and Mr Ford speaks English.'

'Oh, I'll come. I don't fancy being left here on my own.'

Goodall climbed on to the driving end of the bench, while Parker let Deeta into the middle and squeezed up alongside her. No way was there room for his left arm unless he put it round her shoulders. She didn't flinch, but then she didn't give either. He felt her thigh suddenly warm against his. She looked back, behind her.

'Did you have to hurt them that much?' she asked.

In all his Army career Goodall had never before driven a real World War Two General Purpose Vehicle. The reality of the jeep's gear-stick, the big steering wheel, the metal plates for pedals almost like a fairground vehicle, the memories of all those war films, James Stewart, John Wayne, even through to Hawkeye in *M.A.S.H.* – and after a very noisy moment or two some back-of-the-mind memory told him how to double-declutch – it all added up to a small boy's dreams come true.

He was on a high, an adrenalin high. He knew it, and he knew why. It was all very well Deeta asking if they had had to hurt these poor guys in the back that much: when he launched his first kick it had been a calculated risk – the guns were loaded. Why cock them otherwise? Unarmed, faced with a guy toting an automatic capable of putting eight rounds in your stomach with one pull on the trigger, you go for it. You don't mess about. If you've got the adrenalin, you go for it.

In ten minutes, maybe five, he'd come down like a lead balloon. And that's when he'd need alcohol. Serious alcohol. Otherwise it would be deep, deep depression – like when he beat up Jack. And that time he'd kept off the drink and suffered for it too. But that had been different.

'Rum? With coke? Rum punch? Daiquiri?'
  'Just rum.'
  'This is original strength. I guess you know that?'
  Shit, thought Goodall.
  'Ice?'
  'Ice.'
Thomas Ford looked round them, over them, tried to take them in, make sense of them. He saw a beautiful, tall, fit spic lady whose accent when she spoke American suggested Miami-Cuban, though apparently she worked for Bullburger. He saw a lean, medium-height, dark-haired guy with a sloppy grin and a sloppy haircut, though his dark eyes were evil, who spoke like one of those limey actors who keep winning Oscars. He saw a tall, heavily built Viking, red hair, freckles and all, who had almost pulled one of his minder's arms off. He saw trouble.

Ford, fat and ill, what hair he had left crew-cut, in Lacoste T-shirt above Bermuda shorts printed with day-glo sharks, varicose veins and slip-on sandals, sipped from a bottle that said Perrier, turned from the bar and handed Goodall his neat rum on the rocks. Outside thunder growled and then pounced, shattering the stillness of his glassed-in veranda. Rain banged on the sloping glass roof like machine-gun fire.

'I guess we've got another week or two, then we can forget the rain for six months. So, what are you guys here for?'

Parker shifted in a deep cane chair that squeaked then grumbled beneath him. It had a high, shield-shaped back woven in fancy patterns.

'Proper facilities down at the old *finca* that has been rented for us . . .'

'No. I mean, what's the purpose behind your visit? What are you all here for?'

Parker gave his daiquiri a shake, mixing the citrus in with the crushed ice and the rum, and said: 'I want bedding for the three of us . . .' – he glanced at Deeta – 'sleeping bags will do, proper cooking facilities, some food and drink for tonight. We'll go down to the village tomorrow . . . I suppose there is a shop there?'

'A Spar.'

'Fine. I asked Franco up at San José for a four-by-four and I suppose that's what your men were delivering, so we'll keep it. And we want to feel free to use your forest, over to the north, without interference or spying.' He paused, shrugged, and put some steel into his voice. 'Come on. You know what I want. I want what you've been paid for.'

The American thought for a moment, remembering what they had done to two of his own private army.

'You got it,' he said. He'd wait, hang on in, but meanwhile: 'You got it.' He took another pull at the Perrier bottle, and posed with the top just below his pendulous lip.

'But did you have to be so mean with my two boys?'

'They cocked their guns at us. Not friendly.'

'They were fooling, they're jokers, that's all.'

Parker shrugged.

'We weren't to know that. Where we come from we take no chances with guys with guns. Not even stupid guys. Especially not stupid ones.'

'And where's that? Where's that you come from?'

Parker stood and finished his drink. Deeta and Goodall hurriedly did likewise. Clearly the interview, the meeting, whatever it was, was almost over. Parker gave the fat American his most evil grin.

'England,' he said. 'That's where we're coming from.'

13

Deeta was deeply surprised at the way both Parker and Goodall buckled down to sweeping out three of the rooms, laying a fire – for the old *finca* was damp and cold by nightfall at the end of the rainy season – and cooking a passable meal out of what Ford had given them, but she kept her surprise to herself. She knew from experience that if she had been sharing the same circumstances with US Green Berets a broom would have been thrust into her hands and she would have been told to get on with it.

She lent a hand, but kept herself away from any physical contact with them: she had sensed the charge she produced in both of them in the proximity of the jeep; she had seen how they had no inhibitions about wreaking violence on anyone who got in their way; and she did not want to send out ambiguous signals.

Not that she didn't fancy them, especially Goodall, who was big: but if, when, something happened she wanted it to be on her terms and not a mistake, and certainly not a rape.

When the meal was ready, fried pork chops, sweet potatoes, a salad of tomatoes beefed up with chopped green chillies, they took it out on to the veranda. By then the rain had stopped, the thunder receding into the mountains to the west. The tropical heat came back though the sun was already sinking towards the hill behind them: the ranch was far closer to sea level than

San José, though it was thirty kilometres from one ocean and twice as far from the other. Mist gathered in the shallow gullies but lay especially thick above the small river in front of them. The black steers moved through it like slow porpoises in cloudy water, occasionally looming up beneath them to eye them with big, brown eyes above mouths that munched the grass that fattened them up for Bullburgers with Balls. Which, Goodall remarked, was odd, in fact false representation under the Trade Description Act since each and every one of them had had its balls removed.

Deeta failed to understand his Tyneside accent and Parker had to laboriously explain the whole joke, if it was a joke, and actually went a little pink as he did so.

'Balls, you know? They've been castrated so they have no balls, *cojones*, know what I mean? But the ads, the advertisements, say . . .'

He turned to Goodall, who was now beginning to heave with silent laughter.

'Drop me in shit like this again,' Parker growled, 'and I'll pull yours off.'

For a moment Deeta warmed to their schoolboy vulnerability, and they all felt a little safer, a touch more relaxed.

'So, to quote the man himself, where's this Ford coming from?' Parker asked.

Deeta shifted her jeaned buttocks on one of the three folding director's chairs they had brought back from the modern ranch house with the other gear and the supplies Ford had had loaded into the back of the jeep, and said: 'He was one of the first American ranchers out here. There was already a beef farm on the site but about a quarter the size of what it is now, and this *finca*' – she waved her fork around her head – 'was the farmhouse. The story goes Ford won it off the Tico owner at a poker game in the Union Club, a smart venue in San José.'

She chewed for a moment and then swallowed.

'Later, when beef got to be big here, he signed an agreement with our rivals, Macburgers, to sell all his beef on to them. They laid out quite a lot of money in bureaucratic circles, Ministry of This, Ministry of That' − she rubbed her forefinger against her thumb − 'you know what I mean, they got government permission for him to clear more forest, three times what had already gone. He got rich, built the pad on the hill . . .'

'And then?'

'He got greedy. People like that do. He let the land be used by El Pastor, a Nicaraguan Contra, who was training up rebels to invade Nicaragua across the San Juan, and he took CIA money. They say he also let CIA planes use the airstrip for moving drugs, coke out of Colombia and so on. Part of a CIA plot to make the world think the Sandinistas were trading in angel dust. But he wouldn't work with the Contras in the north, and quite quickly ceased to be flavour of the month with the CIA. Who may or may not have arranged for a bomb to go off, giving El Pastor a fright, but killing a couple of journalists who were trying to interview him. That led to a lot of bad publicity which Macburger got caught up in. Next time round they failed to take up their option on his beef and he's been going to market ever since to sell it, on the open market, undercut by the local peasant producers, who are happy to take much less . . .'

'I get it. He wants a contract with Bullburger. So he's letting us use his land . . .'

'Yes. But maybe we won't give him a contract. After

all, we are also paying him to do this for you.'

'Does he know why we're here?'

'No. But perhaps he guesses . . .'

'Do you? Do you know why we are here?'

She smoothed a finger across her lips, put her plate, almost empty but she had left some sweet potato, on the floor. Parker wondered: did she mean him to see that far down inside her shirt when she did so? She straightened, looked out over the gloaming.

'I have not been told either, but, like Ford, I can guess. You, with the men who are coming out to join you, will destroy the research station on the other side of the river, in Nicaragua. It was done before, but not properly. You will do it properly. Yes?'

Parker said nothing. It had all been a touch too flip, a touch too easy. He sensed that she was not guessing, that she knew. But possibly not because Franco or anyone at Bullburger had told her, but someone else – higher up the chain of command? And where did that go? Far beyond Bullburger, that was for sure. They were biggish, he reckoned, drawing on his City expertise, but not that big. He recollected imperfectly something he'd seen on the big glass street door to the company's main office: 'A Member of the AFI Group', something like that. But the 'I' an upright corn-cob, making it a logo. Later it could be something he might have to remember, take account of.

If Parker, in his City role, had traded commodities like coffee, cocoa, maize or grain, instead of metals, he would have known very well who AFI was, and just how big.

Goodall too assumed that Deeta knew more about it than they did.

'So what have they got in them greenhouses? Cannabis? Coca? Definitely it ain't the maize they're growing all over the plantations all around.'

'But those have to be torched like everything else. Especially those,' replied Parker.

'Why?'

'Tim, ours not to reason why . . .'

'Ours but to do or die, like?'

'Or, more hopefully, take the money and run.'

'What do you think, hinny?'

'Hinny?'

'Never mind his funny English.'

They were all getting a touch laid-back on the rum and Cokes they were drinking.

'What do you think, Deeta? What's this all about?' asked Parker.

'I don't know any more than you do.' She stood, pushed her palms down her thighs. 'That was very nice. I enjoyed it. You got it, so I'll wash up.'

'Ah, but just wait till our mucker Gordon Bennett joins us. He really knows how to cook. I'll give you a hand.'

Parker stepped down into the meadow, flipped out a Dunhill, flashed a small gold Zippo at it, inhaled, and looked back up the hill. A sliver of silver moon lay on its back above the crest. Beneath it Ford's smart pad glowed with the electric light they still lacked. The distant purr of a diesel generator disclosed its source. He breathed in smoke, turned into the meadow, said boo to a steer, which backed off promptly, scraping its hooves in the grass before turning and trotting away.

This, Parker said to himself, is not straightforward. But then it never is. Someone up there – he looked up at the now clear sky, Milky Way and all, which, like the moon, was oddly angled in these latitudes – knows what's going on, and someone down here does too. Buggered if I do. But I wish I did.

In the kitchen Deeta too had puzzles to contend with. That these . . . thugs, who could tear men apart, not only swept floors, cooked meals but were ready to help with the washing-up too. She ran cold water from the tap and added it to the boiling water from a pan Goodall had had the foresight to leave on the fire.

'So,' she asked, 'who is this . . . what did you call him? Gordon?'

'Gordon Bennett. Fucking good cook.' Goodall looked around for a drying-up cloth, but there wasn't one. 'We'll just have to leave them to drain. Gordon Bleu, we call him, like Cordon Bleu, get it?'

14

Next day, at nine p.m., UK time, Gordon Bennett welcomed the last of his recruits into a private lounge next to the bar in the Hotel Biarritz, Earls Court. Fourteen of them now, spread across the chairs and sofas, holdalls and kitbags strewn around them, all, almost to a man, with pints of ale or strong lager in straight glasses in their fists. They were already talking louder than they should, swapping reminiscences, catching up on one another's lives, or, if they had not met before, comparing notes about stations they had been on though at different times.

The last to arrive were the Strachan twins, Mick and Jamie, from Liverpool. They were already half-cut, having drunk the InterCity buffet car's whole stock of McEwan's Export.

'Eee-aye-addio, what a fucking load of shit,' sang Jamie as they stood in the doorway and chanted as if at a rival football team. Big men, with straw-coloured hair and red faces, Liverpool-Irish but the Irish a long way back, they rolled into the room, rumpled hair here, thumped a shoulder there.

'Gordon Bennett, our Mick, look who's here, if it isn't Gordon Bennett himself, the fucking old archbishop.'

It was a nickname that went way back and referred to Bennett's sour, withdrawn manner and the pontifical way he had had with new boys during SAS weapons training in Bradford Lines at Hereford, later renamed Stirling Lines.

'All right, lads. Get yourselves a drink at the bar, on the gaffer, and then settle down,' said Bennett.

'Who *is* the fucking gaffer, I'd like to know?' someone bawled out.

'As far as you're concerned, the gaffer's me till we get out there, then it's Mr Parker.' Bennett stood, looked them over and remembered Wellington's words in similar circumstances in Spain in 1809: 'I don't know what effect these men will have upon the enemy, but by God, they terrify me.'

There was Geoff Erickson with his pony-tail and a heart still dicky from the bug he'd caught in Papua; Winston Smith, randy as ever, communicating with lewd gestures the history of his latest conquest. He ended the story by putting out his tongue, giving it a Gazza wiggle, and then placing the tip just on the septum of his black nose. Bennett hardly had to lip-read to guess what he was saying: 'It's all on account of me long dick, know what I mean?'

Round Smith were sat three West Country lads Bennett had rescued from turnip bashing near Dorchester: Mike Henchard, John Crick, and Alfred Stevens. They were glued to Smith's every word, scarcely concealing how impressed they were with his citified street cred. They were a bit of an unknown factor – not long honourably discharged from their units, they were on their first stint as mercenaries.

Behind them Jack Glew, the quietest of the bunch, still nursed the Burton's he'd had all evening. He was still mourning his lost dahlias: not a lot of fire in his belly now, Bennett reckoned, but dead reliable in a crunch situation.

He shifted, took in the other sector. This could be the Wild Bunch, he thought: the Strachan twins and the two cousins from the Welsh rehabilitation centre. It turned out they were Brummies, Bill Ainger and Colin Wintle, and though they were the youngest there by ten years, they looked hard, maybe even hard enough. Lean, dark, wiry like whippets, their movements were sharp and quick, and they said little. If they were impressed by the hardened veterans all around them, they had clearly decided not to show it. They had not drunk much, just half a pint more than old Glew, and they were alert, watchful. The problem was, they were not soldiers. They had killed, and that was a lot, for if you've done it once you can do it again. They had killed on purpose, knowing what they were doing. But they were not soldiers. And no one, not even Gordon Bennett, could turn young men, however ready for it they might be, into soldiers in two weeks.

Were any of them soldiers now? How much had they lost in Civvy Street? Team spirit might return quite quickly – they had all after all, apart from the Brummie cousins and the four foreigners, served in 22 SAS. But could they regain the habit of obedience, of instant, unquestioning, uncalculating response to an order given not necessarily by someone with rank, but simply by somebody who knew a bit more, was better placed to make a decision than they were? It could be a forward guy in an observation post, or someone who had been on the patch only half an hour longer than they had. Could they still do that?

At least the last four, though not Brits, were soldiers, through and through. Two Gurkhas he'd been lucky enough to pick up on his way back from Dorchester. He'd stopped off at Blandford Camp to say hello to an old acquaintance and learnt that they had just finished a tour of guard-room duty with the Royal Signals before being returned to their original unit. It had been their last job before being flown back to Nepal, and their residence permits expired the very next day with the end of their signing-off leave.

They had already been christened Bill and Ben, the Flowerpot Men: smaller even than the Walshes, seemingly carved out of teak, with smiling, flat, olive-skinned faces and slightly oriental eyes, they knew soldiering English, no more, but they knew soldiering. It was not just in their blood – it *was* their blood. Bennett wondered if the old stories were true: that they weren't admitted to the Gurkhas until they had demonstrated their ability to decapitate a goat at twenty yards with a kukri. If they could, he'd do an open-spit roast for the whole squadron when they got there . . . stuffed with tropical spices and maybe yams.

And finally, through a contact who had retired to Marbella, Toñi, but introduced as Tony, Montalbán, and Julián Sánchez, both just out of the Spanish Foreign Legion, skipping bail on charges of taking a Torremolinos bar to pieces when the owner had tried to close it at three in the morning. Bennett reckoned they'd be useful soldiers, for he had a lot of respect for the Spanish Foreign Legion, which was less foreign than its French counterpart and had recently been involved in real fighting. The King of Morocco used them against Polisario, the nomads in the south-west Sahara who continued to resist Spain's secession of the Spanish Sahara to the Kingdom of Morocco. Bennett also reckoned it might be no bad thing if there were at least two Spanish speakers on board for an operation out of Costa Rica and into Nicaragua.

'Right, lads. Bit of hush, please.'

He'd worked at this over the years, getting just the right amount of steel in his voice to bring a rowdy meeting like this to order, without appearing to hector or shout or pull rank. Yet the silence did not fall quite as quickly as he would have liked and Mick Strachan finished what he was saying, something very nasty about Ian Wright, the Arsenal striker, just so Winston Smith could hear him.

Then Strachan looked up at Bennett, daring him to make something of it. It was a warning, and they both knew it: without the threat of being on a charge, the glasshouse, and, at the end of the road, a court martial, Strachan would require something that meant something to keep him in line.

'First of all, the objective. For now I'll keep it dead simple . . .'

'You'll need to if old Smithy's going to cop hold of any of it,' someone shouted.

This was par for the course, the usual bullshit, and Bennett allowed himself a sour grin as the chuckles faded.

'Just a word or two about the objective. What we have to do is occupy a small patch of land just over the border from where we'll be in Costa Rica for long enough to torch the crops around it, bomb the buildings and get back out.'

'Nothing to it then, Sarge.'

'Not a lot. Apart from fifty ex-jungle fighters armed with AKs who've been given the job of looking after it. But like I said, you'll get the details once we're all there. What we're concerned with tonight is getting you there . . .'

'The fucking Strachans can swim. They're good at that.'

Smith, getting his own back, drew a lot of laughter. When they had first arrived at Hereford, the twins had told no one they couldn't swim, and nearly drowned as a result. It took them just three days to learn.

'Right, but only if they've brought their water-wings. Seriously though, we don't want to be too conspicuous about how we get there, so I'm splitting you up into four parties, one on each of four daily direct flights out of Heathrow to Miami, and then on to San José. Each group will have a leader who will look after the tickets, make sure you get the Miami transfer right, generally act as mother to the rest. Once in San José you'll be met at the airport by a guy called Paco Franco who will be holding a placard with

"Bullburger (Costa Rica) S.A." written on it. The first two lots to arrive will be there early enough, so long as there have been no delays, to get the Ticabus, that's the local coach service, on the same day to Los Chilos, arriving in the late afternoon the day after tomorrow. Los Chilos is the nearest small town to where we're going. The other two groups will be a day behind because their planes don't leave Heathrow until later tomorrow, and they can't make the first ongoing connection to San José, so they'll have a longer wait in Miami and a night-stop in San José. Again Franco will look after you. Any questions so far?'

'Who's me mum?' It was Smith again.

'Well, you're dead right about one thing, Smithy, you yourself are definitely not one. Right. Jack Glew is Mum of the first lot and he has Montalbán with him to help with the lingo if necessary, and Ainger and Wintle. Geoff Erickson leads the second lot with Julián Sánchez and Bill and Ben. Mike Henchard the third lot with Mick Strachan and John Crick, and I bring up the rear, hopefully collecting any stragglers on the way with Smithy, Jamie Strachan, and Alf Stevens . . .'

'Shit, man, I'm only travelling with Jamie Strachan if he promises to have a bath every . . .'

'Stuff it, you poncy black bastard . . . Listen, Bennett, why can't I travel with my bro . . .?'

'Because he's dead scared together you'll pull the aircraft you're sharing apart. Ain't that right, Sarge?'

'Yes, frankly. That is part of it.'

'And the other part?'

'You're twins. You look alike. You're in the same small party. That draws attention – immigration, passport officials, that sort of thing. They check out twins' documents, they remember them. Incidentally, both at Miami and San José you must all make very clear to any official that questions you, that you are tourists, on holiday, and that you know your visit is time-restricted without visas. Anything else? Right, the three other mothers can come to me now and collect tickets, schedules, funny money, and so on, and then it's early basha for all but especially those on the first two flights . . .'

'No way.'

'Mick?'

'It's not half nine yet, and this is the first time we've been up the Smoke since Wembley last year. We're off out. See yer in the morning.'

In the event it was two o'clock the next afternoon before Bennett was able to get the Strachans out of the Tottenham Court Road nick, where they had been charged with disturbing the peace. It cost him a grand in bail and it was bloody lucky for all that no mention had been made of going abroad, and that they'd left their passports in the hotel with their bags. If they had not they would have had to surrender their passports and that would have been that.

It was a bad start for Bennett in many ways: he had to juggle the tickets, and get Smithy on the third flight. But worst of all, he had not been able to do what he should have done, which was put the Strachans back on the train to Liverpool after their night of mayhem. They were short-handed as it was, and he knew the operation would no longer be viable if he turned up two short of the minimum. And the Strachans rumbled it: knowing they were indispensable, they sauntered into the departure area of Terminal Four at five o'clock in the afternoon, much recovered after a huge brunch in Garfunkel's, and still singing: 'Eee-aye-addio, Arsenal are wankers.'

15

Sitting on the veranda watching the blood-orange sun grow like a flower over the lowlands that stretched away to the distant Atlantic, feeling its heat as soon as it came clear of the mists and yellowed to gold, Parker and Goodall laid aside the maps they had brought out with them and surrendered to the magic.

'Whenever I see that happen I swear I'll never miss another sunrise as long as I live.'

'The coffee's good too.'

'Fucking marvellous.'

'All right, then.' Enough of that, Parker thought. One thing I don't want is my senior NCO turning into an aesthete, nature-lover or whatever. 'The river down there is a tributary of the San Juan, and the village south of us is called Medio Queso. Which, if memory serves, means "medium cheese". Odd name for a village. Indeed it seems to be the name of the river as well. According to my map there's a bridge there and then a track on to a hamlet called Santa Elena. What I'm proposing is that we take the jeep, buy supplies at Medio Queso, park the jeep at Santa Elena and hoof it from there. If we strike across on a north-east bearing, we'll hit the border between two frontier posts, leaving us about five kilometres short of the San Juan.'

'The San Juan's not the border, then?'

'Not here. Another twenty kilometres or so further east and it is. There's an island in the middle of the San Juan about three kilometres south of the objective, and the map marks a ferry.'

'Which might be guarded. Or at least in use.'

'Absolutely. But we're going as bird-watchers. Or butterfly fanciers. And if challenged, we rely on Deeta to bail us out . . .'

'She's coming, then?'

'Oh, I think so, don't you? After all it's what she's here for.'

There was, at that moment, a sly, almost evil look, certainly an all-boys-together look in Parker's dark eyes that Goodall did not much like.

They made one or two last preparations, then Parker got on to the driver's end of the short, narrow seat.

'Today it's my turn to steer the bumper car.'

He called out for Deeta three times before she came and when she appeared on the veranda he was brusque with her.

'Come on. Get in.' He pushed the nodding quiff off his right eyebrow. 'We've got a lot to do today. I was looking for an early start.'

She looked at Parker, then at Goodall, who was standing on the passenger side, waiting for her to step up. Her brow creased, and then she gave a swift upwards shake of her head, flinging back her stunning dark hair.

'You first,' she said to Goodall.

Goodall knew better than to argue, better than to query her demand with the boss, get his approval. He got in, and she followed him, clanking the low door to behind her. As Parker let out the clutch Goodall glanced across at him — and didn't like the sullen set of his mouth. For her part, Deeta angled herself away from them, drummed with the fingers of her right hand on the top of the door, and tossed her head again as the slip-wind lifted her hair.

During the ten minutes it took to get down the dirt track

to Medio Queso, both sides seemed to have backed off and the uncomplicated relationship of the night before was resumed. The tiny village had three shops: shacks, really, like the rest that lined the fifty-metre-long main street, but with open doors, bead curtains, dark interiors and low counters with shelves behind. In the first, Deeta, following Parker's instructions, bought a dozen soft but cooked tortillas, a tin of spiced beans, a bottle of Nicaraguan rum and a six-pack of Coca-Cola. In the second, she bought a scrawny chicken, which the butcher's six-year-old son went out into the backyard to catch. The butcher chopped off its head and handed it back to the boy, who plucked it in a shower of white feathers in three minutes flat. Dad then chopped it into small pieces, each worth about two bites, and wrapped it in waxed paper. In the third shop they bought a machete, and a small, folding Camping Gaz ring and two small disposable cylinders. Then Deeta went back for a small saucepan to heat the beans in, and then back again for a tin-opener.

By now it was half-past nine and already humidly hot. The purity of dawn had gone, a copper haze was filling the sky and only the breeze created by their progress made it all bearable.

The track jackknifed through beef pasture, but much of it swampy, the grass growing through sheets of shallow water, the steers trudging through it, fighting off the clouds of flies that surrounded them. Tall waterfowl on stilts strutted among them, delving with spoon-shaped bills into the buds and grass, finding worms and snails stirred up by the passing hooves. Stands of timber, primary forest or secondary, circled the low, close horizons – tall trees, all of much the same height and apparently of only a few species. They certainly had none of the grandeur or variety of Borneo's Mount Kinabalu, thought Goodall. More like the stuff they had trained in in Belize. And then, as they approached Santa Elena, the landscape took on a different look, and again one which he could connect with past experience: paddy-fields, the rice plants almost ready to flower, and the peasants, the first humans they had seen since leaving Medio Queso, paddling through them with hoes to weed them.

Santa Elena was much like Medio Queso, but even smaller. Beef production is not labour-intensive and the whole area seemed to be very thinly populated. Moreover, as Deeta explained, they were now entering what had been a war zone, a minor war but enough to drive much of the local population inland. Although most of the Contra insurrection or rather invasion against the Nicaraguan Sandinistas had come from the north out of Honduras and El Salvador, there had been at least two groups operating in the area they were now in. They were gone now but had left land-mines close to where their camps had been, land-mines which occasionally exploded under the feet of the larger fauna or when a self-pruned limb dropped from the canopy. And this was the reason too why there was still a substantial strip of more or less virgin lowland rainforest beginning a couple of kilometres inside Costa Rica and filling the five-kilometre gap between the border and the river, and then again on the other side.

Their appearance did not seem to attract any interest or attention from the few people about in the tiny square, which had one shop, one bar and a small church, no more than a chapel really, with a single bell above the door and a corrugated-iron roof. A couple of ragged urchins had appeared by the time they had unloaded and kitted themselves up.

'We're going to have to leave the jeep here,' said Parker. 'We'll take the distributor, but I don't want to come back and find the wheels AWOL. Tell them I'll pull their heads off *and* torch the village if we find anything gone.'

Deeta hunkered in front of the urchins, a boy and a girl, the girl with her thumb in her mouth. She spoke gently for a moment or two, the kids grinned, answered her, and she handed them a hundred-colones note.

'What did you say?'

'I told them there'd be another of those if we came back and found everything as we left it . . . *¿Qué?*'

The boy was pulling at her hand.

'He says the rain will come in an hour or so and if there's a roof you should put it on.'

'Smart-arse. Thank him very much for me and tell him we were just going to do that anyway.'

Parker led the way, with compass, map, binoculars and bergen on his back, Deeta followed, and Goodall took up the rear. They were dressed in as unmilitary a style as possible: the men in flowered shirts, brightly coloured linen trousers tucked into socks, Deeta in a T-shirt and baggy white jeans. Their jungle boots looked serious enough and were indeed standard US Army issue but in fact had been bought in an ordinary camping shop in San José.

A track out of the village took them on roughly the north-east bearing Parker wanted, through stands of maize and a small banana plantation; there was then a belt of bush scrub where trees had been felled but either the ground had not been properly cleared, or, more likely, cultivation had been abandoned and the area was slowly reverting to wilderness. And then, almost suddenly, the forest gathered round them and any sign of a trail petered out. There was a narrow screen of low growth, forming a sort of fence or vegetable wall on the periphery, made up of brilliant emerald ferns and saplings, but the growth was new, called forth by the sun to fill in the gaps made by the loggers, and they found they could push through it easily enough, with a little help from Parker's machete.

'You been in jungle before?' Goodall called to Deeta.

'Of course. But not lowland forest like this,' she called back, but without turning her head. 'And always as a tourist in one of the nature reserves, where there are proper trails.'

They trudged on into the rainforest proper: it was eerie, like a submerged cathedral, it was so wet. Sodden underfoot, sodden in the air, but hot too, especially where there was a hole in the canopy through which shafts of white light came streaming through the hot haze and made all the flat leaves and fronds they hit burn white and silver.

The floor their boots squelched through was almost clear of growth apart from occasional bromeliads, with thick, waxy leaves in tight rosettes, and lianas and stranglers growing down from the canopy rather than up from the floor. The trees were not large in terms of thickness, few had trunks of more than half a metre in diameter, but Goodall could see, now they were in among them, that there were many different species, far more than are found in temperate or man-managed forests. Many had big buttresses, triangular flanges up to six metres high, supporting them. Very little light filtered right down, and only ever in clusters of shifting spots, saucer-sized or even smaller: sunflakes scattered like daisies on the litter, but strong enough to burn anyone who stood for more than a few minutes beneath one.

Up above was where it was all happening. If they paused for a moment the stillness of the floor closed around them, but as from a distance they could hear the sporadic calls of birds, the crack of a branch, the sudden rustle as some bird or creature in the canopy made its move thirty metres or more above them.

'Easy to get lost,' Deeta said, after a further ten minutes or so during which Parker had folded away his map. There was a note of query, a hint of anxiety in her voice.

'Actually impossible,' he replied. 'We keep on this bearing for ten kilometres and we hit the river. As simple as that. I reckon we should make it just about noon.'

'And then back again – twenty kilometres in all.'

'Well, yes. But I rather hope we can get across the river and up to the objective. Another five kilometres. Ten there and back. Thirty in all. Too much for you?'

'Not really. I suppose not. I am fit.'

But already her calf muscles were beginning to ache: it was not simply a matter of walking, but of managing the extra bit of effort, small in itself, of squelching each foot in turn out of the composted wet morass, which she saw, now that her eyes had become accustomed to the subaqueous gloom, was not just a mulch of leaves, with rotting trunks and limbs of trees. It heaved with the ants, spiders, centipedes, millipedes, bugs and beetles that rustled, scampered and scurried through it. She shuddered, felt grateful for her boots and tucked-in floppy trousers.

'Snakes?' she called.

'Not a problem. Not many poisonous. They keep out of your way if they can,' Parker answered.

Well, thought Goodall, that's what they always told us in Belize.

After another twenty minutes Deeta began to realize it was boredom that might be a problem. Previously in forest she had been with guides who would stop every four or five minutes and point out features: plants, flowers, insects, butterflies, noteworthy spectacular growths high up in the canopy above or whatever – things the ordinary tourist would miss. And always it had been in one of the mountain reserves where the terrain itself was varied, where waterfalls might appear round a corner, or tremendous views open out from an escarpment. But here it was the same all the time, hundreds of thin trunks, dangling creepers, unremitting gloom; and if it wasn't, Parker was allowing no time to sample whatever discreet variety there might be.

Suddenly she sensed how Goodall quickened his step behind her, then felt his hand lightly touch her shoulder.

'Look. Up there.' His hand flew up, pointing way above Parker's already receding head.

A cloud of electric-blue chips of light, perhaps a hundred of them, floated and lazily flapped through shafts of sunlight, each a hand's breadth or more across.

'What are they?' It was Goodall who asked the question.

'Butterflies. Morphos. I've seen them before, but never so many at once.'

He stood behind her, and again and suddenly through the damp heat and with the jewelled insects swirling above them, she was conscious of the sexual energy that was building between the three of them, which might, like radioactive enriched uranium, reach critical mass under the right circumstances and set off an uncontrollable chain reaction. Yet she also felt a little tremor of gratitude that Goodall had thought to bring to her notice something beautiful she might have missed.

'Come on. Why have you stopped?' snapped Parker.

'Butterflies. Above your head, man.'

'I don't think we've really got time for this, Goodall, do you?'

'Sorry, sir. But you did say we were bird-watchers or butterfly fanciers. Just practising.'

'Don't get funny with me, Tim.'

'No, Mr Parker. No way.' He gave Deeta's shoulder a slight push and muttered in audible *sotto voce*: 'Quick march, hinny, left, left, left-right, left.'

Ten minutes later – and Parker almost walked into

them, they had already become so much part of the dark forest — two strands of barbed wire, set at a metre and a metre and a half in height, stretched in a more or less straight, east–west line, right across their path.

'Shit. Nearly had me.'

Deeta and Goodall came up with him.

'What are they here for?'

'Frontier.' Parker slung off his bergen, passed it under the lower wire and then ducked between them. The litter at his feet suddenly heaved, a dome of it nearly a foot across, and began ponderously to shift itself towards a nearby bromeliad.

'What the hell's that?'

'Toad.'

'Fucking big one!'

'Welcome to Nicaragua. Think ourselves lucky it wasn't a claymore.'

16

Matt Dobson prowled the City, not literally but by modem, fax and telephone, hunting out the knowledge he wanted. He already knew Finchley-Camden was in the shit at Lloyd's, and he soon found out for how much. He knew that the operation F.-C. was laying on for AFI was an earner; it was not hard to guess that he was planning to use it to get clear of the mess he was in. He relished the thought that if he could ensure that the two-fifty k F.-C. had put in escrow got lost, then F.-C. would remain pretty much in the shit, at least to that amount.

But he could not for the life of him see what AFI could possibly achieve in Costa Rica with upwards of twenty trained killers (he calculated the number from the amount of weaponry ordered) equipped if not to state-of-the-art excellence then very well indeed. Costa Rica was a stable, relatively prosperous country which, unlike any of its close neighbours, had been at peace with itself since a minor civil war ended in 1949. There was no army, elections were held regularly and without fraud, and there was no guerrilla movement to be supported or wiped out. Eventually he resigned himself to admitting that whatever AFI were up to it was not the sort of meddling United Fruit and the CIA had got up to in Guatemala in 1951 or ITT and the CIA in Chile in 1973.

It was not even the case that AFI were particularly big in Costa Rica: beef was their only major concern there and if for any reason the local industry collapsed or Bullburger was wiped out by Macburgers, it would register as only the tiniest of blips in the graphs that recorded the multinational's enormous profits.

Sitting in well-heeled luxury in what Dobson called his office on the first floor of his Cadogan Place house, his fingers twiddled with an executive toy or two; then he sat back from a desk which, the salesperson at Christie's had asserted, had once belonged to Napoleon. His soft palms and manicured fingers stroked the bull's-blood leather of his big executive chair – purpose-built to fit the desk. What I need now, he murmured to himself, is a spot of lateral thinking. He reached for a telephone: lateral thinking was a commodity Matt Dobson bought when the need arose.

Lunch time the next day, the Star and Garter, Kew Green. Saul Kagan, clad in his usual grubby tweed suit, with his Old Etonian tie pulled in the sort of knot that has not been undone for a quarter of a century or more, simply hoisted in the morning and pulled down at bedtime, sat on a bench seat with sausage and mash in front of him, his brown raincoat and felt trilby on one side, and Ted Brett on the other.

They made a contrasting pair. Kagan was in his late fifties and looked as seedy as only a man could who was expelled from Eton for buggery ('We all did it, old boy – but I did it in Windsor High Street') when he was sixteen and had later worked for MI5, the SIS, the CIA and the KGB and for a time for all four at once. Ted Brett, on the other hand, was the very image of a conscientious researcher: nice pullover from Marks and Sparks, cords, and Hush-puppies. He was eating breaded plaice.

He chewed and swallowed, took a short pull at the half pint of Speckled Hen he had allowed Kagan to buy him. Brett hardly ever drank at lunchtime on working days, but since it was a free meal, something that did not often come his way, he felt he might.

'As I understand it' – this was one of Ted's favourite phrases – 'what you are postulating for the purposes of the book you intend to write is that multinational food conglomerates are vulnerable to attack if the main food staple they deal in fails.'

'Something like that.' It wasn't really like that at all, but Kagan was nearly sixty and he had learnt over the years that experts will not part with a thought or an idea until they can convince themselves it is really theirs and not one prompted by someone else. So he kept quiet and let Brett rabbit on.

'It's not really the case. Booker McConnell for instance depend more on marketing and distribution than actual production. Nabisco are basically processors and if one source of raw material dried up they'd go to another, and if the whole lot disappeared, well, then they'd just diversify.' He was not at all sure about any of this, but it was a lead-in to what he wanted to say. 'However, when we come to AFI, we're talking . . . talking about a different ballgame.'

Brett blushed slightly at the raffishness of this, but felt it was all right. After all, Kagan (which Brett assumed was the real name of a very popular writer of thrillers, for that was what Kagan had hinted at) was, in spite of his age, more than a touch raffish himself.

'The parent company developed ways of processing maize, what the Americans call "corn", in the early years of this century. Breakfast cereals, popcorn, cornflour, and many many more, and corn – maize, that is – remains at the very heart of their operation. Now the maize they use is grown across the US corn belt, and elsewhere too, but it is all hybridized to achieve the specifications they want, though we have provided them, and this is strictly on the QT, please don't mention Kew in this at all, with DNA variants and so on, giving them the possibility of genetically engineered . . .' Ted paused, aware that the sentence he had started still had a long way to go, and he had forgotten where it had started. Another gulp of Speckled Hen set him going again.

That evening Kagan called at Cadogan Square, and after accepting a large single malt, made his report from a repro Sheraton chair set in front of the Napoleonic desk. He wondered if Dobson knew that the Napoleon in question was Louis, the grand-nephew of the first Napoleon, and a spectacular failure. Come to that, did Dobson know the Sheraton was a Maples repro job?

'AFI,' he said, 'depend on corn, almost all of it grown in the USA and all of it, for their processing depends on it, hybridized, or, more recently, genetically engineered. Strains developed in such artificial ways are extremely vulnerable to disease, pests, unexpected climatic shifts and so on, for in the process of creating them the immune systems built into the robust natural forms, over millennia of evolution, tend to be degraded or even eradicated.

'Of course, wherever their corn is grown AFI subsidiaries supply the growers, at a price, with pesticides, antiviral safeguards, antibiotics and finely tuned fertilizers. But these are all targeted on known threats. What would be possible, for someone seriously concerned with doing them a lot of damage, would be to develop a threat – a parasite, a bug which attacked the AFI maize strains and was resistant to the artificial defences they can now deploy. The AFI strains are closely related, so it would not have to have a very wide spectrum, and if it were easily reproduced, or rather reproduced itself very readily, it could do to AFI what the locust periodically does to much of East Africa.'

Dobson, leaning back so that the light from the Venetian-glass desk lamp hardly lit his face at all, just brought a glitter to his eyes (an effect that had been purposely contrived), felt his blood pressure and pulse quicken to the level of a minor palpitation. He took a good pull at the whisky.

'So what sort of facility would be needed to develop such a . . . such a pest.'

'Well, apparently, if they had a viable basis to work on, a nasty insect, or fungus or whatever, if something pretty nasty already existed and it was simply a question of developing one that overrode AFI's already existing defences, not a lot. A research station where they could grow AFI strains of maize, laboratories where they could breed and mutate the pest, a few acres of land, good technicians who know their stuff, the right equipment, but none of it outrageously expensive . . . Two other things.'

'Yes?'

'Motivation and time. My source indicates something on the scale of five or six years for the second.'

'And motivation?'

Kagan shrugged broadly and offered one of his rare smiles. Not a pleasant sight, given the state of his teeth.

'Could be a rival seeking to put AFI out of business. But more probably blackmail. Develop the bug, whatever, demonstrate it on neutral ground, give AFI the chance of buying the patent. They'd pay millions. Maybe billions.'

Silence fell as both men ruminated over what had gone before, and savoured the fumes that lingered on their palates, subtly smoky, peaty, tinged with the sherry from the casks in which the whisky had spent fifteen years.

'Drop more?'

Christ, thought Kagan, I must be doing well.

'Why not,' he said, and pushed the cut-glass schooner towards the decanter.

Dobson poured, then said: 'Costa Rica?'

'I think not.'

'Why?'

'By and large Ticoland has kept the Yanks from interfering with a leftish democracy by keeping their noses very clean. They know damn well that if they show any sort of support at all for the wilder shores of socialism or democracy, the CIA and Pentagon will pull the plug. And a serious threat to AFI would look just like that.'

'So. The borders. Panama or Nicaragua. There are powerful factions in both who would love to pull a real nasty on Uncle Sam.'

'And indeed AFI. You see the whole AFI operation undermines the Third World production of maize, the staple food throughout a lot of it, not only as a cash crop but even as a means of subsistence to the local populations . . .'

But Dobson had little interest in starving peasants – unless their lords and masters needed guns to suppress them.

'Which? Nicaragua or Panama?'

'I favour Nicaragua. If the operation you have told me about is being launched out of Costa Rica the target must be close to the border. Now the border areas of Nicaragua, both north and south, are controlled by an army that is still basically Sandinista and by ex-Sandinista guerrillas. It would be difficult for the Chamorro government to interfere with a research station near the Costa Rican border without getting Sandinista approval first. It would be difficult for them even to know about it. Especially if it was privately financed: and it well could be. Lot of bleeding-heart lefty charities still send money direct to the Sandinistas.'

Silence again, broken by the occasional slurp. Dobson gave Newton's balls a poke, setting them ticking.

'You've done well.'

'Maybe. But it's basically speculation.'

'Makes sense though.'

'*I* think so.'

Dobson gave the sort of sigh that means you're on your way, Jack. Kagan unstuck his backside from the repro Sheraton.

'Cheque in the post, then?'

'Of course.'

At the door Kagan turned.

'I have no idea at all what you're up to, Matt, but either way bear in mind one thing . . .'

'Yes?'

'The Ticos have very strict laws indeed against possession of arms, illegal import of arms, private armies – you name it. There are probably fewer guns per head in Ticoland than anywhere else in the world. What I'm saying is that if the authorities knew there was a rogue arsenal trundling about within their borders, especially with rogues to handle it, they'd get very hot under the collar.'

Dobson pushed a finger out into the light and brought Newton's balls to a standstill. Every action has an equal and opposite reaction.

'Thanks, Saul. I'll bear that in mind.'

It all seemed very satisfactory to Dobson. He topped up his glass, stood, took it to the tall sash window and looked down and out across the railings, the plane trees and flower-beds that constitute what is probably now London's most exclusive square. A plan was beginning to take shape in his mind: the fact was he had bought Finchley-Camden's arsenal outright for a hundred and fifty grand. If he could arrange for it all to be lost he'd make a hundred on the deal, and now he reckoned he could see how he could arrange for it to be lost. And maybe, with luck, found again once F.-C.'s two-fifty had been shelled out of escrow and sent, via a couple of Gulf banks, into his own accounts.

17

An hour later they approached the river. The first sign was a curtain of luminous green in front instead of the receding forest gloom that had surrounded them, a curtain that quickly became a real wall of dense riverside growth, a sudden efflorescence of vegetable and animal life, crowding into the light. There were orchids and many other flowers, huge bees, butterflies, tree frogs, lizards, parrots and macaws – buttercup-yellow and crimson, trailing lapis-blue tail feathers. It was almost impossible to get to the edge, indeed difficult to define what was river and what was bank, so overgrown was it with the twisting roots of mangrove and similar plants, half in and half out of the water.

Parker slashed about with his brand-new machete, and gave them a window across three hundred metres of orangey-grey, sudsy water to the bank on the other side beneath a cloud-stacked sky.

'No way are we going to cross that,' stated Goodall.

'Not here, no. But if we push on downstream for a bit we should come to the ferry station.'

It was now very hot and very humid, and the constant dripping from the canopy above, even though it was not yet actually raining, plastered their clothes to their bodies, forming a laminate they sealed with sweat. Even walking behind her, Goodall was conscious that Deeta wore no bra under her T-shirt, which had been loose but was now moulded against her body. Above and below the small rucksack she carried, the supple movements of her shoulder blades and upper pelvis provoked a dull ache in his groin and the discomfort of a slightly tumescent penis. These though were distractingly pleasurable and occasionally he stumbled over the slippery roots that undulated out of the litter.

Suddenly she stopped and he almost bumped into her. She turned and he could see her large, brown nipples and the domes of full breasts beneath the shirt, and his head swam.

'Sorry,' she said. 'Need a pee.'

She shrugged off the rucksack and walked back away from the bank into the gloom they had left, just far enough to put a huge tree between her and the two men.

They looked at each other. A corner of Parker's thin mouth twisted up in a lopsided grin; Goodall flinched away but not for anything could he have prevented his tongue from slowly traversing his top lip, savouring the salty tang.

'It's not a widdle I want, nor a crap neither,' he murmured.

'Take a grip, Trooper.'

'You too, Mr Parker.'

She came back, threading the end of her belt into the last loop, paused, looked from one to the other, and frowned.

'Don't even think of it,' she said.

'Now that,' Parker said, eyeing the twist of her body as she wriggled the rucksack into the small of her back, 'is asking more than human frailty will bear.'

He turned, and theatrically, like the scout in a western or the leader of the cavalry, raised his right arm and thrust it forward.

'Onward,' he cried.

'And upward,' Goodall murmured in reply.

Presently they could see that a small clearing lay ahead: first just a pool of light, then a shanty set in a tidy little garden with a fenced-off corner in which a couple of black pigs snorted and snuffled. There was a jetty on which an oldish man in a big, floppy straw hat sat with a primitive fishing rod. He already had a metre-long tarpon wrapped in palm leaves on the boards beside him. Occasionally he sluiced a bucket of water over it to keep it fresh and discourage the flies and ants from making a meal of it before he could get it to the kitchen.

'Tell him we want to get to the other side.'

'Please,' Deeta corrected him, thumbs in her belt, dark eyes hard.

'Please.'

'Always "please", whatever you want. All right?'

'Please ask him if he can arrange for us to get to the other side.'

'OK. ¡Hola! Buenas tardes. Señor, por favor . . .'

She rattled on. Goodall and Parker looked at each other and mouthed the word across the space between them: 'Please?'

The old man went into his hut, and came out with a coiled brass klaxon with a big rubber bulb on the end. He squeezed it fiercely and sent an echoing squawk across the slowly moving, swirling river. It was answered by a distant squawk from a similar jetty on the other side and presently they saw a similar old man climb down into a small boat with an outboard motor. A couple of tugs, the motor fired and he cast off. As he did so, thunder rumbled distantly out of the bruise-coloured sky and a sudden gust of wind banging up from the distant Caribbean pushed through the tops of the trees, beating out a flurry of birds and setting a troop of howler monkeys off in a paroxysm of ghostly shrieks. An alligator none of them had noticed slithered into the water a metre or so from the jetty on which they now stood.

The rain began when they were halfway across: huge drops, fired down as if from a nail-gun, marked the surface with thousands of silvery pock-marks like sequins. In the narrow bow Deeta turned on to her back, arched her head, opened her mouth to catch them, stayed like that for a moment or so, clutching the sides of the boat, eyes half-shut, legs spread, facing the three men in the stern. The rain ran down her temples into her hair, splashed on her shirt and jeans, trickled down the insides of her thighs. Then she sat up, shook her head, and grinned.

'Oh boy, I needed that.'

But she had been watching them. She needed an ally, was sussing out the situation, studying them, trying to decide which of them she would have, make her own.

On the other side they found a much larger enclosure with four or five wooden shanties, and a small open-air restaurant with a roof of bamboos and leaves. Four or five people were there to service the small establishment, mostly old, women as well as men, and one small boy. Deeta gossiped away with the old man and then turned back to them.

'They are expecting river cruises from Granada on the big lake to start again when the rainy season lets up. They go right down the river to the Caribbean and sometimes the smaller ones stop here. If we hang about for an hour or so, he'll knock us up a meal,' she explained wistfully.

But Parker already had his map out on one of the wooden tables.

'Let's get what we've come for done first. It's only about five kilometres and across cultivated land.'

'Well, anyway, I'm having a drink: he's got a cold-box. *Oiga, tres colas.* We're coming back the same way? Right? I'll tell him to have a decent meal ready for us at . . .' –

she looked at her watch – 'five o'clock? Three hours be enough?'

Parker shrugged, folded away the map, scowled, and said nothing. Goodall suppressed a too obvious grin.

'It'll be a hell of a lot better than chicken fried over that Mickey Mouse stove you bought.'

'We'll not get back to the *finca* tonight if we stop here.'

'Good. He's got a bunk-house. I checked that out too.'

This time the Tynesider did laugh. The small boy – Juanito, the old man called him – brought three frosty bottles of Nicaraguan cola, not the real thing perhaps, but cold.

The final stage of their trek took less time than Parker had suggested. The enclosure was on an island with a narrow wooden bridge connecting it to the north bank. The urchin crossed it in front of them, and then disappeared, no doubt going about whatever business occupies small boys who can get away from adults for half an hour.

From there a dirt track took them through a narrow belt of secondary forest, barely more than scrub. The rain was intermittent and often heavy. Deeta produced a hooded plastic mac, cherry-red with orange sunflowers; Parker a large Greenpeace umbrella with a shaft in two pieces which he screwed together like a billiard-cue. Goodall had nothing and cursed them, refusing to share the umbrella. Deeta offered to take off the mac and spread it like a cloak across both their shoulders – a very tempting prospect indeed. But he refused, foreseeing how they would stumble in the potholes and huge puddles, how he would end up with the raincoat and she would get under the umbrella with Parker.

As they trudged Deeta began to sing *Born in the USA*,

making a marching-song out of it. Goodall, who was also one of the Boss's fans, joined in. Parker did not.

'But you weren't, were you?'

'What?'

'Born in the USA.'

'How do you know?'

'You're a tico.' Goodall was proud of catching on to what natives of Costa Rica called themselves.

'Do you mind? *Tica*. I presume you know the difference? And, although I wasn't born in the USA, nor am I Costa Rican. Nevertheless it was less than three hundred miles from Miami, and that's where I got this job – Bullburger's boss company hangs out there.'

'So you are American?'

'Sort of.' She shrugged. 'Officially, yes.'

Not much later they rounded a stand of immature secondary forest.

'Christ!' said Parker, making them stop and pulling them back into the cover of the trees.

In front of them the ground dropped gently away into a large flat bowl a kilometre in diameter which might once have been a lake or swamp. Now it was filled with the nine plots of maize they had seen in the satellite photographs, each a hundred metres square, with a compound of small buildings on the far side. But what had made Parker cry out was the fact that the whole square was now enclosed by a five-sided chain-link fence, two and a half metres high and topped with razor-wire, with a watch-tower at each of its five corners. The ground all round had either been cleared or was farmed as paddy-fields.

Parker focused his bird-watchers' Fuji 10 × 50 binoculars.

'Sorry, chaps,' he said. 'Mission aborted.'

He sensed Goodall's reaction.

'No, you dope. Not the whole thing. Just this recce. We

can't get any nearer without being spotted. They could send out a patrol, take us in, question us. We haven't been through an official frontier post — we could be in dead trouble. Sorry, but we'll have to go back.'

And he led them back out of sight of the watch-tower.

Questions flooded through Goodall's mind.

'We can't take it on without a proper recce,' he said.

'No.' Trudge and splash, back through the yellow puddles. 'I'll come back while you're training, do it properly, totally under cover, no silly pretence of being bird-watchers or whatever — they just won't see me. Set up a proper OP, suss out their routines over forty-eight hours.' He thought for a moment. 'And I'll do a fly-over too. Get that Aussie chap to lend a hand.'

'Those photos we saw. They were right out of order.'

'Certainly past their sell-by date.'

'Sloppy lot on that tower, though. Long hair in pony-tails. Revolutionaries, I reckon. Not in fashion right now, I'd say . . . Che Guevara and all that crap.'

Never mind that back in those distant times he had had the Che poster over his own bed for six months or so; until his dad saw it and tore it down.

'Yes. Backward area this, though. I suppose.'

And if Parker's tone was a touch drier than usual, Goodall did not ask himself why.

Goodall had one last question.

'And what was growing on the other side of that fence? Looked like maize.'

This time Deeta answered.

'It was.'

Twenty minutes later Esther Somers, the black lady who had spoken to Goodall at a table on the veranda of the Grand Hotel in San José two days earlier, rumpled her daughter Zena's hair, took off the Russian binoculars she had slung round her neck and handed them to the Commandant.

'Yep,' she said. 'That was them, OK. We done a good job, keeping track of them all the way from San José. And especially you.' This time she rumpled the hair of Juanito, the urchin from the restaurant. 'If you hadn't got the last bit right, it would all have been a waste. All the way from San José.'

She spoke Spanish, but slangy, the language of the streets of the Central American capitals, so the English rhyme wasn't there, though she was aware of it in her head, and grinned at it.

'The Englishman Goodall. And the girl from Bullburger. That's them. The other guy? Boss man, I guess. He was quick about getting them under cover, but not that quick.'

The Commandant pulled off her black beret, let black hair tumble about her shoulders and flung it about, then reached across the camping table she used as a desk, shook a roll-up of Nic tobacco from the Camel pack she kept them in, and lit it with a Cricket. Her face was wrinkled, part Indian, a waxy grey, but with a slash of bright lipstick across her mouth and eyeliner round eyes that had seen too much suffering. That way she maintained her womanhood.

'So this is what? The advance guard?'

She looked round the small square room – an enclosure of dried maize stalks woven between stronger wood, beneath a roof thatched with palm and maize leaves. The question was not just for Esther, but for the three men and two women, all in DPM combat gear with holstered Makarovs on their hips, who stood around her.

'Yes,' said one. 'And probably the senior officers, the leaders of the operation. We could take them out now. Have the frontier guard arrest them for illegal entry . . .'

'They'll have some story. Tourist. Strayed across . . .'

'That'll be their cover,' another chipped in, 'and it'll be difficult to have them held for more than a day or two. Be nice to tourists, that's what the Chamorro government wants. Meanwhile we'll have shown them we're on to them . . .'

'So?'

'Keep an eye on them. And if we can, get a radio beacon in their gear. And there's at least one man on the ranch who'll help if we ask . . .'

Back at the restaurant Deeta, Parker and Goodall shook off the wet as well as they could, and accepted viciously strong Cuba libres from the old man, who promised them the meal of a lifetime, if they could wait.

Deeta suggested: 'Give him that chicken you bought. He'll fry it up a lot better than you could have done.'

Giving in, Parker did so. The old man unwrapped the heavy greaseproof paper, sniffed, and shrugged.

For the next hour the rum and Cokes continued to come, together with fried small fry, salads spiced with coriander and chillies, tortillas filled with spiced minced pork, and eventually the chicken pieces, golden brown and heavy with garlic.

'What did I tell you? Dee-licious.'

Meanwhile the rain continued to sheet down on the thatched roof and the river beyond and the light began to thicken but through it, back and forth, came the little boat that had brought them from the other side. And eventually two huge tarpons, like giant herrings, grilled *a la brasa* and surrounded with sweet potatoes arrived on their table. No individual plates – just a fork each. The old man hung a fizzing pressure lamp over their table and asked them if they would like to stay the night: they could have separate rooms, just like a motel.

Parker was, Deeta decided, holding his drink less well than Goodall. He cajoled the Tynesider into swapping stories, the obvious point of which was to demonstrate that anything Goodall had done during their Army and especially SAS service, Parker had done better. And more brutally.

'You see, Deeta, you get your elbow locked in his armpit, that gives you leverage, your forearm and wrist come back round to the back of his neck, and if you can you get a good hold of his ear, the ear on the other side, that is – that's what you do. If you can't get round to that, then it's the short and curlies. That leaves your right hand free to come up and over and on to the front of his head but on the other side. Both hands then give him a solid yank clockwise, and whoops! you've broken his neck. Ever done that, Goodall?'

'No, Mr Parker. Only in practice. Not for real.'

'Lying bastard! But I do wish you'd call me Nick. Share and share alike. Eh? That's what it's all about. Isn't it?'

They drank beer with the fish, and presently Goodall announced that he needed a slash.

'A what?' Deeta asked.

'A tinkle. A rattle and hiss.'

She decided that the time had come to make her choice, and her move.

'Me too. I'll help you find it,' she said.

The old man carried a lamp ahead, across the sodden ground strewn with palms, showed them two sheds with little plastic cut-out pictures on the doors, a top-hat and a fan. He opened both, lit candles inside, and indicated they should snuff them out when they had finished. She took the fan, found a dry slab of wood with a hole in the middle on the floor. Beneath the hole was a pit, not as deep as she would have liked. A mound only inches beneath the hole heaved with insects. The smell was strong but not heavy or horrible. She pulled down her trousers, set her feet on the wood, squatted, and peed into the hole, hoisted her pants but left the belt and zip undone.

Goodall, next door, for all his experience of roughing it, decided that it wasn't for him. Maybe male effluent smells sourer than female – more animal protein in it, perhaps – and went back outside and pissed against a nearby jacaranda.

As he zipped up and turned she caught his arm, led him a little way to the fence that surrounded the compound, leant against it, cradled his face in both her palms, and put her lips against his and her tongue between them.

He thought of England. Literally. Of Mary and Jack. Of the lad he'd beaten to a pulp, and the wife whom he'd never beaten, not much, not often, but enough. Of whether or not what he was doing now was betrayal. Of whether or not he wanted to live, to get back to Tyneside, where, so Mary and his mates used to say, he belonged. But right now, he thought, as his aching prick rose and pushed against the bare skin of her stomach, just now, just here is where I belong.

'Please?' he murmured throatily in her ear. 'Please!'

'Help me out of . . . all this. Please.'

Somehow they got her trousers, shoes and socks off and hung them from a tree. Her feet squelched into the mud, and wriggling her toes, she guessed she liked it. They got his underpants down but not off.

She sighed, and presently took him into her, leaning against the fence as she was with the steady drip of the rain out of the warm velvet sky falling about them, and a hint of the moon behind the clouds, and the tropical scents mingling with the smoke of the old man's cooking. I think, she said to herself, though her head was beginning to swim, I've picked the right one. And as soon as she saw Parker's face over Goodall's shoulder when the younger man came out to look for them, she felt sure.

Parker had smoked a Dunhill, right down to the filter, picked away at the tired remains of the fish, and then decided they had been away from the table longer than they should have been.

He found them. In the dim light Parker could see that Goodall's trousers were round his knees and his big white bum was pumping against her. She was standing on one bare toe, with her other foot clamped across the top of Goodall's leg while her fingernails tore at his buttocks, not breaking the skin but leaving red weals. Parker wondered what she had done with her trousers, shoes and socks. The rocking, pumping accelerated and then suddenly she cried out wordlessly above the sound of Goodall's panting, then he too shouted, not loud but it was a shout.

'Geronimo!'

Her head came forward, and her chin fell on to his shoulder.

She focused glazed eyes and giggled.

'He did say "please", just like I said he should.'

'Fibber,' Goodall growled, without turning his head, 'it was you who said "please".'

She giggled again.

'Well. We both did.'

Parker turned away, angry and humiliated.

18

'Hi, Jack.'

'Hi, Tim. Good to see you.'

Jack Glew swung down from the coach, slapped Goodall on the shoulder. Round them a brief mêlée of backpackers, mostly American, and peasant women in black, one with a brace of live white hens clutched by their yellow legs in her knotted brown hand, swirled for a moment and began to disperse up and down the dusty main street of Los Chilos.

'Meet the gang. My bit of it anyway.'

Goodall looked them over one by one. First a tall, Spanish-looking guy, very dark, tan not colour, very thin, with gangly limbs, bony wrists protruding from the buttoned-up white cuffs of his shirt, and bony ankles above long feet in flip-flops.

'Tony Montalbán. Ex-Spanish Foreign Legion.'

Montalbán's thin face, with its long, pointed nose, had a melancholy cast. Give him a goatee, Goodall thought, and he'd look like that crazy knight, Don Whatsit. The Spaniard's handshake was long and emphatic, and accompanied by pats on Goodall's shoulder. For an awful moment Goodall thought he was going to get the continental kiss.

'Bill Ainger and Colin Wintle. I know they look like brothers, but they're cousins. Bennett picked them up at Gareth's remand centre in Wales. Tried to persuade Gareth to join us but he wouldn't.'

'You're not soldiers, then?'

Colin grinned up at him.

'Not yet, Mr Goodall. But ready to have a go.'

Brief but firm handshakes.

'We'll see. We'll see. But call me Sarge or Tim.'

Lean, hungry, and tough, all right, he thought. But, Jesus H., they're very young.

'OK. Bring your things. I hope you travel light, 'cos there's bugger-all room in the back of our wheels.'

He pointed across the wide, hot, damp street to the jeep on the other side. The coach roared, spewing diesel fumes. Already it was turning, and would also cross the street to where a small queue had already formed to take a different lot of peasants and backpackers back to San José and points between. Goodall let it separate Glew and him from the others.

'I know what you're thinking, Tim.'

'Fucking right you do.'

'There's some good lads coming on behind.'

'There fucking better be. Else we're in deep shit. Deeper even than I thought.'

He took the older, smaller man's elbow, and almost guided him across the street.

'Anyway, Jack, what brought you along? I understood you'd given up this sort of lark.'

'So I had, Tim. But you know how it is. I just can't take what fucking England's become.'

It was not just the scythed dahlias. It was a government that robbed you blind and then put your taxes up when it had sworn not to, it was a football team that was one-third black and still lost, it was the cold, wet weather threatening sciatica. Not least, it was the fat, foul-mouthed comedienne on the telly, who made him sweat with embarrassment when she came on – and the fact that his wife wouldn't let him turn her off. It added up to promise withered like a frost-bitten rose, and no spring in sight.

'I know what you mean, like, mate.'

Ainger and Wintle were already sitting up in the back of the jeep, with big grins on their juice-smirched faces, and huge slices of puce watermelon clutched in both fists. Montalbán had bought them from the vendor who worked the bus queue, and was now expertly teaching them how to spit out the black seeds. Good, thought Goodall. At least he can crack his face. He swung into the driver's seat and Jack got in next to him.

'Long time since I been in one of these,' he said.

Goodall turned, looked over his shoulder, preparing to pull out, caught the eyes of one of the grinning Brummies. He was still not sure which was which.

'You get the runs off of that melon, don't blame me,' he said.

He steered round a heavily paniered donkey and tooted the horn at an urchin who was capering about, both index fingers raised above his head. He had just scored a goal with an empty cola can, right through the door of the butcher's shop.

The second group, consisting of Geoff Erickson, Gurkhas Bill and Ben, and Julián Sánchez, arrived on schedule in the late afternoon. Night swept down, like a lid on a tin, one of them remarked, over the veranda of the old *finca* even before they had had their pork, beans, and tortillas. When Deeta, with very little help this time, had cleared it away, Parker called them together. They had electricity now, a line had been run down from the generator up on the hill, and also hammocks. All through the afternoon Ainger and Wintle had used a power tool on loan from their American landlord to mount fittings in the walls strong enough to support them.

'Right, chaps, I thought I'd just let you know what sort of schedule we have ahead of us over the next two days . . .'

Parker looked them over. They were quiet, responsive, even eager, sitting on director's chairs, or half-sprawled in front of him. The two Spaniards – Julián Sánchez was short and plump, a sort of fit Danny DeVito – stood at the back smoking cigarettes filled with black tobacco.

It would not be the same when the heavy brigade turned up in the next day or two: Smithy and the Strachans, even the turnip bashers, would follow the SAS tradition of barracking a briefing. But those in front of him now were either too old for such childish sports, too young, or didn't speak the lingo. Christ, he thought, and a wavelet of bleakness which, if the word had been part of his everyday vocabulary, he would have called despair, washed through his head. He pulled himself together. Somewhere behind him he could hear Deeta washing dishes: an angry sound. He too still felt angry at the thought of her.

'Tim, with Jack as second in command, will hold the fort here for three days, along with all of you apart from Geoff. Your duties fall into three parts. You will set up a physical-training programme suitable for the climate and the terrain we shall be operating in. Tim has a pretty good idea already of what we are up against in that respect. Two. There is secondary and primary forest on the other side of the hill, beyond the modern building you can see near the crest. This will be our main training area in the three weeks or so we have before the off. I want Tim and Jack to get to know it in the next day or two, suss out its possibilities, and particularly to look at it in the light of what Tim already knows. Three. You have here the six men in our squadron who have not had experience of Special Services work or at least not in the tradition of the regiment we have served in. You will instruct them in the principles of how three four-man patrols with a fourth patrol as back-up can penetrate enemy territory and work in a self-reliant but mutually interdependent way to achieve a designated objective . . . Yes, Jack?'

'Do we know how we split up?'

'No. That will emerge during training . . .'

Parker was suddenly conscious of a reaction among the men, a focusing of attention away from him. He realized that the washing-up sounds had ceased and that a perfume he had come to hate, though he still coveted it, was close.

He turned.

'Deeta. This has nothing to do with you.'

'Oh, but it does,' she insisted, hand on hip, the other swinging a cloth. 'I am in your army, Nick. As much part of it as any of these soldiers.'

'Very well.'

She moved among the mercenaries. For a moment he thought she was going to sit by Goodall, who thought so too. But she joined the Spaniards at the back, accepted a cigarette from Sánchez, and leant against the wooden post that supported the veranda roof.

'You have one other job, of course. You will meet the Ticobuses and bring in the other half of our merry band as they arrive. Sort out among yourselves who takes charge of that.'

Deeta pushed herself off the post.

'I can drive a jeep. And I can sort out problems that might arise in Los Chilos.'

Parker took a deep breath.

'Ah, but,' he said, and he made the last word sound like a stone dropped from a height into a still pond, 'you are coming with me and Geoff.'

'Where to?'

'Puerto Limón. To take delivery of all our gear, check

143

it out, and supervise its onward shipment to here. Geoff, because he's our weapons expert. You, because you know the lingo.'

She pulled on the cigarette, let the smoke drift through the light from the naked bulb that hung between them. Suddenly the cloth she carried in her hand flashed and she fatally swatted the huge moth that kept banging against it.

'You don't need me. One of these guys can handle the Spanish for you and they know the words . . . to do with weapons and so on.' She indicated Montalbán and Sánchez.

'They speak very little English, and they need to train with the rest.'

She slung the cigarette out into the night, and went back into the building.

Partly to defuse a situation he did not understand but did not like, Geoff cleared his throat.

'OK, boss. But how do we get to Puerto Limón?'

'By plane. Pilot's an Aussie called Doug Harvey.'

'Rather you than me,' Goodall muttered.

'Apropos of which,' Parker went on, 'Bill, Ben, Colin and the other Bill are to be up at first light – with Tim in charge. You clear and flatten a suitable runway so he can land and take off without killing us. Three hundred metres long, fifteen metres wide. Minimum. By nine o'clock. That all clear? Good. Basha now and no messing.'

19

'Problems?'

'Bloody say so. Can't raise airport control, can't clear to land.'

Harvey eased the small plane away from the airport, little more than a strip with a small control tower, three hangars and an administrative building sandwiched between the main road south and the Atlantic. He made a wide sweep out over the purple sea then came back in an arc that would take him south of the port and the town strung over a rocky headland above it, before beginning a second approach.

Geoff, looking down at the town, suddenly exclaimed: 'For Christ's sake, they're shooting at us!'

'What?'

'Look, look down there.'

A large cloud of white smoke seemingly made up of hundreds of cotton-wool balls had suddenly appeared below them, blocking out their view of much of the port. The cloud was filled with small orange flashes.

Deeta grinned at him.

'Fireworks,' she said.

'Fireworks! In daylight? At eleven o'clock in the morning?'

Her smile became broader, and she nodded knowingly.

Parker turned back from Harvey, and snarled at her.

'What the fuck's going on, then?'

But before she could answer, Harvey rattled off a brief sentence in Spanish, then lifted the can from one of his ears.

'Got him now. He's drunk. He says the airport's closed but we can land if we like. Oh, shit. What's the date? Twelfth October? I should have remembered.'

He put the plane into a shallow dive.

'What does he mean, 12 October?'

'*El Día de la Raza*. The Day of the Race, the Spanish Race, the day Columbus discovered the New World. It's big here. Did you see that island off the headland? That's Uvita. His landfall on the last voyage he made. Limón's only claim to fame, so they make a real big thing of it here.'

Wheels rumbled, then settled, and they felt a touch of G as Harvey applied the brakes. The tailplane steadied, the airport buildings came into view with three or four other small planes more or less haphazardly parked close by, and they came to rest. Harvey throttled back, left the prop idling, stood up, pushed between them, and swung back the cabin door. A blast of warm air rushed in – and silence. Then a distant fusillade of small arms, or rather rockets, as another battery of whizz-bangs was released into the sky four kilometres away.

Standing at the bottom of the three folding steps, Harvey held out a hand for Deeta, which she refused.

'OK, sport, that's it for today,' he said to Parker. 'Bullburger will give me a bell that they've got the camera I reckon we need for the job you want and I'll get it properly mounted. Ten days I guess should do it. Till then, *¡Hasta la vista!*'

He raised his hand in mock salute, and climbed back in. As they turned away the engine coughed, the prop accelerated and they felt the slipstream tug at their legs.

By the time they reached the glass doors of the admin building he was airborne and on his way.

The doors were locked.

'I don't believe this,' Parker cried. 'I do not believe this. We're locked out!'

Geoff grinned grimly.

'Or in,' he said. 'Depends how you look at it.'

'In' seemed about right. Like most official airports and airstrips the world over, this one had a solid fence trimmed with razor-wire. The gates were padlocked and there were no cars on the inside, just one battered moped. The hot wind coming off the sea, as the land mass behind warmed up, buffeted round the grim concrete buildings, blowing litter about, and was strong enough to send a cola can skittering. Half an orange windsock, its hem long since shredded into strands, thrashed manically, desperate to be free.

'But Harvey talked to someone. Someone in the control tower said he could land,' Parker complained.

It was a low structure perched over a low cliff with waves crashing below it. A rusty outside staircase led to a glazed door. On the roof above, a radar scanner probed a sky empty of planes though huge gulls faced the wind effortlessly before sliding off into swooping dives at the wave crests. Behind the glass a tall Afro in green, yellow and black T-shirt and red baseball cap worn sideways capered silently to the ragga piped into his dayglo-pink earphones from the Walkman he wore on his snake-skin belt. The console in front of him was littered with half-eaten tortillas and he was holding a bottle of white rum.

He paid no attention at all when Parker and Geoff banged on the glass, rattled the locked door, but when Deeta joined them he found her reflection in the tilted glass in front of him and spun to face them, white teeth filling a mocking grin. Maybe he had been waiting for her.

'Am I glad to see you, man,' he hollered as he unlocked the door. 'You just have to be all my wettest dreams come true.'

His English had the pure, almost Welsh, vowels Goodall had heard in the San José football ground. He pulled Deeta in and slammed the door before Parker could get a foot in. They watched while she moved to the console, hitched her backside on to the corner, laughed and tossed her hair back. The guy sloshed rum and Coke into a plastic mug for her. They chatted some more and she laughed again, then he reached out a hand and stroked the white cotton of her trousers, his black hand moving to the inside of her thigh. She came off the console, put her mouth to his ear and whispered, or at any rate spoke very quietly with occasional glances at the two men outside. He nodded enthusiastically, but stayed by the console while she returned to the door. She shouted through the almost soundproof glass: 'Gascoigne says he'll let me out of here and all of us off the compound if I suck him off or if you give him twenty dollars.'

'You can't be serious.'

'I'm finding it difficult, I must say. To be serious. But, believe me, Gazza means it.'

Parker looked at Geoff.

'She's a whore, you know. Bonked Tim night before last.'

Geoff's thick lips narrowed and a frown line appeared between his large eyes. He flexed large hands, a builder's hands, stretching the stubby, strong fingers.

'Mr Parker, I think you should pay,' he said.

Deeta introduced her new friend as Gascoigne Ambrosia Watts and they followed him back across the windswept tarmac round the cluster of shuttered and locked buildings to the big, steel-framed gates. Gazza walked with his arm round her shoulder, and she with hers round his waist. He was a very big man and she actually had to look up at him when she wanted to say something or laugh with him.

'See what I mean?' Parker growled.

Geoff reserved judgement: in fact he was a man to whom judgement never came easily – he preferred to accept people at their own valuation.

Gazza undid locks, threaded out chain, slipped bolts, and the gates squealed. Parker gave him a twenty-dollar bill and he and Deeta then went into a full and lengthy comic routine, which ended with her sobbing with laughter.

'He fell for it,' she moaned, 'he actually fell for it.'

The whole awful situation was finally compounded when Gazza tore the note in two and gave half to Deeta.

'See you, man,' he called once they were through and he was back on the inside, locking himself in again.

'Is there a taxi, a bus?'

'Bus maybe in three days' time. Taxi you might raise on the phone.' He indicated a telephone blister by the deserted bus-stop. 'But shit, man, you only half an hour hoofing it downtown. Have a nice day. Man, it is a nice day . . . Town's to your right,' he added unnecessarily.

The road was a two-lane blacktop with a pavement only just wide enough to take two abreast, and often ran quite close to the rocky shore. The other side was filled with shanties made of a wide variety of materials from containers through corrugated iron to cardboard on bamboo frames. There were palms, corn, bananas, and pineapple growing among them, plus chickens, donkeys and a cow or two. The very few people about seemed to be mostly black or partly black. Hardly any traffic at all came along and what did was heading for the town ahead, which clustered above a semicircular quay about a kilometre in length. Fireworks continued to climb out of it though always drifting inland on the wind.

Parker made Deeta come alongside him.

'What did he mean: three days before a bus comes?'

'El Día. It's a long day. Things don't truly get back to normal until the seventeenth. And the whole place is closed solid for Carnival, today and tomorrow.'

'Carnival is Lent, before Lent. February . . .'

'Everywhere else. But not here. They have theirs now. Because of Columbus. Columbus was here. Kilroy came later.'

Parker strode on, manically pushing his hair to the right though the wind constantly pushed it back. He was now in a foul temper.

'Why didn't I know? Why wasn't I told?' he raged.

'I didn't know we were coming here until last night. And I forgot about Limón. El Día is a holiday everywhere else too, but not the big deal it is here.'

Parker strode on.

'We were meant to be here yesterday. But we took two days over our trip to . . . the target. That was your fault.'

'Oh, come on!' she said, drawing out the words in anger and scorn, and then dropped behind.

He called back at her. 'You been here before?'

'Sure.'

'Where's the Hotel Maribu-Caribe?'

'Other side of town. Down the coast.'

'Franco's expecting us. He's been expecting us since twelve o'clock yesterday.'

The town closed round them, a severe grid of late-nineteenth- and early-twentieth-century square blocks laid out with scant regard to the rocky topography. In spite of this it could have been, should have been, attractive, but neglect compounded by the ravages of the 1991 earthquake had left it looking shabby and tumbledown – sometimes literally so. The port below looked run-down and seedy: on the two piers derelict cranes rose like praying mantises above rusty railway lines, while behind them the nineteenth-century warehouses were empty and shattered. Only the more inland side, where the fishing fleet unloaded, looked at all used. When Geoff, who was interested in such things, remarked on this, Deeta explained that while what he saw had been the old port, built to export bananas and coffee and import manufactured goods, a new port seven kilometres up the coast had now replaced it.

But the main promenade above the port, lined with rattling palms and tropical ornamentals in front of what had been the houses and offices of the merchant and shipping bourgeoisie, was throbbing with carnival spirit. Floats, not on the grand Rio scale, but just small trucks with a steel or marimba band at the back, all covered in tropical flowers, idled past stalls selling spiced skewered meat and sausages, and chicken quarters sandwiched between tortillas or coarse bread. The wind tore through the clouds of blue smoke which swirled through the palms and shrubs. Others sold Imperial beer, and *guaro*, very cheap rum in small plastic tumblers. Vendors with trays slung from wires or rods offered slices of fruit of all sorts on beds of ice. Geoff fumbled for change to buy something he had never seen before – peachy-pink flesh in star-shaped segments – and offered a slice to Deeta.

'Mmmm,' she cried. 'Fantastic. What is it?'

'I thought you'd tell me.'

'Never had it before.'

The flavour was sort of perfumed, as if with apple blossom and something richer. She used the tip of her tongue to catch a drip from the corner of her mouth, then caught up with Parker, who was pushing his way through the crowd ahead of her.

'Want some?'

'Just get me to the Maribu-Caribe. Somebody should have told me.'

'What?'

'That all this was going on.'

She dropped back and fell in with Geoff, twisting her index finger against the side of her head.

'He's screwy,' she shouted above the din as yet another battery of rockets, connected to a single fuse and mounted on a rack, were fired into the air.

Near the end of the avenue they came to a taxi rank where a very old, battered Merc was just dropping a family of about eight, mostly children, all done up in their fiesta best, and eating candyfloss. They piled out; Deeta, Geoff and Parker piled in, Deeta in the front next to the driver.

'Maribu-Caribe, *por favor*,' said Deeta.

'I think I could have managed that myself,' growled Parker.

'I guess you could,' said the driver, black and therefore an English speaker. He glanced up at his mirror, fixing on Parker. 'I hope you got a booking, man. Hotels are solid for the Carnival. Load a Ticos come in to party here every year, know what I mean?'

He flicked on the radio – hot salsa – and clicked his thumb along with the beat, swaying back and forth, giving the steering wheel an occasional nudge with the little finger of his left hand while his right drummed fingers on the top rim.

They passed shanties on one side, the sea on the other, and within five minutes the driver swung right, down a short driveway and pulled up in front of a neat, low, modern building surrounded by palms and tropical plants. Hummingbirds sucked syrups from test-tube-like containers fastened to the wall near the door. The words 'Maribu-Caribe' were strung across the marquee.

'Is this right? Doesn't look like a hotel.'

'The accommodation, sir, is in attractive, private, air-conditioned bungalows set in the terraces which drop towards the sea. Sir.' The driver turned and grinned from a mouth with a lot of gold in it. 'The brochure says so. I quote: "There are two pools, a restaurant and a bar."'

They were back in Ticoland. Reception, and all but the cleaners, washers-up, and laundry maids were Ticos. Deeta rattled away with the clerk behind the desk, then turned and looked as solemn as she could manage.

'No room at the inn,' she said.

'Tell him we're booked in. By Bullburger. By Francisco Franco, who should be here.'

She rattled again and the clerk rattled back. He made lots of gestures, his elbows held close to his uniformed body, his forearms spread wide and an occasional fore-finger semaphoring negatives across his chest.

This time the grin was beginning to show.

'He says we were booked in for last night. Franco was here. But when we didn't show by four in the afternoon, and things were beginning to close up for the fiesta, he left. He did leave a message though. He'll be back on Thursday when the docks reopen – unless he's heard from us in the meantime.'

'And today's Tuesday. We'll just have to stay here then. Until Thursday.'

'But like I said: no room at the inn.'

'So what do we do now?' It was almost a hiss.

Parker's face was white, and Deeta shivered. She knew he had a temper, and was beginning to suspect that while the fuse might be long, when it burnt through the bang would be very destructive.

'I could ask him to ring round. See if he can find somewhere else.'

'Do that.'

'Mr Parker, there's something you should know.'

'Yes, Geoff?'

'Those kids who were in the taxi before us. I think one of them left a lump of candyfloss on your seat, so to speak.'

With a look of total disbelief, Parker passed his right palm across his backside. It returned with a tuft of sticky pink fluff between thumb and forefinger.

20

Even before the small plane had become a midge in the distance and dropped below the low south-east horizon, Jack Glew had the seven of them lined up, Goodall included, all ready to begin a brisk run-through of the Royal Canadian Air Force exercises, Chart Four, Level B.

'Right, lads, we need to get through this before it gets any hotter. Feet astride, arms up, swing down to the left, touch the floor outside your left foot, between feet, press, outside right foot, swing up, make a big circle above your heads, arms straight as you can, lean right back, then down again . . . One . . . two . . . three . . . twenty-six . . . twenty-seven . . . twenty-eight. On the floor, on your backs. Never mind the ants, ants in the pants will help you move when it gets to the running bit, legs straight, feet together, arms straight above your heads. Sit up, touch your toes, keeping arms and legs straight . . . One . . . two . . . three . . . nineteen . . . twenty . . . twenty-one . . . Turn over, on to your fronts.'

'This is frigging worse than fucking Wales,' Bill Ainger whispered to Colin.

'I heard that. Twenty-five press-ups while the rest of us take a breather. On the knuckles, Trooper, on the knuckles. Next. On your fronts, arms stretched out. If your face is in cow poo, then you may move it. As you were. The poo, that is, not your face.'

Fifteen minutes passed.

'Right, take five. Suck a salt tablet and take a short, I said *short*, drink of water. Then you're going for a run.'

Goodall drifted away from the rest. Involuntarily his gaze drifted to the spot on the horizon over which the plane had disappeared. It was thirty-six hours since it had happened. And during that time she had hardly touched him, and only three times blessed him with a smile more deeply personal than the ones she bestowed on the others. And he hated the way she talked to the two Spaniards in their own lingo and occasionally laughed, even seemed to be laughing with them at the gringos. It was all a pain, but it made him feel alive too. He'd forgotten what being in love felt like, how it was more pain than pleasure, but not an evil pain, just the pain of longing. Grass rustling alongside him pulled him out of his reverie. Glew had come alongside.

'What do you reckon, then?'

'Eh?'

'What do you reckon of this lot, then?' Glew jerked his greyish, cropped head back over his shoulder.

'The Flowerpot Men are fine. You'd expect them to be. Bill Ainger took it in his stride. Wintle seemed a bit stressed. And the fat dago's face was the colour of black-currant juice by the end. The other one, though, he's a bit of a dark horse. Either he's a fucking good actor, give him an Oscar, or he's super-fit. Didn't seem bothered at all.'

'We'll see. Sánchez, the fat one, is not bad. Reckon he'll come through if he can shed half a stone.'

'Not much likelihood he will. Once the master chef turns up, we'll all be eating more then we should.'

'Maybe,' said Glew, laughing. 'This here run – no need for you to wreck yourself doing it.'

'Thanks a bundle, Jack. Tell the truth, the ground's a mite uneven and until I'm a bit fitter, I'd rather not chance me knee on it.'

Jack gave his right arm a light slap and moved off.

'Right, lads. Let's be having you,' he called.

That, thought Goodall, was Jack for you. Considerate. Knew these younger lads would run him into the ground and that wouldn't do the image a lot of good. Discipline was not going to be easy, and most of the squad knowing they could outrun him wouldn't help. His gaze went back to the horizon. She, they, would be away one night, they'd said. Would she fuck Parker? Not Geoff Erickson, anyway. Geoff was totally a one-woman man, devoted to the old biddy he shacked up with – painter, artist, nearly old enough to be his mum. Goodall shook his head. Folks is funny, you can't deny it. But would she? Would she have it away with Parker? Probably. You have to admit it . . . probably.

He shook his head fiercely, swallowed back the rising gall, the spasm of hopeless longing, spiced now with jealousy and a touch evil as a result.

'Then you pass in front of the building at the top, but you don't turn downhill till you get to the corner of the fencing. Follow the fencing down to that big palm almost on a level with us, then, only then, you cut straight back here. Pay no attention to the bulls, but if they do go for you then you'll just have to run that bit faster. I reckon it's about a mile and a half, so I'll expect the quickest back here in ten minutes and nobody under twelve.'

'Count me in, Jack.'

Glew looked at Goodall for maybe a full five seconds.

'Make it fifteen,' he corrected himself. 'Five, four, three, two, one . . . GO!'

They started at a steady trot, bunched up, across the flat plain to the north of the old *finca*, the long, wet grasses swishing against their track-suit thighs, their trainers squishing and squelching in the spongy ground. Crickets like biplanes whirred up at their approach like the planes that buzz King Kong in the old movie; flies with glinting, burnished gold bodies rose in clouds from the steers' droppings. Then, after about four hundred metres, they swung left, according to Glew's instructions, and began to climb the slope. Goodall felt the sweat beginning to break, his heart began to pound. The Flowerpot Men, small, lean, dark, pulled away from the rest, though Montalbán stayed in touch.

The slope steepened, and the main bunch began to lengthen with Bill Ainger at the front of it, then Sánchez, with Colin Wintle and Goodall at the rear. Then, to Goodall's amazement, he heard light footsteps behind, in time almost with his. He glanced round and saw Jack Glew almost on his shoulder. The small Midlander was going well, elbows pumping, head up showing the sinews in his scrawny neck and his Adam's apple.

'Shit, Jack, what you playing at?'

'You'll see. Keep going.' He glanced at the stopwatch in his right hand. 'Got a sight closer to you than I should have done without you rumbling me though.'

They began the sweep round that would bring them on to the level, passing in front of the modern *finca*. All the time they were following a simple double-wire electric fence which pinged every five seconds or so as the current came on: enough to keep the steers from straying into the forest. For most of the way there had been a swathe of scrub between it and the trees, but now, near the top, big almendros, jacarandas, hung with lianas and epiphytes, with swags of blossom, purple and white, came close and occasionally their big branches, spreading wide since they were on the light edge of the forest, dropped welcome shadow as well as magical scents. Birds rose out of them, scarlet, yellow and blue, cawing like crows or screaming like peacocks, trailing long feathers of gold. Wintle hesitated, clearly wanted to slow up, stop, have a look, but caught sight of Glew on his heels and ploughed on.

They passed in front of the American's ranch house. Ford was on the terrace, with a glass of something long and milky-looking in his fat paw. He raised it as they passed in mock salute, and sucked up icy fluid through a straw. A few yards further on there was a group of his cowboys who jeered and catcalled, waving their baseball caps. One still had his arm in a sling, and Goodall felt a tremor of anxiety. They'd need revenge, the two he and Parker had humiliated; it had not come yet but it would.

'OK,' said Glew, 'this is where we leave the pack. After all, someone has to be at the finishing line.'

And he swerved off at an acute angle, back down the hill towards the old *finca* and the patch above the corrals and bunk-house where they had been doing the preliminary exercises. Downhill now but not as steep going through the middle of the bowl as the outer edges had been. The run had not so exhausted Goodall that he could not now enjoy the easier pace, as the others pounded on along the top of the hill.

Standing, panting, then remembering the old routines and doing cooling-down exercises, jogging on the spot, arms stretch, arms down, arms stretch, they still managed to talk to each other as the Flowerpot Men approached the palm that would release them for the final stretch across the flat. Montalbán was twenty metres behind them, Bill Ainger fifty metres behind him, while Wintle and Sánchez jogged along more or less happily a hundred metres or so in the rear.

'What you reckon?' said Glew.

'I guess Bill and Ben will do it,' replied Goodall.

'Take a bet?'

'Now I might have done if you hadn't made the proposal,' said the Tynesider, laughing.

And, sure enough, Montalbán broke away from the palm, with three hundred metres still to go and twenty to make up, winding the Gurkhas in as if on a line. Suddenly they knew they were under threat but, short and tough, built to go on for ever, they had the wrong build for a sprint to the finish. The grey, thin Spaniard, hardly puffed at all, floated in with five metres to spare.

'Shit,' said Goodall. 'You'd have taken me money. And you knew it.'

'Aye. Montalbán ran the fifteen hundred for Spain in the Tokyo Olympics. Came fourth in the final. I was there.'

Of course you were, Goodall recalled. Light middleweight. Made it to the quarter-finals.

21

The manager of the Hotel Maribu-Caribe was profusely apologetic.

'I find you a room. No problem. *Mañana* perhaps, tonight is impossible.'

'We want a room tonight. We believed we had a room here. If you have not got a room for us here, then find one somewhere else.'

There was such an edge of steel, of threat in Parker's voice, that the manager blanched as if he were gifted with second sight and saw his hotel in flames.

'All right, all right. I do my best.'

He reached for his phone. Twenty minutes later he had an offer.

'In the old town, you know? Calle Siete, between Avenidas Dos and Tres. Very nice place, but self-catering. Yes. Self-catering apartment. Fifty dollars US a night, OK? I know it's too much, but well . . .' – he shrugged – 'the fiesta, you know? I call you a taxi, yes? You pay the *conserje* when you get there.'

'Looks all right,' said Geoff, ever the optimist, as Deeta paid off the cab. 'Interesting anyway.'

They looked up a façade of tired stucco, some of which had once been moulded, at rusty wrought-iron balcony railings and at rattan blinds looped out over them in front of open glass doors. Trailing geraniums and more exotic tropical plants were the only things that gave the block a lift. On the top, fourth, floor the shutters were closed and decorated with a poster that read '*Se Aquila*' and gave a telephone number.

'To let,' said Deeta. 'That'll be it.'

She pressed the button marked '*conserje*' and presently the big, cracked old door was hauled open, its bottom edge squeaking horribly on crazed marble tiles. Deeta chatted up the old grey lady in black dress and bedroom slippers, and they all followed her, keys jangling, up the winding staircase. It stank of rotten fruit, old cooking oil, cat piss – though since they saw no cats it might have been guavas past their sell-by date.

At first the old lady refused to hand over the keys, even to open the door until money had changed hands – one hundred dollars for two nights. She pushed the notes up her sleeve, thrust the keys into Deeta's hands and almost scampered back down the stairs, determined to be well away before they had even begun to inspect what they had rented.

Geoff and Parker swung their holdalls on to the one big old bed and looked round. They saw a high-ceilinged room that once might have been grand, but now there were damp marks on the ceiling, the wallpaper below the picture rail had begun to drop and someone had peeled off triangular shards of it, leaving them in crumpled heaps on the uncarpeted black floorboards. The bed had an iron bedstead, a dirty-russet-coloured quilt left in a heap on a bare mattress, stained and thin, and a bolster. There was a small wooden table, on one corner of which the laminate had lifted into a curl, two old wooden chairs, and a large wardrobe. In an alcove curtained with plastic sheeting covered in black crumbs which turned out to be dead insects, there was a basin, a small kitchen dresser and a double gas burner, none of them clean.

There were three windows, all looking out and down

into the street from which they had come. The middle one was larger than the others, with double wood shutters. Parker opened the glass doors, folded back the shutters on to a very narrow balcony. Hot, humid sunshine flooded in, doing little to dispel the foetid stale air.

'Jesus,' he said. 'Where's the loo?'

'On the landing outside,' Deeta replied.

'Jeee-zusss! Let's get something to eat.'

'The best restaurants are always near the market,' Deeta said, and they quickly found a good Chinese, the Chong Kong. Because it was still not yet two o'clock they were able to get a table without having to wait.

'Our sleeping arrangements,' Parker announced as they were finishing their meal, 'could be interesting. Clearly two in the bed and one on the chairs is the only practical way of organizing things. Equally clearly, no gentleman, and I hope, Erickson, we are both gentlemen, would ask Deeta to sleep on the chairs . . . see what I mean?' And his dark eyes gleamed as he pushed the lock of hair off his forehead, which was now covered with a sweaty sheen, not from heat, since the restaurant was air-conditioned, but food and booze.

The proprietor hovered over them, anxious to shoo them out, hoping to turn the table round at least three times through the long afternoon. But when Parker was trying to get him to accept American Express, Deeta announced: 'Right, you guys. Carnival tonight and I intend to party. So right now I'm going back to the apartment' – she waved the key under their noses – 'for a couple of hours' siesta. On the bed. On my own.'

And she left before either of them could stop her. And since the proprietor now had Parker's American Express card in the back somewhere there was no way they could chase after her, or get back to the room before she did.

They did not see her, at least not to speak to, until Thursday midday. They wandered listlessly up and down the quays. The wind dropped and a little rain fell, but nothing like what they had become used to inland. Rocket sticks along with dead fish and living jellyfish heaved on an oily swell against the rough-hewn greasy stones.

From two until nightfall the town, which had been buzzing so frantically when they arrived, turned into a town of the dead, especially in the later part of the afternoon as the restaurants and snack-bars emptied and the revellers returned to hotels, lodgings or their homes for a long rest before the real business of Carnival got under way.

Parker regretted that he had chosen Geoff Erickson, though it was his expertise as an armourer that had really made the choice. There were lads in the troop who would have taken a firmer line with Deeta, joshed her along a bit, filled her up with a few bevvies, got her going, but not Geoff. Now if it had been young Smithy . . . he could charm the knickers off any bint he set his sights on.

At Geoff's suggestion they climbed away from the quays and investigated the Parque Vargas. As they walked among the palms and glorious flowers, Geoff talked about Gina and Parker felt a pang of deprivation. He had no one to ring up or write home to. His mother lived in a grace-and-favour flat in Hampton Court, where she drank gin and tonic as soon as the sun dipped beneath the yard-arm and right round the clock until it dipped beneath the yard-arm again. His father, once a Queen's Equerry – hence his mother's apartment – was now, at sixty-plus, a beach bum in Baja California. No known address.

At the far end of the park they came to the sea wall

again, high now and facing the ocean. A small aircraft carrier had hove to about two kilometres out. Geoff slipped some coins into one of the telescopes that lined the parapet.

'Colombian flag,' he said. 'Called the *Colón*. That means Columbus. But I reckon she's ex-US Class Two. What do the Colombians want a carrier for?'

'Combined operations with the US DEA, CIA and Pentagon to catch drug smugglers. Window-dressing really. Those officers in the restaurant must have been off it.'

He looked at his watch and they turned back along Avenida Dos, seven blocks, and got back to their room just as the two hours Deeta had asked for were up. The door was shut, but not locked. She'd gone, taken her bag with her, and left a note and the keys: 'Back Thursday morning. No way will you get into the docks before then.'

'Fuck,' said Parker. 'Or rather . . . not fuck.'

He chucked himself on to the bed, which wheezed and clanged beneath him.

Two hours later night fell, and was signalled by a barrage of rockets that seemed to be launched from the roof above them. Music burst out all over: bugle bands marching with the floats; fairground hurdy-gurdy music from the roundabouts and rides which had taken over the baseball ground a block away; hugely amplified salsa and ragga from street parties on almost every street corner.

'Can't beat them, have to join them,' said Parker, and led the way down into the pulsating town.

They drifted into the baseball ground, and wandered through the attractions and sideshows. They watched the Ticos driving their Ticas manically in the dodgems, showering sparks from the electrified lattice above. Geoff sussed out how the .22 Winchester-style rifles dropped to the left and won a giant panda which he gave to a small girl, who sucked her thumb and tried not to cry even though she had lost her grown-ups . . . and it was about then that it came to him.

Geoff Erickson knew jungles – both urban like Belfast and tropical like Papua, knew them, killed in them, and had so far survived in them. And he knew when he was being watched. There was nothing mysterious about this, no ESP, though his colleagues, particularly the Fijians he had worked with, were convinced he had shamanistic powers. He reckoned it worked on an unconscious level, but was readily explicable all the same.

In a forest a leaf that moved against the wind, a rustle in bamboo too high to be caused by a snake, a bird's alarm call when there was no apparent cause for anxiety were the sort of signs, barely perceptible, barely perceived, that raised the hairs on the back of his neck. In urban surroundings it was different: a head lifted above the crowd or peering around a taller man's shoulder, a newspaper lifted just too late to hide a face, just as Geoff approached a corner that would take him out of sight.

'Mr Parker, we've got a tail.'

'Sod. Rather thought we might have. But I said to myself, if it's not just my imagination old Geoff will have latched on too and he'll say something.'

'Shall I take him out?'

'Just the one, is it?'

'I reckon.'

Parker stood and thought. He had his back to one of those rides that puts people in pairs in buckets that then hurtle back and forth and spin as well. Two of them had Colombian sailors in them, ratings this time, not officers. And then over his shoulder Geoff saw her: Deeta, and she was with Gascoigne Ambrosia Watts, the air-traffic controller from the airstrip. They seemed to be having a good time together. Geoff wondered if Parker had noticed her, and then again whether she was part of whatever outfit it was they had on their backs.

Parker came out of his reverie. His eyes were sharp now, and he looked leaner, more alert. All of which left Geoff feeling mightily relieved: he had begun to harbour doubts as to his CO's professionalism, for all the reputation he had brought with him.

'If he knows anything about us at all,' Parker said, and the drawl had gone, his speech was clipped and hard, 'then he knows we're not up to anything out here in the streets. His game plan could be something like this: he wants to spend some time in our room, going through all our stuff, whatever, and he wants to know he's not going to be caught at the top of the house if we come back before he's finished. So he wants to see us settled in somewhere before he goes in. Somewhere where we're going to stay put for . . . what? An hour or so?'

'A restaurant?'

'No, Geoff.' Suddenly the little boy in him was playing games; the silly ass was back. He threw a playful punch at Geoff's shoulder. 'Nookie, Geoff. That's what we want. Nookie. Every port in the world has nookie for sale. Question is, where?' Then the voice went hard again. 'And, Geoff, I want this guy alive and talking. I want to know who sent him and why. Here's how we'll do it . . .'

Half an hour later Geoff was outside their apartment block again, having followed the man who had been following them away from the lively brothel, possibly improvised for the Carnival, that the pimp Parker had quite quickly found had led them to. The outer door of the apartment building was ajar, and no one was watching it from the street. The Carnival's racket drowned the short squawk that came as he made a gap wide enough to squeeze through.

The shallow stairs were wooden and worn, so he hugged the wall, knowing that that way they were less likely to creak.

Soon the darkness was almost complete, the light from the street left behind, the glow above him luring him on: almost certainly it came from the crack beneath the door of their room. The rest of the building seemed to be deserted: all out at the party? Or perhaps no one else lived there at all, apart from the old woman in the basement.

The adrenalin was pumping now, and with it a surge of happiness marred only by a brief cold ache in his chest and a tingling in his upper left arm – he was used to that; it was the effect of the heart murmur the medics had discovered when they overhauled him after his Papuan virus, the murmur that had got him the honourable discharge he had just about been ready for. Some time in the future he'd have a heart attack. If it's not now, then it's still to come. He waited for it as patiently as it waited for him.

The Carnival receded as he climbed the stairs, and with it the noise cover. In his mind's eye, he pictured the room he was approaching. The bed, and more important, the bedding, the chairs, the table. All could be used as weapons of defence – or attack. He tried to guess what the intruder was up to. He had got there three minutes ahead of Geoff: presumably he'd be going through their kit – what there was of it. One change of clothing in each holdall, toiletries. Suddenly Geoff had a feeling that there was more to the situation than he had yet cottoned on to – something to do with a breath of fresh air coming down the stairs towards him. But he was close now, and had to concentrate on what was about to happen, so he pushed the thought away.

While the other floors had two doors each, the top landing had just the one, and the toilet opposite. Eyes accustomed now to the dark and aided by the light that seemed to stream from under their door though it came, he knew, from just the one dim, naked bulb above the bed, Geoff paused on the threshold and listened intently. He tuned into sounds above the distant racket. Small things being moved. A footstep. Then the sharp hiss of an aerosol can. In half a second he visualized the intruder firing off a squirt of Parker's deodorant and he was through the door like a bullet.

The trouble was, there were two of them. The first was behind the door. He should have been waiting for Geoff – after all, that was what he was there for. But he'd been looking at and laughing at number two, who was squirting Paco Rabanne into his armpit. Geoff thumped the heel of his hand into the man's jugular with the sort of force that would have taken his head off if his hand had been an axe. He knew that the combination of pain and a serious lesion to a major blood vessel would certainly incapitate him for a moment or two. Or kill him.

The second man, lean, wearing jeans and a sleeveless vest which claimed it had come from Key West, Florida, made a fatal mistake. A long, steady blast of deodorant into Geoff's face could have been a problem. Instead he lowered the can, which was in his left hand, and with the right went for the switchblade tucked in the back pocket of his jeans. Geoff sighted on a point a fraction above his navel and kicked it. Hard. A sort of roundhouse kick but not perfectly executed, since he had a mind to get back round and see how number one was doing. And then the pain came again, stabbing deep in his chest and like a shock down his left arm. He knew he had to sit down. He knew he had to find his pills. And if he was going to do these two things then he had to kill these fuckers first.

He did.

22

Goodall had heard the jeep's horn as it crossed the wooden bridge about a kilometre away. Presently it drew up in front of the veranda and Goodall went down the steps to meet them: Jack Glew driving, back from Medio Queso, with the third party.

Something's up, Goodall thought as the three new men climbed down. Young Smithy shouldn't be with this lot.

And indeed the expression on Glew's face as he came over and stood below him said as much.

'Smith's got a message for you, from Gordon,' Glew said.

'It's the Strachan twins, Sarge,' Winston Smith explained. 'Mr Bennett reckons they've been nothing but a very severe pain in the butt since they came on board, and he wants Mr Parker to lay on something that'll show them who's the boss, soon as they arrive.'

'Mr Parker won't be here until tomorrow. But maybe that's just as well. I reckon we can lay on something for the Strachans without the presence of Mr Parker. What do you say, Jack?'

'I reckon, Tim. I reckon we can.'

The second bus was late, arriving shortly before nightfall. As soon as they were off it the Strachans went straight across the street to the nearest *cantina*, where they bought bottles of beer; then Mick Strachan went round the first corner and relieved himself one-handed against a whitewashed wall, tipping the beer down his throat with the other.

'Jesus, I needed that,' he said, pulling his zip up and strolling down the street to the jeep. 'Goodall, you old fart, how's tricks, then?'

'None the better for seeing you behaving like the slob you are, Strachan,' Goodall said, and turned away.

'Eee, we are fucking la-di-da today, aren't we?' Mick Strachan stuck his finger up at the Tynesider's back.

Bennett sat by Goodall.

'Smithy told you about how they got nicked up West and I had to bail them out?'

'He did.'

'By the time we arrived in Miami, the captain had radioed for a paddy wagon to greet them. Harassing the stewardesses, was the charge. They spent last night in jail, and it cost me a grand in fines first thing this morning. I told them it'll come out of their packets when we get paid off, so they more or less behaved until San José. But there they got a bottle of rum from somewhere and Jamie was sick on the coach. So I hope Mr Parker's got something ready for them and more than a tongue-lashing.'

'Parker's away. At least until tomorrow.'

Bennett looked at Goodall, taking in the firm set of his mouth, the grim look in his eyes.

'Parker out of it? That might be all right then.'

'I reckon.'

'This is where you basha. Only one spare hammock available though. That's for Alf Stevens.' Goodall nodded at the thickset, tall, dark West Countryman. 'You two are out the back. In the stable. Best place for you, when all's said and done.'

The twins looked at each other. Small, blue eyes suddenly narrowed in their big, red faces.

"Ere we go, then?' Mick muttered.

"Ere we go,' Jamie replied.

But that was all. Goodall hoped that might indeed be all. They were big lads. Their heavy upper arms and their broad, burly chests stretched their T-shirts (Kop rules, OK?) to bursting. If it came to it someone was going to get hurt, that was for sure. The three of them moved on to the kitchen, and Goodall pointed out the stacks of dirty plates and saucepans, some on the floor.

'Cookhouse. Maid's day off. Lots of washing-up to be done.' Then suddenly he shouted, bellowed like a bull-walrus, a sergeant-major on parade with all stops out.

'Strachan, M. Strachan, J. Get this place cleaned up. Everything clean and shipshape. *Now!*'

'Aw, come on, Goodie. Give us a . . .'

'Attention before you speak to me, you rotten heap of shit, you. Get on with it, before I hang one on you.'

'Oh yeah? You and whose army, then?'

'*My* army. You stupid little wanker.'

And slowly the room filled with eleven silent men, all holding wet towels, some knotted.

Perhaps they would have given in, then, that time. But Goodall's rag was up, and also he knew that if it ended then not much would have been achieved – apart from a load of washing-up. The Strachans would bully behind his and Bennett's back; they'd also collude, form alliances, remain a subversive source of trouble. He reached out, took a towel from the nearest man, Jack Glew, and dextrously flicked it so it snapped like a snake on Mick Strachan's shoulder. The Liverpudlian swung a DM at his knee, missed, then came in with fists flailing. Goodall took one on the shoulder and a backhander on the nose before ducking out of the scrap, blood pouring between his knuckles.

In spite of the weight of numbers the twins broke

out on to the veranda, leaving two more behind them: Sánchez winded by an elbow to his diaphragm and John Crick spitting teeth. But Mike Henchard, the biggest of the Dorset farmers, smashed Jamie with a thundering right which toppled him through the balustrade and on to the grass below, while Gurkha Ben tackled Mick Strachan below the knees and brought him crashing down the steps, almost on top of his brother. The rest followed now, swinging the towels, clubbing, whipping and occasionally kicking the two men until they finally collapsed: heaps of cursing but unresisting battered flesh.

Goodall and Bennett stood over them. Goodall pulled a towel away from his nose, looked at the blood, shook his head and tipped it back.

'The full treatment, Gordon?'

'I'd say so, Tim.'

Mick rolled on to his back, knees still hunched up to his chest, and looked up at them.

'Don't even think of it, Sarge,' he croaked. 'I'll fucking kill you if you do.'

'Well then, you steaming lump of shit, we might just call it a day, all right? But only when you've done the washing-up. *Move!*'

Slowly, then, catching Goodall's mean eye, a bit more quickly, they both dragged themselves upright and climbed the steps again. Behind their backs a sudden chorus of jeers and catcalls rose like the cries of the monkeys in the distant trees.

In the middle of it all Colin Wintle turned to Winston Smith.

'What's the "full treatment", then?' he asked.

'Pull their knickers down and shave their pubes. Then we all slash on them. Shame really. Could've been fun.'

23

'Oh, dear me. I hope you asked them name, rank and so forth first.'

Parker took in the scene. A young, ratty-looking sort of man in T-shirt, jeans and trainers lay sprawled against one wall. A switchblade was stuck up to the hilt in precisely the recommended place, puncturing, almost severing the aorta, so he had bled swiftly, mostly internally, no mess, until his heart, starved of oxygen, gave out. The other guy, heavier, older, was on the bed, legs hanging over the edge, arms spread; he appeared to be looking over his shoulder at an impossible angle.

'You don't look too good yourself.'

'No? But already I feel better than I did.'

Face ashen, lips bluish, a sheen of sweat on his forehead, Geoff Erickson looked up, raised the bottle of pills that he held in his dangling hands.

'Got to these in time,' he said. 'Silly bastards got in the way, and I knew I was gone if I didn't . . .' He shrugged, then a sort of cold grin filled out his thick lips. 'Sorry. I mean like I'm sorry I didn't get name, rank and number first. Or where they were coming from. But there you go.'

'Ah well. Not to worry. What happened?'

'Well, I was a bit of a silly billy really, wasn't I?' As each moment passed he looked a bit better, spoke more firmly. 'This guy,' he said, pointing at the one whose neck he had broken, 'was already here. Got in through the roof: I think you'll find there's access on the other side of the toilet. And was waiting until this one came back with the news that we were shagging a couple of birds down the road before letting himself in. Something like that.'

'And why's he holding my deodorant?'

'Ah. Saved my life, that did. He was giving himself a squirt with it just as I came in. Then, because I'd taken his knife off of him, he tried to hit me with it. Silly, really.'

Parker sat on the bed. The sudden sagging caused the dead man to release a fart: but neither of the living was much bothered.

'So. What were they up to?'

'Sleepy, on the bed, he brought a small holdall. Have a look.'

Parker found the holdall, really no more than a canvas bag with a drawstring, and pulled it open.

'Set of lock-picks.' He held up a ring from which were suspended about thirty small rods, each about seven centimetres long, and bent at a right angle, but with the bend coming at varying points.

'That figures.'

'And what's this?' He pulled out a small package wrapped in white cloth. He undid the cloth and pulled out a small black box roughly the size of a cigarette packet. The matt-black casing was featureless apart from a short antenna off centre at one end. He passed it over to Geoff. 'Well?'

Geoff slipped his pill bottle into his denim jacket pocket, thinking to himself that he'd been a bloody fool not to have them with him all the time, and turned the box over in his hands, feeling its weight.

'Difficult to say, without busting it open.'

'Not a bomb then, fired by radio?'

'I don't think so. Not like any I've seen before. I mean,

whatever this is, wherever it came from it's not home-made. The casing is factory-produced and factory-sealed. And if it was a purpose-built bomb, you wouldn't use plastic, not this sort anyway. Can't be sure, but it has a sort of Russian feel to me. Anyway, I'd guess it's some sort of a bug.'

'You mean someone's listening to us right now?'

Geoff frowned.

'Probably not. They'd have to be pretty close, and they'd need some pretty serious equipment to pick us up. No, I think this is a battery-operated radio transmitter. Once fired it'll emit a bleep, at intervals. Probably the firing device will be able to control or alter the frequency of the bleeps. Like one every half-hour if they expect us to be stationary, one every five seconds if we're on the move. That way the batteries last longer. Anyway, if I'm right, it's a tracking device. If they found a place they could hide it, then they could keep track of us.'

'Range?'

Geoff shrugged. 'In a built-up area you might need line of sight. In open country, several kilometres.'

Parker paced about the room.

'It's a bit crazy, isn't it? I mean, they couldn't expect to place it somewhere where neither of us would ever find it.'

'Maybe, maybe not. Perhaps they just brought it on spec. Maybe I was wrong and it is a listening device. It would not have been that difficult to hide it in the room. Under a floorboard would have done.'

'You're looking better. How do you feel?'

'Fine.'

'Then I think we had better clear up the debris. In this heat they could begin to stiffen up pretty soon.'

The thin one was not a problem. They carried him down the stairs, Parker first, with the head end. Outside they draped his arms over their shoulders, put their inside arms round his waist and hoisted him up so that his toes barely dragged on the ground. The streets were still alive and frenzied, and would remain so until dawn, so they had to push their way through.

'*¿Borracho?*' an old man shouted, as he stepped aside for them.

'*Sí, borracho,*' Geoff replied.

'What does that mean?'

'Drunk.'

'I thought it might.'

The quays, however, were almost deserted and hardly lit at all. They rolled the body over: it made a splash that was virtually inaudible above the general background of noise. The oily, black water closed over him, then slowly his back broke the surface again. The water churned as fish homed in.

The other one was taller and heavier and Parker began to fear for Geoff's heart again, though he insisted he was all right. Nevertheless they took him in the opposite direction, past the railway station and on to a deserted parking lot waiting for redevelopment, dumping him on a heap of rubble. Not fish this time – just rats.

When they got back Parker again held up the small black box.

'And what are we going to do with this?'

'We ought to try to find out what it is, oughtn't we?'

'But how? Take a hammer to it? And it turns out it's a bomb and blows your hand off or worse?'

'Meanwhile it could be broadcasting everything we say. Or telling someone where we are.'

'The harbour again? I'll take it. You stay here.'

'No.'

'Why not?'

'Someone knew where those two were going. Might

come looking for them. I handled one lot on my own, but I don't guarantee to manage another. From now on I think we should always stick together. And when it comes to sleeping, let's take watches.'

'You're right. Shame. I was rather thinking I might go back and have another look at that bordello place. I don't suppose you fancy coming with me? No? Oh well, I'm knackered anyway, so let's basha down.' Parker chucked the black box up in the air and caught it before studying it one last time.

24

They spent a tedious and difficult thirty-six hours together before anything happened, sleeping uneasily, in turn, on the big bed, and going out together for food and drink. During the day, the heat in the top-floor room became almost insupportable and sleep through the night impossible. The Carnival blared and pounded all around them again, as noisy as ever. They checked out the landing and did indeed find a hatch on the far side of the toilet that opened on to the flat roof. Nothing but a low wall separated their roof from the next building in the block. They speculated endlessly and more and more fancifully about what their visitors had been up to, why they had made the moves they had, what the black box was, and so on, but could come to no reasonable conclusion.

'But it means one thing, and that's for sure,' Parker said and repeated often. 'To some extent, and we don't know how much, we're blown. Someone's watching us. And what that adds up to is that when we go in, they could be waiting for us. That could well be what that device was for. To let them know when and from what direction we make the hit.'

It was a huge relief when around noon the next day, Thursday, they heard the sound of Deeta's footsteps on the stairs. She came in as if walking on air, swung her bag on to the bed, turned and beamed at them like spring sunshine.

'What a party! How'd you guys make out? Well, don't

tell me now. I've spent the morning getting the port authorities to open up the right quay at Moín, which is where the new port is. Franco's flying in and will meet us there. I have a taxi waiting so let's move it!'

The taxi, a resprayed Plymouth convertible with the roof down, cruised through streets still ravaged by the celebrations.

'I did real well, you know,' she chortled, swinging her heavy hair back off her cheeks, first on one side and then on the other. 'I kept saying, it's just a question of getting a couple of guys with the right keys, and someone able to check out the paperwork, and finally they gave in. Gazza was a help – a guy he knows, knows a guy who . . . you know the scene.'

'Gazza?' Parker's face was blank.

'You know! The guy at the airport. The guy who let us out. Last two days I've been making out with him. I thought you knew. Geoff saw me with him. I thought you both had.'

'I saw you. But I didn't say anything,' Geoff confirmed.

Parker turned on him.

'Why the fuck not?'

'No point. You'd have just got aerated about it.'

Parker looked out over the rear door he was sitting against, face sour, lips in a thin line, drumming fingers on the side panelling.

Moín was six kilometres down the coast on the corner where the headland that supported old Limón turned back in and dropped almost to sea level, forming a bay. For a moment, before the road dropped, the long, ruler-straight coast unrolled in front of them, stretching north to the horizon and beyond – emerald sea, white surf, white sand, plantations and emerald forest as far as the eye could see, threaded by silver canals and lagoons.

The driver slowed so that they could take it all in and as they did so three low-flying military jets hurtled out of the distant haze not far out to sea and parallel to the coast. They screamed past on their left then climbed into a loop, trailing red, white and blue smoke.

'Colombian. Dassault Mirages. Bastards,' growled Geoff, recalling the Exocet missions flown by the same planes in the Falklands. 'Must be off that carrier. All part of the Carnival fun.'

They dropped into Moín and the modern port, which was almost deserted, though Deeta knew which gate to direct the driver to. There was a security guard, unshaven and bleary-eyed with the flies of his pale-khaki trousers at half-mast and a damp patch below. With him was Gascoigne Ambrosia Watts. Deeta jumped out of the car, put her arms round his neck and fed him a warm, lingering kiss while his big hands slowly caressed her buttocks through her white jeans. He disengaged his mouth and looked over her shoulder.

'Hi, guys! Meet my mate Marcellus. He has one hell of a hangover but I brought him here, and I stayed to lend the poor mutt a hand. Reckon he needs all the help he can get.'

Marcellus checked Deeta's identity as an authorized employee of Bullburger (Costa Rica) S.A. and went into a small guard-shed and returned with a book in which they all had to write their names, signatures and purpose of visit – the last in Spanish. Francisco Franco's signature preceded theirs.

'What does it say?' Parker asked.

'Take delivery of containerized cargo, the numbers, the ship they came on, move them out of the bonded area into an AFI warehouse,' explained Deeta.

'Will that mean a Customs check?'

'A formality. Franco will be seeing to it right now. We had to pay an officer to come in and do it.'

She rubbed finger and thumb together, patted Gascoigne's cheek, and got back in the car.

'Ciao, sweetheart,' she called, and then turned to Geoff. 'He wasn't always Gascoigne, you know? Apparently there's a Brit footballer who got to be a bit of a star recently . . . He wanted me to ask you if you knew him like personally, and I said yes. That's why he's been such a help. They're football crazy in this country, you know?'

Neither Geoff nor Parker believed a word of it.

The car rumbled over railway lines sunk flush with the concrete, threaded its way through a grid of warehouses, most of which carried the Associated Foods International logo or the Bullburger slogan, '*Burguesas con cojones*', before reaching a second fence and a second gate which opened into the bonded area. Franco was outside it waiting for them in a white Eldorado which also carried the AFI logo. He looked cool and neat in a cream suit and pastel-green tie.

He came over to them, all smiles, briefly shook hands with Parker and Geoff, spoke in Spanish to Deeta, and then turned back to the two men.

'The formalities are already completed and the goods are in one of our warehouses. Please pay off your taxi. We can walk from here.'

Presently they stood outside a medium-sized storage facility. Franco handed a key to his driver, whose shirt and trousers made a blue uniform and whose shirt pocket also carried the corn-cob logo. He unfastened padlocks, pushed back a heavy but well-oiled sliding door and stood back.

Franco sent him back to the car.

'Right,' the Mexican said. 'Time at last to check out . . .'
– he looked at a yellow flimsy – '. . . platforms, ladders,
ropeways, etc. for the construction of an Ecological
Observation Centre in the canopy of the rainforest. What
do you English say? I should cocoa?'

And he laughed, pulled down a lever to turn on electricity, flicked a heavy-duty light switch to turn on high
lamps threaded across the ceiling, and closed the door.

The place was empty apart from three three-metre cube
containers all on one transporter. They sat there in the
harsh light like alien goods dumped by passing visitors
from another galaxy. Geoff strode purposefully towards
them, his large blue eyes gleaming.

More keys, real ones and numbers keyed on the number
pads that released electronic locks. The side of the first
container was released and lifted to one side by Parker
and Geoff. Franco seemed unwilling to have anything to
do with anything hinting of manual labour. Inside the
container, stacked metal cases, dark green with stencilled
numbers and letters, had been strapped to hooks on the
walls so that they could not shift in transit.

The mercenaries lifted the first case down and set it
on the concrete floor of the warehouse, then went back for
the next.

'You're not going to check out every single item?'
Franco's voice expressed anxiety and disgust.

'Definitely. Every single item.'

Parker was his professional self again. He knew how
easy it was in this business to send in five good rifles to
cover fifteen duds, and he knew too that there would be
no possibility of doing anything about it once they were
back at the *finca*.

'How long will it take you?'

Parker looked at Erickson, who smoothed a broad hand
along his pony-tail, his head on one side.

'Five, six hours.'

Geoff opened the case and disclosed five rifles, mounted in expanded polystyrene to hold them secure during transportation.

'Not seen them packed like this before,' he muttered. 'Makes sense though.'

'I have,' said Parker. 'In Dubai, I think it was. One of the Gulf states anyway. I think they pack them like that for small shipments.'

Geoff lifted one clear of the polystyrene. It was the first of fifteen SLRs, the self-loading rifles which were made at the Royal Small Arms Factory, Enfield, under licence from Belgium's Fabrique Nationale d'Armes de Guerre. They were the semi-automatic rifle supplied as standard issue to British forces from the mid-fifties to the mid-eighties, and so would be familiar enough to the whole squad, apart from Wintle and Ainger. Even the Spaniards would have used the very similar FN-FAL.

'Well, that's OK, I suppose,' said Parker.

'Anything wrong?' asked Geoff.

'The younger ones anyway would have been hoping for the Colt Commando. Shorter, easier to handle in jungle, lighter, and it's the one they will have most recently trained with. And it's a neater piece of kit.'

'No Colt Commandos. But there are five M16s somewhere.'

Geoff handled the SLR almost lovingly, ran his palm over the furniture, let the butt sit in his shoulder for a second so that it seemed that cybernetically he'd grown a third arm. Then very quickly he stripped down the main moving parts, held them to the light, sniffed at them, put them together again, and moved on to the next weapon.

'Well?'

'It's OK. They've been used. A fair bit. But well cared for. I see no problems.'

An hour later and Geoff was ready to move on to a larger box. It contained two General Purpose Machine-Guns, L7A2s. He unpacked the first gimpy, lifted it against his body, half-supporting its eleven kilos on his bent knee.

'This really is a lovely beast. Best since the Bren. Absolutely no nonsense at all, every bit, every shading of an angle here, the placing of a screw or a rivet, has a purpose, makes sense, and does its job. Nothing unnecessary, nothing silly. You know how it is with more modern weapons. It's all so fucking competitive now. Bolt-ons here, bolt-ons there, optional extras – you name it. But this is the business.'

Parker had heard Erickson was a bit of a nutter about guns. And his appreciation of the weapons he was handling seemed to have more to do with art than the battlefield. But he clearly knew his stuff, and that was what mattered.

Knew it too well.

'Hang on a sec. Sixteen of us in total. Yet already we have two L7A2s, and fifteen SLRs and five M16s. The gimpies need two experienced men each and that leaves us very short-handed in experienced blokes elsewhere.'

He looked at the other boxes now revealed in the second container. 'And I can see there's more specialized stuff to come. Couple of mortars? What else? So what's going on, then?'

Parker shifted about, almost as if he needed a pee.

'I suppose F.-C. knows we're going into a pretty severe training period. Perhaps he ordered over the top to cover any damage or loss . . . during, ah, training.'

Geoff began to strip down the second machine-gun.

'It's getting a bit hot in here, isn't it?'

As the afternoon wore on a heavy heat had begun to envelop them and both were sweating profusely. The source was the clouded glass of a row of skylights in the girder roof.

'Yes. I'll see if I can get Franco to do something about it.'

With some relief Parker wandered across the wide, echoing empty spaces to a small, half-glazed cubicle where Franco and Deeta were smoking, chatting listlessly, listening to the radio: the *Ode to Joy* from Beethoven's Ninth Symphony, played by a steel band to a samba beat. He pushed open the door. It was like walking into a refrigerator, the difference was so great.

'It's cool here. Can you make it cool out there?' He took in a table littered with beer and Coke bottles, coarse brown paper bags that must have held food, and suddenly he felt angry. 'And get us something to eat and drink, would you?'

He slammed the door and went back to Geoff, who was repacking the second gimpy.

'The Colonel,' Geoff said, 'F.-C., and we all know what that can stand for . . . is not only a fucking cunt – he is now a businessman. Once a soldier, I grant you, but now a businessman. And businessmen are fucking cunts. So no way did he over-order. He ordered for a task force of what? Twenty-five, even thirty men?' He shook his head. 'I only hope he knew what he was doing when he cut us down to half that.'

Franco came out of the cubicle, trotted across to a corner of the warehouse, and threw a couple of switches. Fans began to turn, pumps pulsate. The temperature dropped in minutes. Bananas and coffee need to travel chilled, and those were the commodities usually stored there. Deeta brought them tortillas stuffed with cold, spiced minced pork, beers and Cokes.

Geoff was now breaking open the largest package of all.

'Shit,' he said, half-dragging, half-lifting a large contraption out of the big cardboard box. It looked like four stove-pipes, or mortars come to that, welded together on a box which housed a firing mechanism.

'It's an M202 flame weapon. Launches incendiary rockets . . .'

'I know what an M202 is,' said Parker through a mouthful of tortilla.

Geoff turned away, stamped across the concrete floor, then turned on his heel.

'So what do we want one of these for?' he muttered.

'Set fire to things.'

'People?'

Parker shrugged.

'If they get in the way,' he said.

'They'd better not. I've seen people die lots of ways, but being torched must be just about the worst.'

But he had lost Parker's attention. Parker was now staring open-mouthed at the glassed-in cubicle. Deeta was facing them with her elbows on the table, her chin in her hands. Her eyes were closed, but she was smiling beatifically. Why? Because head up, eyes also closed, jacket off, tie at half-mast and trousers too presumably, Franco was humping her slowly and gently from behind.

'That bitch is rutting again,' he growled.

'I could see you were upset,' she said later, 'but I don't see why you should be. We just got bored, that's all.'

25

With the second container checked, the weaponry was complete. Fifteen SLRs, five M16s, two L7A2s, two M202 flame weapons, two 51mm mortars, twenty 9mm Browning High Power Mark III handguns in Len Dixon holsters, five Heckler & Koch MP5 sub-machine-guns, and finally – and this was the weapon that moved Geoff Erickson even more deeply than the gimpies – an L96A1 Accuracy International sniper rifle with a Schmidt and Bender 6 × 42 telescopic sight.

The way he caressed it irritated Parker, who was still in a temper over Deeta.

'Stop creaming yourself over the fucking thing. It's only a gun after all.'

Geoff looked at him with narrowed, slightly glazed eyes.

'It is a small miracle of totally dedicated precision engineering. Basically very simple, as all non-automatic bolt-action guns are, but refined to near perfection. Why do I say 'near' perfection? Because no one likes to admit anything man-made is perfect. But this bloody near is. I just hope we, preferably I, have an opportunity to use it – there's no point in having it if the target is less than five hundred metres away.'

Parker remembered the watch-towers on the corners of the maize fields.

'That can be arranged,' he said.

'Good,' Geoff grunted. 'What's more, this is brand-new, ex-factory. So how the hell did he get hold of it? I mean, everything else' – he waved a hand over the warehouse floor – 'is here because it's no longer service-issue. It's all kit, good kit I grant you, that's being or has been replaced, and that's how it leaks into the sort of markets F.-C. can get into. But not this.'

Parker shrugged, unable to enlighten him as to the rifle's provenance. He did not know that an oil sheik had bought it so he could stalk mountain lions and then sold it on when someone blew the whistle on him.

At the front of the third container there were two boxed Gemini eight-man inflatables. No outboards as far as Geoff could see, but four single-bladed paddles to each craft. Next came the ammunition: boxes of 7.62mm, tracer and incendiary as well as conventional; 5.56mm for the M16s (not enough); shells for the mortars, HE and white-phosphorus; twenty preloaded, four-round incendiary-rocket clips for the M202; 9mm parabellum for the Brownings and the Heckler & Koch MP5s. There were also large kitbags filled with fatigues in a variety of sizes and printed in jungle disruptive pattern, and belt kits with double magazine pouches on the left, and on the right a compass pouch, a survival knife like a small machete, water bottles with filters, and a bayonet.

'Christ, you don't need to check those.'

'Just counting. Twenty-seven, twenty-eight . . . That's about what I thought. Some early stage there must have been, when you, maybe with Bennett and Goodall, decided thirty was the minimum requirement to do the job with no or very little risk of casualties. And now we're down to sixteen. I don't like it, Mr Parker. Not at all do I like it.'

'Why not? We have good intelligence. Aerial photographs, inside info. Sixteen can do it – if they do as they're told.'

'You know fucking well what I mean,' Geoff barked as he stooped to pick up a Browning, which he hefted from hand to hand. Small though it was, it was as much a piece of sculpture to him as the Accuracy International. 'In peacetime or involved in a minor war, operations are planned and conducted on a no-loss basis. Your voter back home wouldn't countenance anything else. Of course there are losses, there always will be, especially if you have the Yanks on your side, but no one goes in on an even Stevens basis expecting superior training and equipment to carry the day. But mercenaries, soldiers of fortune . . .' – he let out a bitter laugh – 'we march to a different beat.'

Parker eyed Erickson warily as if the man were a dog presumed reliable and faithful over the years but now suddenly showing all the symptoms of rabies.

'It's the fucking market with us, ain't it? Sixteen go in, four come out. Mission accomplished, and you've only paid for sixteen and only risked sixteen lots of kit. That's how it works . . .'

Parker attempted anger and upper-class, know-it-all bravado.

'Listen here, Erickson. Finchley-Camden is no monster. And another thing too: he values us as assets, not, even though we're freelance, as expendable assets but as ones he can call on again and again. He wouldn't stay in business very long otherwise. Come on now, there are still a few things left to sort.'

But Geoff was not through yet.

'Sure. You, Bennett, Goodall, maybe Smithy and me, even the turnip-bashers, and Jack Glew of course . . . he'll want us back. But the others? The youngsters? The Spaniards? Bill and Ben? They're expendable. And the Strachan twins – who wants them back? It's a dirty business . . .'

'But someone has to do it.'

'I'm not so sure about that. But there will always be some poor bugger who will.'

Footsteps echoed across the concrete. Franco slipped a comb through his shiny black hair. Deeta pushed an errant flap of her black silk blouse back into the top of her white jeans, and pouted a kiss in the general direction of the Englishmen.

'We have to go now,' Franco said. 'Doug Harvey is waiting for us at the airport.'

'Why? What do you mean?'

'I have a business to run in San José, remember? And I needed Señorita O'Donnell with me for a day or two.' Impossible not to detect the smugness in his voice. 'So we shall say *adiós*, and er, leave you to it. Come along, *cara*!'

'What about this lot?'

'I have a driver for you. He'll be here in . . .' – he looked at his watch, a chunky affair on a wide gold-and-platinum bracelet – 'in about an hour. You should have it all back in the containers by then, as he should not see what he is carrying. He knows where to go. You can travel with him if you like, or make your own arrangements – hire a car, a taxi' – he shrugged – 'what you like. But we must go.'

'You're leaving us without an interpreter . . .'

'Don't worry. The señorita will be back with you the day after tomorrow when Harvey flies over to do your little photography mission. OK? So, *adiós*.'

When they had gone, Geoff said: 'They only say that when they don't expect to see you again.'

'What?'

'"*Adiós*". Well, we'd better get through the rest.'

Six medical kits and six radio transmitters – the latter the detachable part of a PRC319, with the electronic part left out. What was left was a very light and practicable RT unit. Geoff checked that the medical kits were adapted for jungle warfare. He held up a mucus extractor designed to suck out debris from a bullet wound.

'I hope that if I come to need this, there's someone around who knows how to use it. And six of everything? We'll need an elephant to carry it all.'

By now Parker was fed up with Erickson's whinging, and said as much, though he wondered if perhaps he was suffering a delayed stress reaction to killing the two men a couple of days earlier. Possibly. Yet there had been nothing cold-blooded or unnecessary about it. Things like that did get to some men. But for the life of him he could not fathom why.

Presently they heard the towing vehicle pull up, and went out to look at it. There was room for both of them in the cab, and they decided to travel back to Medio Queso in it. The driver, pointing at his watch and miming there would be no need to sleep, indicated that they would get there early the following morning.

26

The beef savannah, then the plantations of sugar cane, bananas and maize on the Costa Rican side of the border, slid away behind them like a pancake slipping off a plate, the plate being the forest they had been carved from. Ahead the San Juan river uncoiled like a yellowish-brown snake. Over to the left they could see the immense expanse of Lago de Nicaragua, filling the western horizon. To the right the shores of the Caribbean were lost behind the dense mist that hung over much of the forest. Most of it was dark, though occasional shafts of sunlight picked out brighter colours where holes in the cloud canopy let it through. Presently they crossed the river and, looking down, Parker recognized the island hugging the north bank where they had stayed too long, eaten and drunk too well, where Goodall and Deeta . . . And then, quite suddenly wisps of grey cloud drifted past, and occasionally blanked out the land below.

'Shit,' said Harvey. 'We'll have to go lower than we need, lower than I want. Bloody rain's early today.'

A few heavy drops splattered against the windscreen as he switched on the wipers.

'What difference will it make?'

'Without the height we'll have to make four sweeps across instead of the two I was hoping for . . .'

'And?' Parker sensed he'd left something unsaid.

'I expect you know there was an earlier attack, five years ago.'

'Yes.'

'I was part of it. Spraying defoliant. And the bastards had a Stinger. Damn near got me. I don't think they'll do the same again: this time I'm not so obviously hostile. Here we go.'

Harvey had already explained to Parker that the Japanese aerial-photography system he had bolted to the fuselage beneath them was fully automated. Activated, it would focus on the ground below, determine the best aperture setting, and fire at one-second intervals, exposing up to three hundred and sixty frames of fine-grain, military-standard negative film.

'All you have to do is sit back and watch,' he had concluded.

Watch, yes; sit back, no. Parker shifted back and forth and from side to side, trying to capture in his mind's eye all he possibly could of what lay below, first through the windscreen then through the side windows. He knew from experience that a visual survey often retained information which would aid interpretation of the photographs later on.

The trees became patchy, there was more land under the plough, and then there it was, rushing towards then up at them, the perspectives broadening until it slipped by beneath them like a map. Parker was appalled.

The plantation, a square kilometre divided by dead-straight paths into nine equal lots of maize, was just as he expected, just as it had been in the photographs Bennett, Goodall and he had seen on the billiard table at Wrykin Heath. The crucial difference was that it, and the small compound beyond, including the greenhouses and other buildings they were now passing over, was not only enclosed in a pentagon of high fencing with watch-towers at each corner but that the towers were set in diamond-shaped redoubts in what is one of the classic patterns fortifications have taken ever since the invention of gunpowder. Any assault on any one of the sides could be covered by enfilading fire on both flanks from fortified positions.

As they climbed out of their first sweep they passed over a steel bar gate and a track that wound round a low rise of higher, forest-clad land. Parker recalled there was a village two kilometres down the track and then an unmetalled road that led to what passes for civilization in one of Nicaragua's less accessible backwaters.

And then they flew over the compound again, but this time on a different trajectory, so that it was framed in the south-facing passenger window. Again there were differences. As well as the controlled-environment units and the two-storey building with lab, records and whatever else they had been commissioned to destroy, there were four long huts, made of preformed construction units with windows, but with the usual thatched roofs, and one smaller one, of corn stalks on a bamboo frame and fitted with radio antennae. It did not need much imagination of the military sort to guess what they were: barracks and a control centre or HQ. Yet it's not often that a barracks is surrounded by neat rows of beans, tomatoes and peppers flourishing on bamboo canes.

Parker suddenly remembered the meeting at Wrykin Heath, the glib awfulness of the little speech he had made, and Goodall's and Bennett's subdued but boyish excitement at the thought of the mission they were about to embark on.

What had he said? 'They make bad defenders, they won't like sitting around on their arses for months, and they won't take to routine garrison discipline.' Something like that. 'They're barracked two kilometres away in the village, and only fifteen or twenty are on site at any one time . . .' What he had not allowed for, because he had not visualized himself in the garrison commander's position, or remembered his own basic staff training, was that the one thing you get a defending garrison to spend every waking hour on is maintaining and perfecting your defences.

There was a final factor he had not faced, but he now knew he would have to. A factor he had kept from Goodall because he, not Goodall, had been the one with the binoculars. The neat orderliness of what he had seen, the vegetable patches, were all part of it. He knew, and the others did not, that at least some of the garrison's complement – it could even be the entire garrison – were women.

The sun winked briefly back at the plane like a heliograph, and like a heliograph it spelled out a message. You're watching us – but we're watching you. I hope you got sun-blindness as a result, Parker muttered to himself, visualizing someone using binoculars to track the plane into the sun.

Doug Harvey leaned across to him: 'I reckon they're on to us. Do you want me to go on?'

'Yes. Unless you see them lining up a Stinger.'

Of course the garrison was on to them. Who else could the two men Erickson had had to kill have been working for, if not the garrison? And again the doubt gnawed: what the fuck had that little black box been for?

As they came back for the fourth and final run they could see small groups of figures in combat fatigues gathering outside the huts to watch them. Some even waved. At least they weren't pointing Stingers at them.

'Go as close as you can to one of those watch-towers. I need to suss out just what factors are involved.'

'Well. Let's hope, or anyway pretend, that ground-to-air missiles don't form part of it. Or an M60 firing tracer.

She's only a little old bird, and it wouldn't take a lot to knock her out of the sky.'

Nevertheless, he took the Beaver down another thirty metres and nudged her to the left. The watch-tower rushed up at them, then flashed away to the side and was gone, but the brief glimpse – the photographs should confirm it – had been enough. The timber that supported the tower was set inside a bunker solidly constructed out of hurdles and sandbags. Again, the figures on the ground and the watch-tower platform waved.

'I reckon some of them could be sheilas.'

'If they are, it's something to keep to yourself.'

'I can understand that.' Harvey was grim. 'I'd have to feel pretty menaced by a woman before I'd point a gun at her and pull the trigger.'

He put the plane into a shallow climb, banked on to the bearing that would take them back to the *finca*. Parker felt pissed off by a lot of things – not least Harvey.

'You've flown combat,' he said to the Australian.

'How'd you know?'

'The way you fly this crate. Nam? The RAAF flew combat in Nam. Napalmed the odd village or two, did you?'

Harvey looked sour as well as grim.

'I was a youngster. Barely out of my teens. I believed them when they said things like: "They're just little yellow folk. Not like us. Not quite human."'

The 'not quite humans' gathered in the square hut, or at least the ones with 'extra responsibility', for that was how the ones with rank saw themselves – rather than as senior officers. Most of them sat on folding wooden chairs round the central table. The Commandant, sitting in the middle, coughed on her roll-up as she smudged a shred of black tobacco away from her thin, orange lips.

'Daniel?'

A handsome dark man in his late twenties briefly smoothed his glossy black moustache before speaking.

'The registration letters. It's the Beaver that belongs to the Australian. Harvey.'

'The one that sprayed you in the attack five years ago?'

'That's right.'

'So what was he doing this time?'

'Photography. You could see the camera underneath the plane.'

The Commandant breathed a rattly sigh.

'Does this help us at all?'

'Not really. It'll help them. A lot.'

Esther, the black woman from Brixton, spoke abruptly: 'We should have foreseen this.'

'What . . . and shot him down? We no longer have Stingers. The Chamorro government took them away from us.'

'We could have disguised things. Made the place look stronger than it is. Or even weaker . . . lured them into a trap.'

'Señora, not even you thought of that until now, so how do you expect us to be so clever?' A smile and spread palms defused the sarcasm. 'Still nothing on Manuel or Juan?'

She looked across the small space at a thin old man with white stubble on both his chin and head.

'I'm sorry, Carmelita, but yes. I was going to tell you, but the plane came over . . .'

'All right . . . I think you have bad news.'

'Yes. We have definite confirmation now that the two bodies found in Limón, on the waste ground and in the harbour, were them. The Tico police are treating them as routine Carnival casualties. Eight people died during the week, so why should they do otherwise? But that's not all.'

'Go on.'

'Our source there checked out the room they had been renting. All their stuff was there but not the radio signaller. The only conclusion we can come to is that Juan took it with him . . .'

'Why would he do that?'

'And they, the Englishmen, found it on him when they killed him. I don't know why Juan took it with him. If he did . . .'

Another woman chipped in from the back. The words were muffled, strained through the handkerchief she held to her eyes and mouth to restrain her tears.

'Juan knew it was very valuable, the only one we had. He would have been afraid to leave it behind – in a public rooming house.'

Silence fell over the crowded room. Then the Commandant smashed the table with her palm.

'*¡Hostia, sangre de Dios*! If they found it . . .'

'They might not know what it is,' said another voice, male this time.

'They'll know. And that means that they know we are watching them. They know we know what they are planning.'

'Well. That explains one thing,' Esther put in.

'What?'

'Why they were so blatant, so obvious about their fly-over just now. They know we know who they are – else why should we be planning to plant a tracking device in their kit?'

The Commandant began to stub out her roll-up, thought better of it, shook out another, and lit it from the first. Shards of flaming tobacco dropped on to the table in front of her.

'It's worse than that. If they know what it was, and guess that we were going to plant it not on them in Limón, where they would surely have discovered it, but among their weapons at the *finca*, then they will have worked out that someone over there . . .'

She left the words unsaid. Esther filled them in.

'. . . is on our side.'

As the Beaver touched down on the now much improved airstrip, Parker could see that a small group of his men were clustered around Sánchez and trying to wake the steers up into some action. The rest, stripped to shorts and jungle boots were playing a fast and furious game of five-aside football. Montalbán was weaving his way towards a goal improvised out of a couple of fence posts hammered into the soft earth when one of the Gurhkas brought him down with a vicious late tackle from behind. The field exploded into a well-orchestrated and entirely play-acted storm of abuse which Mike Henchard ended by placing the ball on an improvised penalty spot, from where he scored through an empty goal.

Four survivors out of sixteen? Parker thought. We'll be lucky if it's no worse.

27

Bill Ainger had relished the pistol practice they had been through an hour earlier. First there had been the wonderful feel in his hand of the hard, compact gun, seen so often in the sort of films he liked best; then the shock of power that went through his palms and wrists when, double-handed in the approved fashion, he pulled the trigger; the smack the report gave his eardrums; and finally the tiny, dark hole that appeared in the target twenty metres away. Now he took his right hand away from the stock of the SLR he was carrying across his chest, butt up under his cheek, thumb behind the pistol grip, fingers stretched over it towards but not touching the trigger assembly, muzzle lying over the crook of his left arm pointing at the ground, just in the way the squaddies always hold them on TV as they move through the streets of Belfast. And he sniffed his fingers, briefly savouring the lingering smell of cordite and refined machine oil.

He grinned at himself, for the action had triggered the memory of how, after his first girl, his first playground fumble, he had not washed his fingers until he was quite sure the smell of her had gone, a smell not unlike that of some of the flowers around him now. First girl? Only girl, because the next four years had been spent uncomfortably female-free at Her Majesty's Pleasure.

The memory, and what he was doing, and what he was experiencing, and the excitement of the gun across his chest, and where he was – all of it suddenly produced a strange choking feeling in his chest and throat, the hair on his neck stiffened, his penis thickened, and tears pricked his eyes.

'What the fucking hell's wrong with me,' he muttered, for the word that might have done had had no real meaning for him until then. The word? Happiness. More than a small cigar.

Concentrate. Get back on the job. Remember where you are. He glanced forward and to his right. Fifteen metres away he could see John Crick easing his way through a tangle of lianas, and beyond him, even further forward the blackie, Winston Smith. And behind him there was Julián Sánchez, the fat Spaniard, always a laugh, but moving now as silently as a cat.

Not much noise but in the distance, a couple of kilometres or more away, a machine-gun barked in short, five-round bursts, and birds stirred uneasily high in the canopy, releasing a brown leaf that slowly floated down ahead of him. But when it just about reached his eye level it drifted into a spotlight of sun, spread pure metallic-blue wings and lazily began to climb back to where it had come from: a butterfly, the biggest and most beautiful he had ever seen.

Big Mike Henchard slid forward from the firing position and slipped the hinge-clip off the foresight of the gimpy's barrel. He then took the foresight blade between his thumb and forefinger and screwed it down to counter the error. His first burst had clipped the top of the improvised target.

'Now look, sonny,' he said to Colin Wintle, 'chances are you won't have to do this, not if I keep my head down anyway, but you'd better cotton on in case . . .'

Colin glanced across the space, less than a metre, that separated them in the sangar they had improvised from fallen tree trunks on the edge of the forest. His grin was hesitant, hopeful. So far his duties as number two in a gimpy position had not gone beyond humping some of the peripheral equipment that went with it, a tripod weighing nearly fourteen kilos and a thousand rounds of 7.62 link weighing twice that much over a kilometre of savannah, hauling the branches about to make the sangar, and then holding the belt at the angle Henchard prescribed, while the dour West Countryman shot pieces off a lump of cardboard they had set up two hundred metres away. Was he at last going to shoot the thing himself?

'Right. Notice correct firing position. Always sit if you can − if the cover makes it safe to − with the butt in your right shoulder, left hand clamped over the waist to keep it steady and control the recoil, second pad only of the right index finger on the trigger and only the thumb behind the pistol grip. If you wrap all your fingers round it you'll grip it when it fires and sure as hell you'll pull to the right. Now you try.'

Henchard stood and helped Colin into the position he'd described, swivelling the lad's shoulders to the correct angle, checking the grip of his left hand. Then he reached round and unclipped all but ten of the linked rounds from the belt Colin had been feeding for him.

'I want it in two bursts, five each time, ten seconds between. *Go!*'

Although clamped by the tripod, the dead metal and wood suddenly seemed like a howling wild animal, pummelling Colin's shoulder and desperately trying to wrench itself out of his grip. He remembered though to release the trigger, count to ten and then fire again. But this time there were just two shots left − he'd fired off eight in the first burst. And the cardboard sheet, stapled to a frame improvised out of three strips of timber, looked exactly as it had before.

He looked up at Henchard.

'Where'd it all go?'

'Christ knows. But don't be surprised if Gordon serves up monkey stew come supper time. Look, we'll try tracer – give you an idea what's happening.'

But Gordon Bennett had other ideas. The day before he had scrounged timber and corrugated iron off the *vaqueros* who looked after Thomas Ford's cattle and he had rigged up what looked like a sort of makeshift bus shelter but was in fact a place where he could spit-roast large chunks of meat. He stacked the driest logs and branches he could find along the floor of it, lit it at dawn, made sure it was going well, then damped it down. Then, with Deeta beside him, he had driven the jeep up to the modern ranch house, bargained with the fat American for a steer and still ended up paying fifty per cent more than the market price. Though Bennett was normally a very careful shopper it didn't really bother him – it wasn't his money.

Then back to the bunk-house where Deeta asked for and got a *vaquero* who knew how to butcher – in both senses of the word. With Augusto's help, for that was his name, Bennett selected an animal of about six months, with a touch more fat on him than the others. He was still suckling, but eating grass too, and he reckoned the combination would add up to flavour with tenderness.

Augusto was small, bandy and barrel-chested, yet roped the bullock with one easy sweep of his lasso, and together they hauled him away from the corrals and towards the old *finca*. His mother lowed after him three or four times but made no attempt to follow. By the time they had him behind the *finca* she was cropping the long, wet grass again.

'You may not like the next bit,' Bennett told Deeta.

But she watched. Augusto pushed his palm up and

down the steer's broad, hard face, murmured soothingly, then Bennett grasped the small, stubby beginnings of horns and yanked the head back. The *vaquero* cut the jugular, releasing an avalanche of dark blood which instantly attracted a swarm of large black flies. They waited until the last kick of his back leg, already a purely nervous galvanization, for the animal was clinically dead within two or three minutes, had taken place.

'Where I come from,' Deeta said, 'we would have kept the blood.'

'For black pudding?' Bennett asked. 'I thought you only used pig blood for that.'

'No. For fertilizer.'

She turned away, and climbed the back steps into the big kitchen. She supposed she was relieved that they did not expect her, as the only female around, to do all the cooking, but she also felt she'd like to help. She found a big sack of yams and began to slice the red skin off the yellow flesh, then sighed. Seventeen was an awful lot to feed at one sitting.

Augusto had brought his three principal tools – a cleaver, a saw and the big knife he had already used, and he used them now to sever the head and the legs at the hocks. Then he skinned and gutted the beast. Suddenly he began to jabber away in Spanish at Bennett, who had to go back into the kitchen and call Deeta out.

'He wants,' she explained, 'to take all the bits and pieces back to the bunk-house: they'll use it to, um, beef up the bean stew that's their basic diet.'

Gordon thought for a moment. He'd had in mind, for the next day, a splendid tripe dish in a sort of goulash sauce that he rarely had a chance to make: the Strachans, even perhaps Glew and Goodall, would relish it, but he suspected the others, especially the younger ones, would reject it. So he agreed.

Now came the moment of decision: should he break up the carcass or broil it whole? He looked at his watch: they had made good use of the time and there were still four hours available, so he decided to go for the second option. He and Augusto ran two spits he had prepared through the carcass, rubbed it inside and out with coarse salt, and hoisted it into position over the fire, which was now burning slowly and very hot. In the event some parts would be charred to a cinder, while others would appear to be almost raw. But he knew there was no danger – meat that freshly killed can be eaten raw with very little risk.

And the cooking needed very little attention, leaving time for him and Deeta to chop pineapples, mangoes, prickly pears, cherimoyas or custard-apples, guavas and passion-fruit, and other fruits he did not even know the name of into a plastic bucket which he laced with brown sugar and rum, and on top of which he placed blocks of ice, also brought down from the ranch house.

'You'd make a good husband,' Deeta said.

'I nearly did. But she buggered off with someone else while I was in the Falklands.'

'Las Malvinas.'

'Yes, well . . . Where do you come from, then? Tim said Miami, but I don't reckon they save beef blood for fertilizer in Miami. Stockyards yes, but not ordinary people. What I mean is, where in Miami do they kill their meat the way we just did?'

'In Cuba they do. We did.'

Then she fell silent.

The lads voted it the best meal they'd ever had. Only Geoff demurred, refusing to eat any.

'Burnt meat smells the same, whatever the animal. And it's a smell I've had in my nostrils too often.'

'Jolly good, Gordon, and never mind our resident whinger,' Parker added. 'Maybe we should do it again, the day before the off.'

They had eleven days left. Not enough, and he knew it. What he did not know was how many other things were coming together to destroy them.

28

A circular storm stacked cumulus above a horizon where bruise-coloured cloud base fused with black sea. Nearer, the crowns of palms thrashed in sudden gusts of wind and the scarlet and purple bougainvillaea shivered and shimmered as fingers of air pushed through the blossoms. Fitful sun struck rich white gold from the chrome of cars and a darker glow from bronze-tinted glass. A rolling bank of dark vapour coming off the sea pushed back the sunbeams and left the six octagonal towers that clustered asymmetrically round a taller pentagon looking almost black. Only the giant sign on top, its 'A' and 'F' in gold, thick and round, then a stylized chunky corn-cob in flashing green for the 'I', continued to catch the diminished light.

Shallow steps, glossy and dark, climbed to toughened-glass doors which slipped soundlessly open as a tall, lean man, immaculate in a black silk Armani day suit, trotted up through them and into an atrium filled with ferns and ornamental palms, lit by concealed spots. A fountain tinkled and a tape on an endless loop played the opening bars of the slow movement of Beethoven's 'Pastoral' Symphony. There was no receptionist, no guard, but each of the six black doors had a thin slit through which a plastic card could be swiped. The man chose a door and took a lift to the offices that clustered in the top of one of the towers. There men, mostly men, very few women, sat at huge desks beneath more palms and ferns. They murmured to each other over cordless phones, keyed in commands, and mused over the green glowing data that pulsed or streamed across their screens. They paid no attention to the cloud palaces that formed, shifted, tumbled on the horizon, to the endless succession of spume-crested rollers, or the dance of storm-tossed palms. They heard nothing but each other's voices, laid-back and cool, and the ticks and bleeps of shifting displays.

Higher still was the office of the Vice-President (Latin America). Its enormous windows filled three sides of the pentagon and all looked out on to the ocean. The Vice-President alone of all who worked there did likewise, using high-powered binoculars, but only when nubile girls were surfing. He was a lean, grey, cadaverous man, quite different from the fat oaf who had preceded him and who had been murdered by Esther Somers, from far-away Brixton, five years earlier. A bleep. He touched a key or two, and information scrolled down. He touched another button.

'Jethro? I guess you just got in. The entry log says so. You'd better come up.'

The man in the Armani suit arrived three minutes later. They shook hands, briefly.

'Matt.'

'Jethro. How's it going, then?'

Neither sat down. Corporate etiquette demanded that interviews at executive level should be conducted on the hoof for the first ten minutes, at managerial level twenty, while below that you did not sit down at all. Management consultants had calculated that twenty-five thousand hours a year were thus saved by keeping the chit-chat to a minimum.

'Not good.'

'Tell.'

'Tom Ford tells us that there are only sixteen combatants in our corner. Admittedly they are well equipped, almost too well equipped. Moreover, at least eight are not the ex-SAS we were promised. The ones who were are training the rest, some of whom are very raw indeed.'

'Prognosis?'

'Failure.'

'Who says so?'

'Patton and Powell – the military consultants we usually use. They've seen these . . .' – he tipped the photographs Harvey had taken from the Beaver two days earlier over the big desk – 'and they reckon a committed, battle-hardened garrison of fifty, even with the lousy armament they've got, could hold it against a brigade for ten hours. By when the Nic army would have moved up to relieve the garrison. They reckon the guys we actually have will back off in half an hour – if they're not all dead.'

'What happened, then?'

'Cowboy outfit. That firm Maud went to in London must be cowboys. Cutting costs all the way – except in equipment, which, as I said, is not only good but about double what they have the manpower to use. I'm afraid Maud was taken. We'll have to activate the back-up.'

Vice-President Matt Annenburg took a turn towards the window. Down below, a surfer staggered along the deserted walkway above the heaving sea, struggling to hold on to his board as great gusts of wind plucked at it.

'These . . . cowboys. Will they make enough noise, start enough fires to cover the back-up?'

Armani suit grimaced. The back-up had been his idea. It had to work, or else he would be in the shit with Maud Adler – instead of in her shoes, which is where he wanted to be.

210

'I guess so. Yes, I guess so.'

When he was gone, Annenburg picked up a phone as secure as any line can be in the country with the most advanced and comprehensive surveillance potential that any nation has ever had.

'Kramer? I want a line to the Colombian military attaché in Washington DC. Then the CIA Central American desk at Langley. And when I'm through with that, one to Tom Ford at the Hacienda Santa Ana, Costa Rica.'

Since he was the best private investigator in San José, Celestino Márquez was not only a member of the Union Club, but was even welcome there. Inside, the atmosphere was one of wealth made comfortable by an indefinable shabbiness. It was the perfect place for the wheeling and dealing which went on between the old-money, coffee-rich members of the oligarchy, brash new entrepreneurs in construction and the tourist industry, government ministers and senior civil servants.

Márquez had worked for most of them at one time or another, sorting out the merry-go-round of marital infidelity, uncovering just who was on the take from whom, passing on information and disinformation for a fee, and so on. He was a hunchback, with one leg in a brace on a raised boot, and he suffered from chronic asthma – which helped the people he worked for to tolerate him. They might fear him, they certainly needed him, but they could also despise him.

He had arranged to meet a senior official from the Ministry of Internal Affairs, the Minister of Law and Order. Don Diego had corrugated black hair, silvered at the temples, a perfectly aquiline face, and wore a turtle-neck sweater of wool as light as silk and as blue as the ultramarine of deep seas, over perfectly tailored grey trousers. He was drinking coffee in an alcove of the main club-room when Márquez hobbled up to him.

He waved the investigator into the pale-grey buttoned-silk chair next to him, and poured a black stream of coffee for him.

'What can I do for you?'

Márquez sucked briefly on his pocket ventilator, then sipped his coffee. It was good; the best in the world.

'I'll come straight to the point. A group of British mercenaries are training on Tom Ford's land. They are well equipped with mortars and machine-guns as well as small arms, of which they have more than they can possibly use . . .'

Don Diego smiled quietly to himself.

'How could they possibly . . .?' he began, but Márquez waved him silent with a claw-like hand.

'As I am sure you already know, they came in through the AFI facilities at Limón.' Márquez's voice was hoarse, crow-like, yet strangely quiet. 'And you will know that they aim to attack and destroy the maize research and development station on the other side of the San Juan. AFI is paying a lot of money to have that done, just as they did five years ago. Now, I have a client . . .' – Don Diego smiled uneasily to himself: Márquez generally did have a client – usually one with a lot of clout – '. . . who wants the mission to be carried out but who is very interested indeed, for reasons of his own, in seeing these arms confiscated as soon as it has been completed. Many of them will not even leave Ford's land, the rest can be picked up as the men return to Costa Rica. I understand this will all happen on or around 5 November . . .'

'My dear Don Celestino, I am not quite sure why, just supposing there was any truth at all in what you are saying, I should want to confiscate these arms. Clearly they do not represent any threat . . .'

But Márquez had fallen into an asthmatic fit which anyone who did not know him and his tactics would have diagnosed as terminal. Don Diego knew better and waited until the ventilator had done its work.

'I am not sure how I would interpret the presence of a large number of military weapons on our soil,' the investigator wheezed, 'in the hands of a gang of mercenaries employed by a Yankee corporation . . .'

'International. AFI is international. It's what the "I" stands for.'

'. . . a corporation as powerful as United Fruit, and far more secretive and ambitious, but I am sure I know how journalists, not only our own but the foreign press too, would interpret this. Some at any rate might suspect the possibility that a coup was planned, a rerun of the Chile experience . . .'

The Minister of Law and Order thought it through for a moment.

'Don Celestino, clearly you can arrange for the press to discover those arms and those mercenaries if you want to. Can I be certain that if I do what you ask, the press will definitely *not* discover them?'

'You know I can speak for the editors of *La Nación* and *La República*. If some broadsheet journalist stumbles on it, then you will have to deal with it.'

Don Diego conceded the reasonableness of this. The number of desktop publications that hit the streets of San José every week varied from ten to fifty: mostly produced by fascists, racists and elements on the further shores of socialism.

There were details to be worked out: the commander of the Rural Guard in the province of Alajuela would have to be paid to get the timing right, Don Diego himself would want to cash in a handful of Brownie points owed to him by Márquez for past favours, and so on. Nevertheless, when he returned to his office a couple of blocks away up Calle Dos, Márquez was able to confirm by fax to Saul Kagan in London that the confiscation of the arms was in place for 6 November. Kagan passed the news on to Matt Dobson, who took an hour off work to celebrate with Bollinger '90 and quail's eggs.

'Gordon, I am sorry but I shall have to be quite brutal about this.'

Parker moved uneasily about the veranda. Some dim recollection of a house-master at his public school nudged his mind. Also a major in his original unit who used to have a swagger stick to bolster his authority when telling chaps news they might not want to hear. He took a breath and went on.

'The thing is, you are not on board as cook. Don't think I'm not very grateful indeed, as we all are, for the wonderful meals you turn out for us, under the most difficult conditions. I only wish we weren't on the point in the map of Costa Rica furthest from both oceans . . .'

'Lake Nicaragua and the San Juan are both full of excellent fish, sir.'

'. . . so you could regale us with some of your seafood dishes. However . . .'

Bennett lengthened his thin lips in a grimace of resignation.

'However, you are here not because you are an excellent cook, ah, chef, but because you are a soldier, a trooper, and of all the ones here the one who is best at night-work, and also a wizard with a 51mm mortar.'

A distant crump a couple of kilometres away said for him where he wanted Bennett to be.

'So I'm afraid I shall have to limit your cooking duties to half an hour at the beginning of the day, during which you can instruct Deeta, and an hour before serving. I understand that this will mean a drop in the quality of . . .'

'It will also mean you will lose the services of Deeta,' Bennett interrupted. 'In the kitchen, anyway. She's a lousy cook, hates the work, is intelligent, a linguist. She'll just push off if she has to do it all on her own.'

'What do you suggest, then?'

'Augusto, the cowboy who helped me with the barbecue. Get Ford to let him work for us while we're here. Maybe two of them. It really is a job for three. Put Deeta in charge, that will restore her self-esteem.'

Parker was relieved.

'Good thinking, Gordon. Will do.'

'We are getting very much better information out of Santa Ana than we did.'

The Commandant looked round the small table at her inner committee of four. There was Daniel, charismatically handsome, old Jesús with his white stubble and arthritic hands, Emilia, a large, motherly soul who looked after the domestic side of things, the food and water supply, the crèche, and suchlike, and finally Esther Somers, whom the Commandant valued as an adviser on anything involving gringos. Esther's daughter, Zena, played with a tortilla press and some thick mud in a corner, stamping out pancakes of mud.

'First, it seems likely the attack will be a night one. The commander has relieved a night expert from cook duties to step up night training. Second, the attack is scheduled for around 5 November. We should of course get confirmation of that nearer the time, but I think we can safely prepare ourselves with that date in mind. So I want to be sure all civilians are off the site by 1 November. The workers can stop coming in from the village at that date, the lab technicians with all their data, anything that has value and can easily be moved should be well away, back to Managua University . . . Daniel?'

'If they're taking all their stuff why don't we just all pull out?'

'Do you really need to ask? What we are protecting is ninety thousand rhizomes of perennial maize in nine different strains. They are mature. They have reached a stage where they can be divided to reproduce themselves. Which is why this attack is coming now. If it is successful it will again put the work back five or more years, even though a few specimen rhizomes and other genetic matter and all the records are safe. That is how long it takes to develop ninety thousand viable rhizomes. But it is not so simple as that. It is likely the Americans are developing similar strains which may be coming close to viability. If they get in ahead of us they can patent those strains under the new GATT rules, and neither we, Nicaragua, nor anyone in the Third World will be able to grow or harvest what we were the first to develop unless they have a licence from AFI. And AFI, whose whole structure depends on selling the maize it grows in the US, will not be dishing out such licences.'

She pulled in a big breath, let it out in a sigh, and went on.

'It is not too big a thing to say that millions may be spared starvation, that millions may even live in tolerable comfort, growing a cash crop that feeds them as well as sells abroad, if we save these nine hectares from destruction. It's a cause worth fighting for, yes?'

She stubbed out her cigarette, considered having another but thought better of it, then got up and pushed through the beaded doorway into the compound. In front of her and unfenced here, the vivid-green spears of waving corn leaves, and among them the paler-green leaves that tightly folded the hidden riches of the cobs, stood dense and proud in front of her. But instead of growing straight out of simple annual plants, they sprouted from heavy rhizomes, rather like those that large irises grow from, partly visible above the yellowish soil. In some cases two or even three tall, cob-bearing stalks rose from one rhizome.

The others followed her out, and looked at the crop in front of them which could produce corn-cobs in abundance all the year round.

'We shall fight,' said Daniel. 'We shall fight like tigers.'

29

Weapons training assumed less and less importance as old hands quickly rediscovered old skills. What Parker now began to concentrate on more and more was jungle craft and physical fitness. Day by day he moved them in four patrols of four each, deeper and deeper into the forest, varying the loads they carried and the personnel in each patrol. Deeta went with them in case they ran into border patrols or any other trouble.

When Parker protested that Montalbán could do the job as well, she replied, just as Bennett had predicted she would, that she was paid to be an interpreter not a kitchen maid, and anyway Montalbán's English was not up to anything complicated and his Spanish was from Spain and would excite suspicion, even hostility.

On the fifth day Parker took them through the border, about ten kilometres east of where they had crossed before. A couple of hours later they reached the river, again about five kilometres east of the ferry and the island with its restaurant. Here Parker ordered them to inflate one of the Geminis, and hide the other vessel. He then told them all to sit down and listen.

'Right,' he said. 'Bennett, Sánchez, Mick Strachan, and Colin Wintle will basha here for two nights. You can train under Bennett deeper into the forest but you must not be seen by anyone, and especially not by anyone on the other bank. The rest of you, under Jack, Tim, and Mike Henchard, make your way back to the *finca* by separate routes, without contacting each other on the way, and remaining under cover, unseen by the locals. Jack and Tim will then organize a two-day schedule of thorough jungle craft, day and night, but especially night.

'Meanwhile I'm going on a personal recce of the target. Bennett and Mick Strachan will paddle me over the river now and be ready to fetch me back in exactly fifty-two hours' time, that is at fourteen hundred hours the day after tomorrow . . .'

'You're going on your own?'

'Yes, Gordon. But I shall maintain RT contact with you at all times, so you can come and get me out if I run into trouble . . .'

'I don't think you should go on your own.'

'Nor do I,' said a voice from the back. It was Deeta, now leaning against a tree and pushing her damp hair off her cheek. Like the rest, she was dressed in disruptive-pattern jungle fatigues and boots and her face was painted with camouflage cream.

'I'm coming with you,' she went on, to a chorus of catcalls and whistles, accompanied by clenched fists above pumping forearms.

Parker went bright crimson as he stared across the men, who had turned from disciplined troopers into a pack of sex-mad imbeciles. Although furious, he knew better than to shout them down. Bennett, Goodall and Glew would sort them out at the appropriate moment, though he noticed that Goodall's face, half-turned away from the rest, was almost black with mortification.

'Certainly you will not,' Parker said when the noise at last died down.

'Certainly I will. In the first place Gordon is quite right: it's against every rule in the book that you should be on your own in enemy-held territory. Second, if things do go wrong you'll need a Spanish speaker. Third, you are the top of a command pyramid. Take you away, add a few beers and some rum, and I could end up the wrong end of a gang-bang . . .'

Through the renewed chorus of howls and whistles Goodall bellowed: 'No chance, no way. Anyone who messed with you would have to put me out of the way first . . .'

'That could be arranged,' called out another voice sarcastically.

In spite of the noise, everyone heard it, and most guessed, though no one could pin it on him definitely, that it was Jamie Strachan who had made the unforgivable challenge. The racket turned off as if by a switch and you could have heard a leaf fall.

'See what I mean?'

Deeta dropped the words into the sudden silence. And everyone knew there was no way out of it: she was going with Parker. Indeed the one objection they might have made, that she would be a liability, was not valid. They all knew she moved in jungle with a lithe economy of sound and movement that was beyond most of them, and she could outshoot them too – at least with the Browning High Power she wore on her right hip.

'Right,' said Parker. 'Let's get that Gemini in the river.'

He could not keep the smugness he felt out of his voice.

On the other side Parker got out first and put out a hand for Deeta, which she ignored. As Bennett pushed off and he and Mick Strachan paddled back across the wide orange river, Parker slipped off his bergen and from the map pocket took a map and a small sheaf of photographs.

'We are about here. Five kilometres south and down-stream of the island. As you see, the river takes a loop south just below it. The target zone therefore lies about eight kilometres north and then north-west of where we are now. It's in a hollow bowl and to the east the ground rises to between fifteen and twenty metres above the surrounding plain and is covered with virgin forest. We'll move across this high ground until we have the east perimeter fence in full view. We'll hide up in the curtain growth on the forest edge, which we should reach at about midday. And there we stay for forty-eight hours – though we may move around a bit if I think it necessary.'

He folded up the map, slipped the photographs back into their plastic envelope, and slung the bergen back on. He took the compass from his belt kit, took a bearing, let it hang outside its pouch so he could check it every hundred metres or so, then, giving the MP5 a hitch on his left shoulder, set off with his survival knife swinging in his right hand. Deeta followed, feeling a touch under-equipped with just two days' emergency rations in the small rucksack which also held the small black box none but her had seen.

He was still talking and she caught up so she could hear.

'The point of the whole exercise is to see if I can establish over forty-eight hours what sort of routines the garrison follows, what their weaknesses are – and their strengths. I was going to record my impressions on a microcassette and probably I still will. But since you are here you can jot down written notes in case the recorder cocks up . . .'

He was going on like a schoolboy explaining his train set to a married aunt, taking an occasional swipe with his little machete at passing lianas. Why? Embarrassment at being on his own with her at last? Maybe. Would it wear off later? She grinned to herself. Almost certainly.

*　　*　　*

Two and a half hours later they were established where Parker wanted to be: in the inside edge of the thick forest curtain on a corner of the low bluff. First he very carefully, and with a neatness that surprised her, used the machete to trim the curtain to give them more or less clear views at about half a metre from the ground, so they had to crouch or lie to see through the gaps. All this was done without disturbing the outside screen of leafy saplings and tall grasses beyond. Behind it he spread a light and thin but strong groundsheet, two metres square.

Crouching on it, Deeta could see how the track from the village ox-bowed to a gate three hundred metres away. The first huts of the compound were another hundred metres beyond that. Intermittent sunlight glinted off the glass of the controlled-environment facilities. Twenty metres north of the gate a watch-tower stood over its jutting redoubt. In the other direction the fence and the maize behind it ran in a straight line from the gate for nearly a kilometre south to the next watch-tower, which was about eight hundred metres from their hide. Between them and the fence the ground dropped through scrub and then rose slightly across stubble to the fence. Parker carefully recorded all these impressions and made Deeta write them down in a little notebook he had brought with him.

As he finished, the first drops of the afternoon rain began to splash down, and although not much of it would reach them from the canopy in the first twenty minutes or so, he knew it soon would.

'Keep an eye on the watch-towers and the gate and tell me if anything moves.'

He handed her the lightweight Zeiss 10 × 50 binoculars he had been using. They were of modern design with declivities underneath which cradled the balls of her thumbs, and the focusing controls lay easily under her fingers. She had to make a slight adjustment, which meant he had twenty-twenty vision, which did not surprise her, and slightly angle out the two halves as his eyes were set rather close together.

Meanwhile he swiftly cut ten wattles each about three metres tall out of the saplings on the inside edge of the curtain growth, trimmed them and with strong twine bound them into a bender over her head. Over this he threw a dark-green, lightweight but waterproof sheet which unfolded to three metres square, and fastened it down. Finally he covered the structure with the largest leaves he could find. By now water was plopping on to the leaves and the cover and in places falling in a steady stream, but none of it reached her.

'That,' he said, and the boyish pride was still there, 'is a genuine prototype basha.'

'They've just changed the watch on the far tower,' she murmured as he drew himself in next to her. 'Three off, three on.'

He looked at his watch.

'Fourteen twenty-five.'

Eight minutes later a group of fifteen or so in fatigues, carrying AK47s across the crooks of their elbows, came down the alleyway that separated two hectares of maize, crossed the track behind the gate, and approached the watch-tower that was nearest to them. Three of them were carrying umbrellas painted in green blotches – which seemed funny, really, though sensible enough.

'The 'nocs, please.'

Reluctantly she handed them to him.

'I just want to see if the guys being relieved have anything to report, anything to be excited about.'

'Like they spotted us?'

'That sort of thing, yes.'

For a moment she felt the coldness of fear in her diaphragm.

'No. If they've seen anything untoward they're not talking about it yet.' He flipped on the microcassette recorder, and indicated she should back it up with note-pad and pencil. 'Watch changes shortly after fourteen hundred. Relieving guard move round the perimeter anticlockwise, last detail reaching the gate watch-tower at fourteen thirty-five. It takes that long because they go back into the maize each time rather than exposing themselves along the inside of the fence. The group now returning to the compound is nine men and six women. The new detail on the gate tower is three women. Oh yes: at the moment of change-over there were six people all together on the tower at one time.' He snapped off the recorder.

'What do you make of that?' he asked her.

She shrugged.

'The women cook the meal, eat their share, the men come back to eat it.'

She seemed unsurprised and unbothered that a lot of the garrison were female.

Nothing happened for half an hour. The damp heat blossomed between them in the cramped space, sweat poured down their backs and fronts, collected in crevices and crotches. To begin with, when either shifted they were overcareful not to touch each other and when they did they muttered almost silent apologies. In the meantime Parker continued to record details as they occurred to him in short staccato sentences: changes in the light, the intensity of the rain, wind direction as indicated by the black-and-red Sandinista flag that for the most part was a sodden rag but occasionally stirred.

At last he shifted more abruptly, bringing his knee against her thigh.

'Sorry. Touch of cramp.'

'It's all right.'

He drew in breath a touch more sharply and cleared his throat.

'I would, you know, feel more comfortable with you if I knew more about you.'

She laughed.

'Why are you laughing?'

'Sometimes, when you are both serious and embarrassed, you sound just like those limey actors who keep winning Oscars. Sir Anthony . . . you know? So?'

'Really? When I first saw you you were a typical office bimbo, silk blouse, pencil skirt with a slit in the back that practically went to your buttocks, high heels . . .'

'Black tights and Impulse perfume.' She laughed, sat back from him, pulled in her heels, and clasped her knees.

'Quite. But it seems there's more to you than just that.'

'You reckon?'

'You're bilingual, street-wise, confidently sexy, put it about when you have a fancy too . . .'

'And you want a bit of the action, soldier. Is that right?'

'Trooper, if you don't mind. Yes, of course. Who wouldn't?' He was getting very hot and bothered, wiping his brow and the lenses of the binoculars, and scanning the fences again. As he did so he went on: 'But that's not all. You're jungle-trained, weapons-trained, and something tells me you have combat experience. So. Just where are you coming from? As the officer in charge of this operation, I think I ought to know.'

She shrugged, pouted, and moved the Browning slightly so that it didn't press into her hip.

'All right. I am twenty-nine years old. I expect you thought I was younger than that. Most men like to think the chicks they find attractive are in fact chicks. My parents are Cubans, took the option Castro was offering twenty years ago and got off the island, ended up in Miami. Dad was, is a lawyer, but he had a couple of smallholdings as well – all the commies allowed him to keep of what had been a family estate. I used to run wild on them.' There was nostalgia in her voice now. 'Bit of a tomboy, you know?'

'I bet.'

'In Miami I got by, got the right grades, kept out of trouble or anyway wasn't caught. But generally hated the whole set-up after Havana and holidays on the hacienda. Joined the Army, got a transfer to the Marines, you know the whole Goldie Hawn bit, won my Green Beret . . . The idea was I should be first off the landing-craft when we go back . . .' Her voice trailed off.

'Then what?'

'Well, Trooper, you'll just have to guess the rest, but you're right: I've seen combat. Let's just say that right now I'm on secondment from my principal employers to AFI and through the parent company to Bullburger. Your turn.'

'My turn?'

'Why not?'

'All right. But this won't mean much to you.' He pushed back the lock of black hair. 'All very British, you know? Family with posh connections but no money. Minor public school, what you would call a private school, but not a good one. Army as soon as I could. Royal Buff Caps, Rifle Regiment. Not tall enough for the Guards. SAS. The Falklands. Jungle training in Borneo with a bit of a shindy on behalf of the Sultan of Brunei, privately taking apart some freedom fighters he didn't like. Northern Ireland. Plain-clothes work. Got a bit fed up when the Provos took out a couple of our chaps and looked like getting away with it though we knew who they were, so I went, um, solo. Head Shed didn't like what I did . . .'

'Head Shed?'

'The bosses. Offered me an honourable discharge if I kept quiet. Connections got me a seat on the London Metal Exchange, where I trade for a firm run by a guy called Dorf. End of story.'

'Married?'

'No.'

'Why not?'

'Never really appealed to me. Nor to you apparently.'

'Gay?'

'Lord, no.'

But, she thought to herself, he's not one hundred per cent sure about that. She was then surprised when he went on the counter-attack, and rather forcibly at that.

'And what about you? Basically I'd place you as bi or a closet lez.'

'Really?'

They listened to the rain for a couple of minutes, both overconscious of warmth, dampness, the rich smells, bodies too much in contact with clothes they did not need.

'Jesus, what's that?'

A high-pitched concatenation of squeals, rising and falling, like fingernails dragged across several blackboards, reached them from the distance to their left: it was a small procession of four bullock carts winding round the corner, from the village. The mushroom-coloured animals huge-horned, with hump-like necks and great dewlaps, pulled carts that were gaily painted in brightly coloured intricate patterns. Each had a single driver in vest and cotton trousers beneath wide sombreros which kept off most of the rain. The carts were empty.

Parker pulled out his recorder and looked at Deeta with his most boyish grin.

'Back to work, then,' he said, with obvious relief.

30

Jamie Strachan had forgotten that Mick was to be left out in the jungle as part of the patrol that would bring Parker and Deeta back across the San Juan. And he had not realized that Goodall was in a turmoil of disappointed rage, jealousy and frustration. He had also forgotten that Goodall had made the tabloids, front page in some of them, as the ex-trooper who had gone berserk and hospitalized two young men, both very fit, one of them his son, just because, so he was quoted as saying, they had threatened him when he told them off.

As soon as they arrived back in front of the veranda of the old *finca* at Santa Ana, Goodall turned on him.

'Say it again, Trooper.'

'Come on, Tim. It was a joke,' said Jamie. Then he made another silly mistake. Neither twin was that bright, but the fairies left out a proper sense of self-preservation when they handed out their gifts at Jamie's birth.

'She's only a tart, Tim. Not worth the . . .'

And he reeled away, struggling to keep his feet, ears ringing, pain exploding from the vicious backhander Goodall had put across the side of his face.

Jack Glew stepped in quickly, hands up, palms spread.

'That'll do, lads. We'll do this right or not at all.'

The others around them cottoned on. They drifted away from the bergens they had been shedding, the arms they had been stacking, but brought with them the cans of Coke and beer they had already untabbed.

'Fight, fight, fight.' The word went round just as it does in a school playground. But here there were formalities to be observed.

John Crick seconded for Strachan, Geoff Erickson for Goodall. Each helped his man to strip to the waist, then wound torn strips of cloth round his fists and inspected the other's for horseshoes or belt buckles. Meanwhile Henchard, Alf Stevens and Winston Smith did their best to explain to Bill Ainger, Bill and Ben, and tall, lean Tony Montalbán what was involved in 'holding the ring'.

'You don't need to be told,' Glew said, speaking to the antagonists loud and clear in the centre of it all, 'what the rules are. But I'm telling you anyway. No rounds. This is through to the finish. Strict boxing, face in front of and including the ears, body above the belt, nothing behind. Break the rules and I say you have, then the ring kicks the shit out of you. When one of you stays down for my count of five it's all over. Smithy?'

'Boss?'

'Break out a medi-kit and put a kettle on for tea.'

'Shit, man. Why me?'

'You're the only one I can trust to make a decent pot.'

Strong, sweet tea. Glew knew what he was talking about – it was the best thing for men traumatized both physically and psychologically, and both might well be by the time this business was settled.

'Three, two, one.' He ended in a hurry, otherwise they would have started without him and whatever authority he had would have gone.

Or perhaps not. Jamie Strachan had been ready for a whirlwind of an attack from a man he now knew to be seriously angry. He had told himself to be ready to run and run, dodge and weave, pick off the odd jab when he could, wait for the older man to get a bit puffed before moving on to the offensive. But now, contrary to his expectations, Goodall was waiting for him, with a relaxed, open guard.

It bothered him. He danced around a bit, essayed a jab which Goodall did not even try to block. He just swayed back on to his heels, let it brush his ear. Jamie did this a couple of times and, with variations, the result was always the same. Then the fourth time a thunderbolt came out of nowhere, hit him in the midriff, brought his head forward and . . . nothing. He knew at that moment that he was a goner. Goodall could have taken him out – but he hadn't. Why not? Because, and the realization sent a surge of fear across Jamie's mind, Goodall did not just want to win: he wanted to hurt him. All Jamie wanted now was to be able to drop his guard and say: 'Hey, mate, I'm sorry. I was way out of order, my fault . . .'

But the younger lads, Ainger, Crick, Jamie's second, and Henchard, who should have known better, were urging him on with shouts and chants and screams. And whenever he fell back into the wall of bodies that made the tiny, fluctuating ring, they bounced him back out into the middle.

The torment went on. He jabbed away, scored the odd hit, and then took another blaster in his chest, on his upper arm, or again in the midriff. He had never boxed like this before, just with bandages. And he began to realize he had something to learn. Gloves are not there to soften the blow for the receiver. Oh no, they protect the knuckles of the bloke who is handing it out. Which was why, without them, Goodall went for the soft parts.

Jamie was learning, just as a doomed bull does in the arena. And just as the bull does, he learnt too late.

He used the tactic that goes with modern boxing, the one the Victorians never used: the clinch. As Goodall's routine retaliatory thump came in he folded on to the older man's shoulders, and, in the tiny ring of men, with darkness falling like a wick suddenly turned down, brought his knee up into the older man's goolies.

In a way it was what Goodall had been waiting for. Overriding the pain, he stayed in the clinch with his left hand round Jamie's neck, and smashed his right into the pit of his stomach. As Jamie sagged, Goodall got a grip on his red mop of hair, hauled his head back, head-butted him between the eyes and on the chin, and let him drop. Then he stamped on his balls. And he was still wearing his jungle boots.

Glew should have turned the ring on him, but it was already melting away. Any road, he said to himself, Jamie broke the rules first.

Goodall, rubbing his knuckles first on one side and then the other, pushed through the men and climbed the steps into the kitchen.

'Where's the tea, then, Smithy? And Jack, I want a word with you before basha.'

The forest at night was different, as alive as it was in daytime but in a very different way and for Bill Ainger the magic was different too – it was an evil, threatening magic now. He hated it, and was frightened of it. Again he was moving through the dark as part of a four-man patrol, but this time they'd left him to be back marker. Glew was directly ahead of him, about a hundred metres away. Twenty metres behind and forty to the side came Crick, and then Gurkha Ben at the same spacing. Their left arms steadied the SLRs slung over their left shoulders. In their right hands they had small torches focused to a beam just large enough to show them where their feet were and which they also used to signal their positions to each other. But at those distances Bill could hardly differentiate the occasional flashes from the moon catching a distant white flower, fireflies or even glow-worms. A rainforest glow-worm at ten metres was as bright as a dim pencil torch at a hundred.

And the sounds. While most of the canopy dwellers, both birds and mammals, were diurnal, the ground dwellers tended to be nocturnal. Rodents as large as small dogs scuttled through the litter; racoons and squirrels searched it for fallen nuts; a fox, grey and but for its large ears rather wolf-like, paused as it trotted past, its eyes red in his torchlight. And in the air fruit-eating bats many times the size of the British pipistrelle, flitted mewling through the spaces above his head. Vampires, in the form of bloodsucking bats, did exist, he recalled, somewhere in Latin America, but he could not remember where.

He heard them coming from behind: stealthy footsteps, breathing, and jungle terror seized him. Thoughts of jaguars, tigers even, rushed through his brain, a dread too of something he had never heard of, so it was a relief when he turned, opened up the lens of his torch and saw two men, only ten metres away now, coming towards him. They were wearing dark clothes and their faces were blacked up, and they were carrying short iron bars.

At five metres Ainger realized they meant him harm; at two he knew he had to defend himself, but with what? He was still trying to swing the SLR off his shoulder when the first blow came, a vicious swing at his knees. Pain shot through him and he managed a strangled cry as he went down, but the others were too far away to be of any use. By the time they found him the attackers had gone, leaving him in pain like nothing he had ever known and with both kneecaps smashed.

They never found out who his attackers were nor why they did what they had done, but Parker and Goodall knew it was probably revenge by or on behalf of the two men they had humiliated and one of whose shoulders they had dislocated on their first day at the ranch house.

They were right, but only up to a point. It had indeed been the same two men but they had been instructed by their employer, Thomas Ford. And the instructions Ford himself had received had been simple and clear: make sure that one man is taken out, leaving a vacancy that has to be filled.

That night Goodall waited with Jack until all was quiet. Then, sitting at the kitchen table, he pulled out the jewellery he'd bought in San José and a postcard. First the earrings and brooch.

'Jack. Look after these for me. And if anything happens, anything untoward, like, see wor Mary gets them. No. Shut it. Don't argue. I'm not myself these days, and I might make mistakes. Should never have got in that scrap.'

He turned the postcard over. It showed a black VW Beetle, 1954, but customized with twin carburettors and a lot of chrome.

'You can buy one for two grand. Use me dough, and buy one for wor Jack. All right, man?'

Ten o'clock on the morning after the first night, and Nick Parker and Deeta were not at ease with each other. She had been disgusted with the food he produced: precooked rice and chicken curry in vacuum-sealed packs, eaten out of the plastic envelopes with plastic spoons, followed by Mars bars, with only tepid water to drink. The basha had remained very hot, even after nightfall, and inevitably, in the darkness, he began to grope.

She could tell him to fuck off and if he didn't she reckoned she knew a trick or two in unarmed combat which might surprise even a guy who was SAS-trained. But that way either or both of them could get badly hurt. She could give in and let him screw her. She could give him a hand-job and hope that would do. She chose the last option. He mistook her efforts to undo his trousers as the symptoms of unbridled lust, pulled them off, pulled hers down and flopped down on top of her, fumbling to get inside her. When she realized she had made a mistake she first got him to wear a condom – she always carried some with her – then tried to go with the flow, lie back and enjoy it. But her enjoyment was not apparently on the agenda. She was used to Latin or Afro lovers, whose manhood would have been deeply compromised if they had allowed themselves to ejaculate before she had at least simulated an orgasm. However, he seemed to believe that his climax was all that was needed to trigger hers, and the sooner he got there, the better it would be for her.

It was very soon.

Pulling her nether garments up and wriggling as far away from him as the basha allowed, she reflected that she had heard tales about Anglo-Saxon lovers, but had never believed they could be this bad.

And now, at ten o'clock in the morning, they heard again the raucous squeal of the bullock carts.

They were pulling out of the gate. Parker focused the binoculars.

'Shit,' he said.

'What's the matter?'

'They're taking out all the stuff we're meant to destroy. Filing cabinets, laboratory equipment, all sorts. They know we're coming. We might as well go home.'

'Let me see.'

He handed over the glasses.

'Yeah. You're right. But not to worry.'

'What do you mean?'

'It's the crop that really matters.'

'Are you sure?'

'Yes.'

'Why?'

'Just take it from me. I know what I'm talking about. And they can't take that with them.'

They watched on as the morning heat increased, saw the guards on the watch-towers change at half-past ten, and then a little after eleven they witnessed another exodus. At nine the technicians and fieldworkers, twelve in all, had arrived on foot from the village. Now they left again, and the technicians, clearly distinguishable because of the shirts and denims they wore rather than the floppy cottons and sombreros worn by the manual workers, were carrying bulging document cases.

'I really don't like this,' said Parker.

'Why not?'

'Clearly they do know an attack is on the way.'

'But doesn't it make it all a lot simpler if all you have to do is fire the maize? Can't you do it from outside?'

'I doubt it. It's green, very wet. We'll have to occupy the whole site, make it ours and work through it systematically. It could take at least an hour to make sure it's effectively destroyed.'

They stayed where they were right round the clock again and by the time they had to return to the river they were thoroughly sick of each other's company. As night fell for the second time Deeta was straightforward and firm: no more sex. Parker wasn't bothered. He'd scored. That was all that mattered to him.

She also gave up on trying to conceal from him what her real purpose was in being there. Just before they were ready to pull back into the forest she produced a black and grey plastic case which looked almost exactly like a serious scientific pocket calculator except that the display was larger than that on most calculators. Parker knew instantly what it was, and watched as she keyed in commands.

'How far away from us is the fence?' she asked as she worked.

'Three hundred metres.'

'And the centre of the plantation.'

'Another five hundred.'

'Direction?'

His irritation at not knowing why she was doing what she was doing was burning up into anger, but he answered her.

'From here to the centre about three degrees south of west.'

She made some more commands, then pressed a memory button.

'I know what that is, you know. It's a Magellan GPS NAV 1000M receiver. By using the three nearest satellites in the Global Positioning System you have just recorded to within twenty-five metres the exact position of the centre of the plantation on the US military grid.'

'Clever boy.'

'But who for? What the hell for? You've got to tell me.'

'No, I don't. But I will tell you this. It's not something you need bother about if you get that corn burning properly.'

On the morning of the second day, the day on which Bennett's patrol was to bring Deeta and Parker back across the river, Glew took Augusto in the jeep into Medio Queso for supplies. He had done this before, but, after a brief conversation with Montalbán, he took the Spaniard along too. Augusto looked worried when he saw Montalbán ready to leave with them, but said nothing.

Every time they had been into town before, Augusto had excused himself once the jeep was loaded and had gone to the only bar and used what seemed to be the only payphone in the hamlet. Jack Glew wanted to know who he was talking to and what sort of things he said.

This time Montalbán followed him into the tiny bar, took a stool against the counter and appeared to be immediately transfixed by the football match on the TV perched above the entrance to the unisex toilet. When the barman suggested he might like to drink something, he asked for a beer in a very loud voice and indicated with his hands that he wanted a big one. Seeing Montalbán engrossed in the match and from time to time swapping a few words about it with the barman, Augusto pulled the payphone towards him, fed three ten-colones coins into the little tray and dialled. Montalbán drank his beer, ate peanuts, watched the screen intently, chatted – and listened hard.

Back at the *finca* he was brief.

'He asked for someone called Daniel. He said the operation was definitely going to begin in the dark. He said we had lost a man, and another man is hurt. That is all.'

31

'Good man, Jack. You did well. So did Tony. Right. Gordon, does our nasty little spy speak any English at all?'

'I don't think so.'

'So he's picking up his information from what he sees rather than what he hears. For instance, he knows we've been doing a lot of night training – that sort of thing.'

'I'd say so.'

Parker looked round the big bare room he was using now to brief the senior men of his team – and Deeta, who insisted on being there too. They'd improvised a table out of a door they'd taken off its hinges and some timber borrowed from the corrals, and across it were spread a 1:10,000 map of the area round the research station and most of the aerial photographs.

'Since you see more of him than the rest of us I'd like you to devise a way of getting him to think the attack goes in two hours before dawn on 6 November.'

'I'll do my best,' Bennett promised. 'The two hours before dawn bit won't be easy.'

'While in actual fact' – Parker's grin as he looked round at them was his most boyishly excited – 'the balloon goes up at half-past ten on the morning of 5 November.'

He paused, looked round at them: Bennett, Goodall, Erickson, Glew.

'Gunpowder, treason and plot,' Geoff murmured.

'Precisely. But there are good reasons, apart from

historical precedent. It's the time when they change the guard at the gate watch-tower, which means there are at least eighteen defenders in one small area: the three who are being relieved, the three who are relieving them, and twelve being brought in from the other towers. With luck we should take out a third of the garrison in the first few minutes. There's another factor: our prime objective now is to fire the nine hectares of maize. It's got to burn and burn well. Any other damage we do to the site is peripheral to this, which is now the main purpose of our visit. The rain comes in the afternoon so this is about the time, after four hours or so of sun, that it will be driest . . .'

He kept quiet about the third factor. There were fewer women in the towers on this particular watch once it was in place than any other, and he reckoned Deeta had been right: from half-past ten to two, some of them at any rate were cooking up the main meal of the day. And he was afraid there might be some in his troop who would be reluctant to fire on women – at least until they had been fired on by them.

'Right. We move into forward positions during daylight on the fourth and into final assault positions during the following night . . .'

'Having first of all disabled our friend Augusto,' Bennett remarked laconically.

'You can just hand him over to Ford,' Deeta said. 'Before we leave.'

'Could turn out drastic for him, but why not? Let's get on. I shall lead the mortar detail from the OP Deeta and I were in. Mick Strachan will support me, and Bill and Ben will cover for us. Our objective will be to take out the watch-tower nearest the gate at the moment of greatest concentration of the garrison there. We'll then mortar the plantation with mixed-fruit pudding, concentrating on the area in front of the compound and hopefully setting up a fire they can't get through.

'Meanwhile Geoff, with Sánchez and Montalbán covering for him, takes the L96A1 to cover about here.' He prodded the map and then one of the photographs. It showed a substantial stand of secondary forest quite close to the one of the five sides that ran on a north-west, south-east axis – the one he, Goodall and Deeta had ended up close to on their first aborted recce. 'The moment you hear the first of my mortars go in you pick off all you can see in the two watch-towers and as far as possible pin down the survivors. There's a slight rise in the ground – not as much as I shall have on the other side – but enough to give you some advantage.'

Parker paused and cleared his throat.

'As you see from these photographs each watch-tower rises out of a lozenge-shaped sangar made, as far as I can tell, from sacks probably filled with earth, piled against wattle frames to a height of about a metre. They have firing ports, normally three to each side, and I reckon that anyone in the watch-towers we don't take out will drop into them and continue to defend themselves from inside – while hoping to be reinforced from the compound. However, the mortar on one side, and the M202 flame weapon on the other, should make it very difficult for that to happen.

'Right. Jack will have the M202 on the next sector up, supported by Jamie Strachan and John Crick. The cover's less good there, so I shall ask you, Jack, to hang back behind this sugar cane here until the action's been running three minutes or so. Then you can move forward down this ditch. Remember, Geoff should be keeping any heads there may be left in the redoubt to your right well down if not actually neutralized, but you can expect some aggro from the one on your left, so you'll use your first rounds in that direction. After that, if all goes according to plan you should be able to bombard the plantation until it's burning nicely in an arc across the middle.'

He looked over them all, from face to face, took in how they had suddenly gone serious, though there was a light in their eyes too, and clearly Goodall and Bennett were anxious to know how they fitted in.

'Tim, you'll be long-stop and in charge of casevac, with Stevens, Henchard and Wintle. You'll position yourself here, about four hundred metres south-east of Geoff, among these palm trees, with two RTs and stand ready to move up in support of any of the three forward groups if they call for it. Tim has Wintle and the gimpy. Henchard says Wintle has done well with it. Stevens and Henchard will have extra medi-kits and four stretchers. As you know, we're very thin on the ground and if things don't go too well you may have to split, the gimpy crew one way, the stretchers another, hence the two RTs. All wounded, walking and otherwise, should fetch up initially at the spot you started from, which we'll equip as best we can as a forward aid post.'

At this point Parker felt a wave of excitement flood through him which left him dizzy. He reached for a glass of water and as he drank he realized just what had brought it on: they were pretending. It was all a big pretence, trying to make it like the real thing. But it never could be. So much was missing: choppers to casevac the wounded, field hospitals with fully trained paramedics, pension funds, regimental spirit, Queen and Country, the threat of court martial and the firing squad if you deserted in the face of the enemy. None of that here. This was naked, pure in a way, what it really was all about. And if it all went wrong, without that deep infrastructure they had had behind them, even in the hairiest of situations in the Falklands or the backstreets of Derry, then they were in deep shit. He cleared his throat again, aware that they were waiting, watching him.

'Finally, as I said, you'll be inserted across the river at nightfall on the fourth, at the point where we left the Geminis. During the night and early hours of the fifth, Gordon and Smithy will get the craft up-river to the island, which they will occupy and hold. Final withdrawal will be to the island and . . .'

'This is crazy, you know? Totally dumb.' Deeta took gum from her mouth, rolled it and flicked it into the fireplace, then went on: 'Two men to paddle two inflatables, upstream? Take out or contain up to five or six men and women? Civvies maybe, but hostiles, for sure. *And*, possibly, cover a forced withdrawal under fire?'

'I can't spare any more. I was going to put Ainger in with them . . .'

'Yes, you can. Give them Wintle. I can feed Tim's gimpy for him.'

Goodall looked up, eyes suddenly brighter.

'Have you ever handled one?' the Tynesider asked.

'No, but I trained with an M60E3 – not so very different. And we've got a couple of days you can wise me up in.'

Parker looked at Bennett.

'What do you think, Gordon?'

'Obviously I'd prefer to have two men with me rather than one.'

'I don't suppose Tim has any objections?'

Goodall blushed, and shook his head.

'Right. That's it in outline,' Parker said, looking at his watch. 'We've got three days to polish up the training. Night of the third we'll have a bit of a *hangi*, eh, Gordon? But not too much booze. And that morning we'll let Augusto make his phone call. We'll have another briefing tomorrow evening at nineteen hundred, when you've had time to digest this one. Right. That's it.'

'What the fuck's a *hangi*?' Deeta asked.

'Fijian for feast. A knees-up,' Bennett replied.

Geoff raised a finger.

'Yes?'

'Gordon – not burnt flesh this time, OK?'

'Curried goat, all right? Smithy'll give me a hand.'

32

'Best-laid schemes,' Parker muttered to himself. Nine-twenty and a lot of things had gone wrong. In the first place, although he had cleared up the basha he and Deeta had used, leaving the space as if no humans had ever been anywhere near it, Mick Strachan had found the one thing he had overlooked.

'Only the one, Mr Parker?' he had said, only ten minutes after daybreak, and two minutes after they had arrived.

Squeamishly using a twig, he had let the used condom swing between them before flicking it back into the vegetation behind him. It had been almost covered with big red ants and a lot of it had gone, but it was still clearly recognizable for what it was.

Instead of the usual clear, deep-blue sky above, and sudden heat drawing up white mist from the plantations, savannah and forest, the dawn was overcast. Distant thunder in the east rumbled and there was a hot stillness to everything that made Parker feel irrationally nervous. And the others too. Bill and Ben muttered incomprehensibly in their sibilant, high-pitched dialect and Mick Strachan began to eat Mars bars like there was no tomorrow. Which, Parker thought to himself, unusually gloomy as he was, may well be the case.

Finally, and again he realized he had failed to get into the mind of the garrison commander, the routine had broken down: from nine o'clock onwards there was movement up and down the grid of alleys between the nine squares of maize. He couldn't clearly make out what was going on since the corn was high, and he got only brief glimpses as men and women in fatigues crossed the narrow spaces between the plantation and the perimeter fence. But he made a guess: they were reinforcing and equipping the redoubts – against the pre-dawn attack they now expected would take place tomorrow, thanks to Augusto's last telephone call.

He was left with an agonizing choice: to stick to the plan, and go in in an hour's time when the relief squad reached the gate watch-tower and meanwhile allow the strengthening of the outer redoubts to continue; or to pre-empt the reinforcement by setting the show on the road an hour or so earlier. But if he did that he'd have to break RT silence and speak to all four patrol leaders first. The sets they were using – the radio transmitters from the PRC319 pack, adapted for voice transmission and the most economical system weight-wise – were set to operate at the upper end of VHF. The problem had been that, with so few men, he had not wanted to encumber one man from each patrol with the full system, particularly as it needed training and expertise to handle. The result was that transmissions would be interceptible, and, supposing the garrison had the equipment, the RTs could be jammed or even used to pinpoint their positions. None of this was going to matter if everything went according to plan, since he did not expect to have to use RT until the operation was well under way, if at all. But now . . .

The garrison had their own RT system, communicating between the watch-towers and the compound – he had seen the antennae – and it would just need someone to be constantly scanning the most likely frequencies to cause the whole operation to be blown. Sweating more heavily than ever, Parker glanced at his watch. Nine-thirty. He'd wait. At any rate until he had received confirmation from Bennett that the island was occupied and their withdrawal secure.

And at that moment his set burbled. He unhooked the handset, and pressed the 'receive' button.

'Island occupied. Out,' Bennett's voice said.

He was half an hour early. For Christ's sake, why?

The answer was that Bennett, Smith and Wintle had found the going much easier than they had expected. After inserting the assault patrols across the river just after nightfall, they remained on the north bank, hid one of the Geminis and paddled the other five kilometres upstream to a spot just short of the island, arriving at ten o'clock. The night was clear, with a half moon on its back almost directly overhead to begin with. Later, as it slid towards the south-west horizon, it still gave them plenty of light. There had been some luminous white mist but nothing serious enough to make navigation difficult. They kept nearer to the bank on their right, but not too close – the river was wide, and the current no problem. Their paddles dug smoothly and rhythmically into the water, making very little noise.

There was, though, the occasional splash and scurry in the roots and tangles that formed the amphibian middle ground between river and land.

'Crocs?' suggested Smith.

'Alligators,' Bennett replied. Being the sort of man he was, he had read a couple of guides borrowed from the Bognor Regis Public Library before he left. 'And more beside. Sharks.'

'Get away,' snorted Smith, confident the piss was being extracted.

'Yes. They come all the way up from the Caribbean. So

if you've any idea of taking your boots off and having a paddle, forget it.'

As he continued to spade the water, Wintle's thoughts drifted back to Bill Ainger. His cousin and mucker. The medic the fat American had choppered in to see to him said he'd probably limp for the rest of his life. Bastards. Colin Wintle had no doubt, and no one had told him otherwise, that his cousin's attackers had been from the mob they were now about to sort out. It would be a pleasure to waste them, if he got the chance, and do it personally too, not just feeding the belt for Tim Goodall.

They made the landfall Bennett had sussed out from the other side a week before, a little gravelly beach formed by one of the many streams that fed the river from the jungle, tucked away the deflated Gemini, and made their way back. This might have been the tricky bit, negotiating jungle none of them had been in before, but it turned out easy enough, keeping the dense forest curtain and the river always on their right. There was very little undergrowth beneath the thick canopy and they had the beam of Bennett's powerful light to follow: a luxury he reckoned they could afford since the risk of getting lost or bogged down could jeopardize the whole withdrawal, while the chances of the bright beam attracting attention were very remote.

By one o'clock they were back where they had started, to repeat the whole process, but this time with all their arms, equipment and ammunition. They were getting tired by now too, so it wasn't until gone five and with a hint of dawn behind them, that they made it again to their beach. With the rising cacophony of the dawn chorus – parrots, macaws and howler monkeys for the most part – ringing in their ears, Winston Smith took first watch while the other two slept for a couple of hours before Bennett relieved him.

In full daylight now, Bennett did not like what he saw. Instead of blue sky, mist off the river and the strong sunlight they expected each morning, there was no mist, no sun, but an overcast ceiling which pressed the heavy sultriness of the air on their foreheads.

It made Bennett anxious. By nature a careful person, anxiety tended to hype him up: he wasn't due to take the island until ten o'clock, but now he felt he should move on the safe side. He ordered the Geminis reinflated and relaunched at nine, and twenty minutes later, towing the second craft loaded with gear other than the rifles, which were across their knees, they approached the landing-stage.

Juanito, the nine-year-old orphan of the Contra war and grandson of the old man who ran the restaurant, watched their approach from behind a pepper tree. As they pulled in to the landing-stage he saw that they were armed, and made his decision. The Commandant had been quite clear: he was to report to her or Daniel any arrivals at the island who could be interpreted as a possible danger to the research station.

Using the bunk-house and latrines as cover, he darted from one to the other, no more than a dark shadow, and, anxious not to make the planks ring with his progress, ran tiptoe in bare feet across the bridge which joined the island to the river bank. Clear now, and believing himself safe, he pelted down the track between stands of sugar cane, maize and banana but still kept the noise to a minimum.

Then, with only a few hundred metres to go, he saw them, a hundred metres in front of him, and right beside the path he was following. Among the ferns and other low undergrowth beneath a stand of coconut palms, they were hidden from the perimeter fence and watch-towers beyond them, but not from someone approaching from the rear. They had their backs to him and were concentrating on what they could see of the fence, some three hundred metres further on: three men and a woman, and even at that distance he recognized her, and possibly one of the men too, from the build of their bodies. He almost skidded to a stop, stood, panted, wondering what to do.

Pretend you haven't seen them, he said to himself. If they think I haven't seen them they've no reason to do anything. 'Do'? He knew he meant 'kill': he had seen war often enough during the first five years of his life and remembered what it meant. The back of his neck went cold, his throat dry. Suddenly he just wanted to run for cover the way they used to when the mortar shells began to drop in his village, and wait for it all to be over. But he knew he must tell Daniel and the Commandant first. And he thought of little Zena Somers, with whom he often played.

He would, he decided, saunter off on a north-west tangent across a small paddy-field and thus keep his distance, and he would whistle, and pick up a stick, and without seeming to care swipe the small panicles of rice as he went. The shallow brown water closed over his feet and he squeezed his toes to make the mud squirt between them.

Deeta heard him, knew the tune from her childhood in Cuba, 'La Marcha de los Pobladores', always sung at processions and state events. She turned on to her backside and focused her binoculars.

'Jesus. It's the boy from the restaurant, remember?'

She handed the glasses to Goodall.

'You're right. Has he seen us?'

Pause. She took back the binoculars and studied the little brown face beneath its mop of black hair.

'I reckon. He's got no call to walk through a paddy-field

when there's a path he could follow between us and him. And he's putting on an act.'

Goodall reached for the RT.

'Mr Parker. The boy from the restaurant is on his way past us, heading towards the fence. We think he's seen us, but is pretending he hasn't.' He replaced the handset.

'No action required from us,' said Goodall.

'I suppose he knows what he's doing,' remarked Deeta.

'He usually does.'

'There are some things you do better. A lot better.'

And the smile she gave him turned his knees to jelly.

Parker swore. The boy had not only seen Goodall and his patrol, but he must have seen Bennett's premature landing too. Swiftly he considered the options: an early launch of the attack was not on – not without checking that everybody was ready for it. He shuffled the photographs, found the one on which he had marked with a red cross the start positions of each group, located the paddy-field, and reached for the RT.

'Geoff? There's a hostile coming into your sector at about four o'clock, three hundred metres. I want him taken out using a subsonic round before he gets in sight of the watch-tower to your right . . .'

'I have eyeball. But he's only a kid.'

'Who knows we're here, and he's on his way to warn them.'

'Shit. I'm not kitted up for a silent shot.'

'Do it.'

Geoff quickly rejigged the Accuracy International, ejecting the round already in the breech and feeding in a new one taken from his pocket. He felt the nausea rise at what he was about to do, but concentrated his mind, his whole being on the how rather than the why, on the perfection of the matt-grey aluminium-alloy frame with its high-impact plastic furniture and long, stainless-steel barrel, the exquisite engineering of the Schmidt and Bender sight. Steady now. He hoisted it round on to a log they had heaved into place, positioned the forward biped, and wriggled himself in behind it. Range 315 metres increasing. Jesus, he's breaking into a trot . . . anticipate the jog of his head . . . sharp focus now as he scrambles up a bank out of the paddy – he'll pause at the top. Nice-looking lad. Squeeze . . . oh shit, I got him. Just behind the ear, I think . . .

Geoff leaned out of the sangar they'd pulled together out of fallen timber and vomited heavily. And when he had finished there was still, thirty-six hours later, a tang of gamy goat, spices and cheap rum up in the sinus passages at the back of his nose and the top of his throat. And a deadly weight in his chest which he knew could blossom into pain.

'*Muy bien*,' Montalbán muttered behind him. 'Nice shot.'

'What was that?' asked Maria Pilar. 'Pili', a small young woman, dark-skinned with high cheek-bones, showing both Afro and Indian descent, clutched the barrel of her AK47, peered out across the stubble left by scythed sugar cane towards the paddy-fields that lay behind banks designed to keep the flood-water in.

Beside Pili in the watch-tower, plump Marisa put down the stick she had been using to tease a lizard in the thatch above her head, and lifted the cumbersome East German binoculars from her ample chest.

'Bough breaking in the forest? There's a bit of a wind getting up. A hunter's gun maybe. One of the villagers out after monkey.'

'It came from over there.'

'OK. If it was a gunshot, where did it end up?' Marisa slowly scanned the area, sector by sector, then cried out: 'Holy Mary, Mother of God,' and crossed herself. 'Juanito. I'm almost sure.'

She saw the last pulse of black blood swell from the hole in the side of his head, then subside as the pump in his chest squeezed for the last time.

The hot wind moaned through the watch-tower supports and as it reached the trees a cackling gaggle of birds rose from their upper branches.

'Is he dead?'

'I . . . think so.'

'Why?'

'He was coming from the island. To tell us they're here already.'

'We must tell Daniel.'

'Marisa? Pili? Move slowly, casually out of the watch-tower and into the bunker. Don't hurry. Don't draw attention to yourselves. Remember your training. Do not cry now for Juanito. We will all weep later. You have done well.' Daniel threw a switch and turned to the others in the command centre.

'They're here,' he said. 'They're already here. We should move. You all know what to do.'

They moved out into the compound. Emilia took little Zena by the hand and trotted as quickly as her weight would allow to the commissary, where three younger girls waited with prepared stacked tortillas wrapped in damp cotton, plantains, still on their stalks, and five-litre plastic bottles of water. She shooed them through the huts, towards the north perimeter – the only one Parker had not recced properly because the aerial photographs showed only very open farmland with crops not fully established, and no real cover.

Meanwhile twenty men and women now piled almost silently out of the bunk-houses, armed with an assortment of weapons: AK47s, RPKs – Kalashnikovs converted into light sub-machine-guns, US M16s captured or surrendered by the Contras four years earlier, a variety of pistols and grenades. They split into three groups: eight went with old Jesús; eight, including Esther, with Daniel; and four with the Commandant herself, one with a cumbersome RT system on his back. Concertedly they followed a previously prepared plan, filing down the inside of the perimeter, out through gaps in the fencing. The Commandant, with her communications people, caught up with the girls from the commissary and headed due north for nearly a kilometre and a half across the paddies towards cover on higher ground beyond a prepared OP. The others fanned out east and west across the fields to well-camouflaged dug-outs and slit trenches five hundred metres or so behind the research station.

The first of Parker's shells fell south of the compound, close to one of the controlled-environment units, shattering its glass just a minute before the Commandant reached her position. She quickened her step but did not run. Three more shells crumped into the compound. Two were phosphorus, scattering balls of pale-green fire, intensely bright, and pumping out white smoke. The command centre she had left ten minutes before blossomed with flame and the thatch crinkled into black ash and whirled away with the wind.

33

Indecision had fallen like a cloak on Parker as soon as he had given Erickson the order to take out Juanito. He looked at his watch. He knew that everyone should now be in position, and that he should be able to start it there and then. But the arrangement was that each group should give him a single password – 'weedkiller' – at ten-twenty, and until they did he would not know for sure that snags had not occurred, problems arisen.

He heard the subdued crack of the L96A1, and decided he must wait at least for its outcome. It was some time before the RT bleeped.

'Hostile eliminated.'

'Good chap, Geoff. Any reaction?'

'None I can see. But he reached the top of the paddy bank and it is possible they can eyeball him.'

Hot wind pushed past Parker's face, rattling the leaves and branches. He looked up at the dark-grey sky: it was almost uniform but clearly there was turbulent movement within the thick cloud. He realized he should have organized a 'wet rep' – but the weather had been so consistent ever since they had arrived it had hardly seemed necessary.

Montalbán touched Geoff's arm.

'¡Mira!' he murmured.

Geoff followed his pointing finger. The two women on the watch-tower to his left, first one then the other, were slowly descending the short ladder into the bunker below. Should he tell Parker? RT silence except in emergency had been the order. He'd wait to see if they were replaced. Meanwhile he allowed himself a moment of sick, cynical relief – even though he had already killed a small boy it was nice to know that ladies were for the time being off the menu: the watch-tower to his right was occupied by men.

The other factor, Parker remembered, was that the ten-thirty start had been dictated by the probable presence of a substantial percentage of the garrison at that time in and around the watch-tower by the gate. But already routines had been altered and unexpected movements had taken place. There was no guarantee that relief of the watch-towers would take place when he expected it to.

He turned to Mick Strachan.

'I don't suppose you could get up a tree for me.'

'No way. I thought that was why you had the little brown men with us.'

'Yes. But I doubt they can tell me accurately enough what I want to know. Ben,' he called, *sotto voce*.

'Sah!'

'Tree. Up. Tell.'

The small, lithe Gurkha shinned up a grey trunk into the canopy. The problem was, his vocabulary was very limited – word-perfect in all that was needed for routine soldiering, but not much more.

Presently, from above, a disembodied voice, said: 'Sah. Peoples. Leaving. Go way.'

'Guns, Ben. With guns?'

'Yeah, sah. Guns.'

Did that mean they were pulling out? No contest?

*   *   *

255

Geoff waited, and then turned his attention to the watch-tower on his right. It was empty. His heart lurched. He reached for the RT. But at that moment Parker too realized that the towers he had in view were also deserted. Had they been evacuated? The bunkers as well? Or were the guards now behind sandbags and safe from everything except pinpoint mortaring? He had a sudden awful feeling that the whole game was slipping through his fingers, and at that moment the first small flurry of rain, drops as big as marbles, scattered like shot across the thin screen in front of him.

'Right, Mick, let's go for it. Instead of the watch-tower by the gate, we'll go straight for the compound. Two HE, two phos.' He glanced at his plotter board. 'These are the new co-ordinates.' He rattled off the numbers then called up into the tree. 'OK, Ben. The compound first, all right?'

Furthest away from Parker's position, on the west side of the enclosure, Glew, with Jamie Strachan and Crick, had got the M202 flame weapon, together with two hundred 66mm incendiary rockets box-mounted in fours, in place just before dawn. With one of the heaviest loads and only three men, they had had to cover the last two kilometres outside the forest in stages, always keeping one man unencumbered and on the look-out, patrolling between the two doing the donkey work and the distant fence. Like the others, they then rested, took watches turn and turn about, expecting to get a good four hours in which to recover. They were well protected by a stand of high and very thick bamboo behind them into which they had cut a bay with their survival knives. In front, between them and the enclosure, was a plantation of sugar cane almost as impenetrable as the bamboo. A straight mud track separated the plantations — any farmworker coming down it would be seen well before he reached them, and could easily be taken out if necessary. But no one came.

The hours went by; the wet heat grew round them beneath the iron sky; flies, bugs and millipedes, all huge compared with their English cousins, became a nuisance. Jamie Strachan, still with eyes half-closed behind rainbow-coloured bruises, seemed unable to control frequent curry-induced farts, noisy and noxious.

Not surprising, then, that at about eight o'clock Jack Glew decided he'd like to eyeball the target he'd so far only seen in aerial photographs, and perhaps suss out the exact right place to station the M202. Picking up his MP5, and muttering a command or two to Crick, he walked down the track, crouched at the end, saw the ditch he was meant to use to get to the eastern edge of the sugar cane and decided it was not as deep as they had hoped. Instead he unholstered his small machete again and eased himself through the cane, chopping only when he absolutely had to. Soon he could peer through the screen at the fence, separated from him now only by a hundred metres of gently descending cane stubble.

He thought about it for a bit. The rockets had a low trajectory and a maximum range of seven hundred and fifty metres, which meant he should theoretically be able to cover all of the nine hectares except perhaps the one in the furthest south-east corner – which lay comfortably under Parker's mortar. There were two problems though. First, without an OP he'd have no idea just how effective his distance shots were, and anything closer he'd have to drop the sights and fire first to skim the fence and then later perhaps just into it. And that, at just over a hundred metres, could be dangerous.

And then there was the problem of the target itself. Banks of rich green maize growing out of mud. Would it burn? Yes. If they got enough rockets in and the wind was right. Would it all burn? Well, maybe. But only if they could get in among it and direct the blaze on the ground – and that would mean the garrison would have to be completely eliminated or at any rate neutralized.

Glew focused his binoculars on the maize. A good healthy crop, in this hectare anyway. Tall, strong shafts, lots of broad, spear-shaped leaves, and two, even three cobs on each stem. Odd though, the cobs on adjacent stems seemed to be at very differing stages of growth.

He shrugged. No one seemed quite sure why it all had to be torched: an earlier theory that it was a cannabis plantation developing particularly strong hybrids to raise money for the Sandinistas was clearly way out. A later one, floated by Parker, that the Sandinistas were developing pests, microbes, fungi and insects that were resistant to US pest control, and they were testing them on the nine hectares, didn't seem right. Or at any rate they'd so far failed, since the examples in front of him looked uniformly healthy.

But the varying maturity of the cobs was a mystery. Glew had grown maize on his allotment one year, just for the hell of it. He knew that the plant is an annual – once it fruits it dies. On the banks of the Trent you could only get one crop a year, ripening in late August. He presumed that in the tropics you might get three crops a year, but you'd have to rotate them over the available land if you didn't want to wear it out. So how come stems close up to each other had flowers, male and female, cobs just forming, and others – he could see the tell-tale tassles of dark-brown fibre at the tips – ready to pick, all close together in one crop?

He pulled himself on to his haunches and focused on the ground out of which the maize grew. Unable to see quite enough, as there was grass in the way, he hoisted himself to his feet. The green, grassy spears of the sugar cane clustered and rustled round his head. Again he adjusted the focus.

The maize appeared to be growing out of elongated turds. He supposed it was some sort of manure or fertilizer. And lower down there were new shoots, just like the ones he had nurtured in his greenhouse, before planting them out. English farmers grew them *in situ* but under strips of plastic to force germination. But these weren't growing through the turds, he was now almost sure of it. They were growing out of them. And they weren't turds at all. They were rhizomes, much like the ones his dahlias grew from, or the tall irises he brought on in June. And maize does not grow from rhizomes. Feeling quite disturbed, though for the life of him he could not see why, he made his way back through the cane and then up the path to rejoin the others.

On the path he looked up at the featureless sky.

'It's a bugger,' he said aloud. 'A right bugger. And where's the flipping sun today, then?' An hour or so later he was still trying to puzzle it all out when he heard the first mortar shells go in, and saw smoke puffed into the air above the sugar cane.

'Jesus. He's started early. Come on, lads.' He heaved up the four-barrelled rocket-launcher by its straps and set off back down the track. Crick followed, stumbling beneath eight sets of boxed rockets, as much as he could carry in one go, while Strachan covered behind them with his SLR. As they approached the end of the track, he went to the corner while Glew and Crick hacked their way through the cane.

'Twenty metres up, and two degrees left, sah,' Ben called down to them, his voice high-pitched with the sudden surge of battle madness. Parker quickly checked off the change on his plotter board, then the adjustments Mick Strachan had already made.

'Go, go, go,' he shouted, and turned away, hands over his ears as Strachan fed the tube with four more shells. As the third went off and while it was still in the air, the leaves above his head shredded, and a sliver of bark flew from the tree to his left, and with it came the sonic crack of M60 rounds, a staccato drumbeat in his ear, and a second later, as he hit the deck, the crackle of automatic rifle fire.

'Shit. That was close. Ben, Ben? Are you all right?'

'Sah! Sangar under watch-tower on left. Two, maybe three fire.'

'Right.' Parker pushed back the errant lock of hair. So the garrison hadn't pulled out after all. 'Mick and Bill. Can you see the firing ports?'

'I reckon,' said Strachan.

'Well, stop them up while I move this fucker.'

Strachan and the second Gurkha spread-eagled themselves at the front of the forest curtain, and began rapid fire, forty rounds a minute, using up four magazines in the time it took Parker to shift the mortar fifteen metres to the left. Return fire lasted five seconds and then stopped: a hit? Parker hoped so. Certainly they'd given the bastards a fright.

Quickly he made the necessary calculations to allow for the change of position.

'Aren't you going to mortar the fuckers?' Strachan asked.

'Not yet. We're paid to get the maize burning. You just make sure they keep their heads down.'

He scanned the enclosure. At least two of the buildings were burning, pumping black smoke which the warm breeze spread across the corn. And the maize was burning – white smoke showed that – but not well and only in a couple of places near the exploded controlled-environment units. At least the rain had held off after that first squall. And Glew . . . surely he . . .?

But before the thought could form, the first salvo of rockets streaked low over the maize, dipped, skimmed the male flowers, and exploded in a shower of bright chemical fire. Parker reached for the RT.

'Jack? Do you read me?'

'Mr Parker?'

'We're having a problem with the watch-tower and bunker to our left. It should be on the far edge of your range. See if you can get close enough to give the buggers a fright. Should be two degrees east of south-east.'

Seconds later the second batch came through, on a slightly higher trajectory, two in the south-east corner of the maize, two in the narrow space between it and the watch-tower and outer fence, where there was nothing for the flames to take hold of.

'Well done, Jack. If you can move fifty metres to your right then you should get just the gain you need.'

He switched off before Glew could remonstrate: he knew the move would bring the M202 dangerously close to the most westerly of the bunkers.

'Right, Bill, steady fire, keep their heads down for us. Right, Mick, four more in the compound, then we'll zero on that damn bunker and take it out if Jack hasn't done it for us already . . .'

And at that moment, Ben, up in the tree above them, let out a screaming stream of words, which, on the ground, only Bill could understand.

Back on the island, Bennett lifted his big head, more skull-like than ever after the exertions of the night. He was sitting at one of the tables beneath the thatch, drinking icy Coke from the dispenser Smith had smashed his way into. Ten yards away Wintle fingered the safety-catch on his SLR, eyed the now padlocked door of the bunk-house into which they had herded the three old men and two women twenty minutes earlier. All three were suddenly alert, apprehensive, as Parker's first salvo thudded in the distance.

'Bugger's gone in . . .' – Bennett looked at his watch – 'nearly an hour early. Could've told us. We'd better get sorted.'

Fucking lucky we got here early, he said to himself as he strode through the little enclosure towards the end of the bridge, pushing through weeping bougainvillaea and trampling a bed of strelitzia with its strangely bird-like blooms. The others followed him.

'Winston, you hold the far side. Get your black arse across, fix yourself a sangar with a good view down the track so you can give covering fire if need be and get yourself and your kit into it. Colin, you and I'll do likewise at this end.'

Bennett pushed back his jungle hat and scratched the balder parts of his pate.

'I wish I knew why the fuck he's gone in early.'

'You could ask.'

'No, Winston. I think Mr Parker has got enough on his plate. He'll not be wanting nuisance calls from the likes of us.'

34

Jamie Strachan was in the ditch at the end of the path between the bamboo and the sugar cane, SLR at the ready, covering the most westerly of the bunkers with its empty watch-tower, though routinely, every fifteen seconds or so, he cast a glance over his shoulder. His head hurt, the swelling over his eyes was getting worse not better, in fact he was pretty sure the bruises behind the broken skin were building up a very nasty infection, and his guts had still not recovered from the hammering they had taken from Bennett and Smithy's goat curry. He was in a foul temper and wished he had someone to kill.

Over his shoulder again, and shit, three hundred metres away at the other end of the path, three figures had just entered it – it was like a dead-straight alley really – two men, one white-haired with a red-and-black bandanna, and one woman. Strachan did not hesitate. He took out the woman because she was in front, double tap, one in the centre of the forehead, the other smashing her collar-bone, shifted and got in two more rounds as the men split, one into the bamboo, the other into the cane. He rapid-fired the rest of the magazine, chucked the box, slotted in another, waited, then shouted.

'Glew! Glew, you old fart, hostiles up our arses, coming from behind.'

But even as he spoke Glew and Crick slid into the ditch beside him, dragging the launcher and six unused rocket clusters behind them.

'What the fuck . . .?'

'Shut it, Jamie. Boss wants us fifty metres south. We were just moving . . .' – he was cut off as Jamie loosed off four more shots at a movement near the body of the woman – '. . . when this happened.' He turned to the big West Countryman. 'What do you make of it, John?'

'It's a bummer. We don't know how many there are. They could be working round the back of the bamboo. I reckon we've overstayed our welcome.'

Glew activated the RT.

'Nick? We've got hostiles coming out of the woodwork behind us . . .'

'Join the club. Fall back on Geoff's position. I'll tell him to cover for you. But listen, Jack. Take the M202 and as many rockets as you can manage with you.'

Glew and Crick scrambled back into the cane and loaded up. Carrying the launcher between them, they could each manage eight rocket clusters on their backs. Just as they were ready Strachan pushed in with them.

'Here, I can take the last two of the bleeders.'

For a moment they struggled with the webbing harnesses and clips which bound the rockets together into manageable loads.

'I'd rather you were out there covering us,' Crick grumbled.

'They'll lie low,' Glew put in. 'They're coming round the back or through the cane, but either way they won't be shooting at us for a bit. Come on, then.'

But as they broke cover a burst of rifle fire crackled out from the bunker beneath the watch-tower. Strachan dropped and loosed off another magazine at the ports while the other two broke into a stumbling run towards a small plantation of bananas. Safely there, they put down the launcher and, albeit ineffectually since they were on the very edge of maximum useful range, sprayed the general area of the bunker with 9mm parabellum from their MP5s. Strachan joined them and they took stock.

The patch of secondary forest which concealed Geoff was seven hundred metres due south of them, but the most westerly bunker, projecting from the fence, came between them. Moreover the land here was divided into small paddy-fields with almost no cover unless they crawled – which was why Geoff, with the Accuracy International, had been put there. They'd have to make a loop, a detour out to the west and back, a good fifteen hundred metres if not more, using what cover they could find in the taller crops and larger copses of secondary forest. And coming at them from the north all the time would be who knew how many hostiles. And with Glew and Crick chained by the launcher between them, they'd make an easy target.

'Well,' said Glew, once they'd got their breath back. 'We'll just have to do the best we can.'

'I'd rather knit fog,' said Crick, his voice thick as Dorset cream.

Jamie Strachan pulled a banana free from the bunch that was at his shoulder, and looked around with wonder.

'I never knew they put them on crutches,' he said, referring to the peeled forked branch that had been pushed into the earth to support the fruit. 'And them flowers ought to be banned. They're fucking rude.'

He began to peel the fruit, strip by strip.

'One skin,' he chanted. 'Two skin, three skin, *fore-skin*!'

Geoff eyeballed them a moment or two later, heading off west, keeping the bananas between them and the bunker.

'Tony. Keep an eye on them for me so I know where they are. Julián. Fire at will on the bunker. I know they're on the other side but if you can get a round through the ports or close over their heads every now and then it'll upset their aim.'

Using binoculars, he scanned the bamboo and cane and the more broken land to the west. Smoke was drifting across it on the hot east wind, and occasionally a flurry of rain tossed the palm tops, ran shadows through the plantations like a comb, and ruffled the muddy water in the paddies. There was a lot of small-arms fire over to the right but behind him too the clatter of Goodall's machine-gun. Christ, he thought, if Tim's got something to shoot at, that puts us in the front line and we may be a touch exposed from more than one side at once.

But now, there, coming round the back of the bamboo and heading towards the banana plantation Jack and Co. had just left, were two, three, four of them. Nicely spread out, looking for cover, but wary of the men they were pursuing rather than anything else. Of course, thought Geoff, it's the flame weapon they're really after. Five. Six. I'll take the fourth — that way I might get one of the ones in front too. They'll react by turning back, see what's happened to their mucker.

He put aside the binoculars and with swift, deceptively neat movements, got his eye to the rubber-padded eye-piece of the Schmidt and Bender sight. Eight hundred metres but with that sort of magnification and lens clarity a picture as clear as ... Then, with the figure of a man, young, bearded, with a red-and-black scarf round his neck just filling the vertical axis, he squeezed off a round and was already zeroing on his neighbour ten metres away as the bullet smashed into his chest just below his left collar-bone. No need for head shots at this stage of the game — just put the buggers on the deck.

That pain again. Time for another pill.

* * *

Five minutes earlier, after a brief chat with Parker on the RT, Goodall was shifting the gimpy so it could now traverse the short sector, not much more than two hundred metres from and including the watch-tower and bunker that had been on Parker's left, and which so far had kept quiet, and the primary forest on the higher ground out of which he expected Parker's unit to emerge. They had agreed on the RT that one bleep from Parker would be the signal for him to lay a firestorm into the bunker, using tracer and incendiary – at eight-fifty metres it was well within the tracer's eleven-hundred-metre burn-out. Meanwhile Bill and Ben would blast it from the other side with their M16s from the shelter of the forest curtain. Under this covering fire they hoped Parker and Mick Strachan would be able to get the mortar across open ground and into cover on the left. It was downhill, through scrub, so they should be able to make it. No way was Parker going to try to take out the bunker with the mortar first, not with what was obviously the second, easterly prong of a concerted circling counter-attack up his arse.

The move had involved lifting the tripod, relevelling the cradle it made, lifting the gun into position on the cradle slot projection, and locking it with the front mounting pin. In all this Deeta helped with the precise easy movements Goodall had taught her over the previous three days.

He opened the top cover and without being told she loaded a belt of two hundred rounds of mixed ammunition, while he cocked the action and applied the safety-catch. Then he grinned at her across the metre or so that separated their faces and the kick in his diaphragm came again as she grinned back. Although her face was painted up like a jungle Indian's on the warpath, and she was wearing baggy jungle DPMs with her hair tied back, he could not forget for one second that she was a woman, and a woman he desired like he'd never desired a woman before. Even the smell of her – sweat and sex, for the excitement of war got to her as readily as to any man, beneath the pleasant, unperfumed smell of the soap she used . . .

'Wake up, lover. We've got company.' She gestured to their right.

Nearly a kilometre away to the north-east the primary jungle fronted a shallow escarpment, where broken rock formed mini-cliffs three metres high covered with creeper in exotic blooms such as giant morning glory; beneath it broken ground fell towards their sangar. This broken ground was filled with scrub, some secondary forest, and abandoned fields or plantations, but none of the growth was so high that it concealed more than a metre or so here and there of the ground beneath the escarpment.

Six figures filed along the bottom of the escarpment, fanned out down the slope, clearly preparing to catch the mortar detail in enfilading fire from two sides at once.

Goodall's thumb closed on the safety-catch, and out on his right Stevens and Henchard had their painted faces towards him too, waiting for the order to move forward the four hundred metres or so that would put them within effective range of their SLRs. But Deeta's thin but strong fingers closed on his wrist.

'Wait.'

He could feel the warmth of her breath on his ear.

'Why?' he said.

'Wait till you know Nick can see what happens. Your tracer will show him where they are.'

He wasn't sure about this. Already the six hostiles were sinking into the scrub, finding immature trees to snuggle up to. But at least they were shielding themselves from the wrong enemy: the one they expected to emerge from the forest above them. He didn't like the way she called Parker 'Nick'.

Then the bleep came.

The machine-gun leapt into life. It was set on five-round bursts and he sent six into the areas where he knew or thought he knew the intruders were, then switched to automatic and finished the belt in six seconds, laying down tracer and incendiary over the whole area. Deeta had the next belt in place in five seconds and this time he switched to the bunker, loosing the whole belt off in twelve seconds while the tiny links fountained around them.

Stevens and Henchard knew what to do without being told. They moved forward swiftly, jumping ditches, splashing through the paddies, finding cover where they could until they were close enough to loose off a double tap whenever anything moved beneath the escarpment.

Meanwhile, out of the forest to the left of the escarpment, bursts of M16 on automatic raked the opposite side of the bunker, but, and it was clear to Goodall nearly a kilometre away, there was only one of them. His heart sank, the joy of battle ebbing — almost certainly one of the Flowerpot Men had copped it.

On the other side Geoff was beginning to enjoy himself. Glew and Crick were circling in on his left, almost always well covered from the hostiles back up in the area they had left. Jamie Strachan was covering their rear, and every time they did show themselves and drew fire, Geoff caught the flash, often sideways or oblique to him, and located its source in the Schmidt and Bender. The joy of it was that he was way out of range of the M16s and AK47s. Within five minutes all firing had ceased in the sector: either he'd taken them all out or they'd learnt that exposing their positions was an invitation to sudden death.

And now here they came, Glew and Crick, in from the north-west, sloshing through the paddy with the M202 between them, only two-fifty metres to go and well out of range of the mob up on the slope beneath the bamboo and cane, and a hundred metres behind them Jamie, the muzzle of his SLR snouting at the thickets they'd left. Jesus, thought Geoff, we've got them down safe and sound and I never thought we would.

At that moment a hail of M16 fired at something close to the limit of its range cut Jamie almost in half. Geoff was on to it, letting off four rounds in five seconds, but what was the use? Some bastard had after all tracked them down almost the whole way, never daring to fire because of Jamie's vigilance until the very last moment, the last chance he'd have.

And then something very weird happened.

Jamie's body twitched and seemed to rise from the mud it had fallen in, smoke and sparks fizzed and then whoosh, whoosh and whoosh again the incendiary rockets he was still carrying on his back arced up into the leaden sky, belching smoke behind them, and the force of their thrust pulled his body up too, now lolling like the broken scarecrow it had become. For twenty seconds the firework display continued as the heat of each ignited rocket set off its neighbour, finally leaving a charred, etiolated, smouldering black statue that slowly toppled back into the swamp.

'Well. It is 5 November.'

Geoff collapsed in hysterical laughter. Glew was in there with him at last, but seemed not to appreciate the joke. But to Geoff it was real enough: the ultimate sculptural happening that said it all for the twentieth century, better than bricks on the floor of the Tate Gallery, better than sheep in formaldehyde: man as a self-destructing Roman candle.

35

'We lost Ben in their first attack. Clean through the head.'
Parker, safely in Goodall's sangar with Mick Strachan and
Gurkha Bill and the mortar with all but one box of its
shells, was still breathless. 'But we held them off enough
to allow us to pull back. They left a couple behind us
to make us think they were following carefully, then the
other six got round in front of us. And, bless you, Tim,
you saw them, and I reckon just about wiped them out.
So. How are we doing?'

Deeta resisted pointing out that it was she who had
seen them.

Parker glanced nervously at Mick, who was sitting on
the ground outside the sangar with his big head up, his
normally rubicund face ashen. He had said nothing when
they told him his twin had gone, but now with a slow but
demented firmness he was going through the standard
routine of thoroughly cleaning his SLR. Parker went on:

'I think we did OK. Perhaps we should have foreseen the
possibility of counter-attack from prepared rear positions,
but when it came you all handled it very well. They
suffered a lot, a lot more than we did, and they'll need
some time to regroup. I imagine they'll take the guys
from the more distant bunkers and then again try to pull
a flanker on us. But I think we should be on our way
by then.'

He scanned the enclosure, the nearest point of which
was now six hundred metres away.

'Still a lot of smoke. I think the far side is burning quite well.'

He was suddenly aware of the silence around him, knew that they were all experiencing the terrible drop that comes after the exhilaration of battle, and that they needed beefing up again. But he was as spiritually exhausted as any of them.

'Right. Our principal objective has yet to be achieved but we still have the means intact. Jack must rocket the maize until he's used up all the ammo he has, concentrating on the middle, then he, with Geoff, can fall back on us here. I'll use up all the phosphorus on the near side. And that's really all we can do. If the maize takes, we've won. If it doesn't, well, as I said, we'll have done our best. Anyway we'll pull back to the bridge and the other side of the river, hopefully before they can come at us again.'

He left Stevens and Henchard out on their right flank, then he looked down at Tim Goodall, who was servicing the machine-gun, checking out the moving parts.

'Tim. I know you can manage that thing on your own . . .'

'Of course I can . . .'

'Take as many belts as you can carry, fall back a bit, take that bit of high ground over on the left and see if you can't cover our arses for us as well as you did before.'

The position he was pointing at was overexposed, but what the hell. He had the range – he'd just have to be sure he didn't let anyone get in under it. Goodall looped four belts over his shoulders, and swung the gimpy across and then behind his neck, with one hand dangling over the stock, the other over the barrel. He marched off, looking like a walking crucifix.

Parker then opened up the RT to tell Glew to recommence rocketing the maize.

*   *   *

Glew snapped the RT off and looked at Crick.

'What do you think, then, John?'

Crick, sitting on the rocket boxes, knees spread wide, shrugged heavily, said nothing.

Geoff looked from one to the other.

'What's up?'

'You tell him, John. You understand it better than I do.' Glew turned to Geoff. 'John's a farmer.'

Over to their right the first of the phosphorus shells whistled down to crump in the maize behind the southern-most watch-tower. They could see the sudden, piercingly bright greenish-white flare, and then the flames red-dened as the leaves shrivelled up, and the cobs became torches.

'We reckon they've found a strain of perennial maize and they're developing it.'

'So?'

'If it works it trebles the output of the land its grown on.'

'So?'

'It's food, you crazy bugger.' Suddenly Crick was angry. 'Food for hungry people. Maybe for millions of hungry people. I don't burn food. And take a look. They know what it's worth.'

Geoff turned, then grabbed for binoculars. Two women dressed in combat gear but unarmed had already reached the burning corn and were batting at it, quite effectively, one with what looked like a sleeping bag, the other with a broom; and now they were joined by a man, running across the short space from the bunker they had deserted.

And then, whether or not it was deliberate was hard to tell, Parker dropped a shell within twenty metres of them. Phosphorus stuck to one of the women's jackets and ignited. She backed off, and they could hear the screams as the other tumbled her into the wet soil, rolling and rolling her in it, but phosphorus doesn't give up that easily. Geoff didn't have to be there: the smell came to him from the back of his mind and he swung the L42A1 round through a hundred and eighty degrees, adjusted the tripod and the sight and put a round, a supersonic one so that Parker would know what it was when it cracked past him, within a metre of his commander's ear. Then he reached across, grabbed the headset of his RT, and snapped the system open.

'Parker. Drop another shell anywhere near those people and I'll take your head off . . .' And the pain came again, screaming out of his chest like an express train out of a tunnel and he knew why: mutiny did not come easily to Geoff Erickson, not when the lives of the men he fought alongside might be jeopardized by what he was doing and the whole structure of command and obedience he had been so thoroughly indoctrinated in was being torn apart – by his own hands.

'Geoff, you stupid fucker, what the fuck's going on? And why isn't Glew firing?'

The pain was even more searing now, but somehow distant, as if behind a roaring wind or the boom of distant surf. Geoff fell back, twisted on to his right side and as he did his vision began to narrow as though a lens iris was closing down; he could hear waves crashing on a shore and knew it was the sound of the huge breaths he was trying to drag in, each more of an effort than the last. And then, there on a bright shore circled with darkness was the small boy he'd shot, waving his arm, beckoning, welcoming . . .

Montalbán and Sánchez looked down at his body, then across to the enclosure. Glew and Crick were running towards it, their hands up, no weapons. Montalbán grimaced, stooped, pulled a groundsheet that doubled as a cape that someone had left on the ground over Geoff Erickson's contorted face. He straightened, shrugged, pursed his lips again at the madness that he knew sometimes descends on Anglo-Saxons. Then he and Sánchez gathered up their equipment and set off across the paddy-fields and down the track Juanito had taken, back towards Goodall's sangar.

'What the fuck is going on? What the fuck are Glew and Crick up to?'

Parker's voice was taking on the hysterical tone of a spoilt and tired boy who has been denied a second slice of birthday cake.

Mick Strachan, satisfied that his SLR was factory-fresh again, came and stood at his elbow.

'Got tickets for the Firemen's Ball?'

Parker glared at him.

'If those rockets don't go in we don't stand a chance. And fuck it, here comes the rain again.'

'Leave it to me, Mr Parker. The more of those bastards get torched like our Jamie was, the better.'

And pulling his jungle hat more tightly on his head, and with his SLR held across his chest, he loped off through the sudden rain, splashing through the mud, crossing with the two Spaniards on the way.

Deeta raised the binoculars she'd been using.

'I can see his gun. But I can't see Erickson. I'll watch while you go on firing: you need to get as much in as you can before the rain ruins everything.'

She glanced round the horizon of tossing trees, and then towards the east, where the sky above the billowing smoke was blackest and riven with distant lightning, and slowly she began to bite her lower lip. Decision time.

'I do?'

Parker reached round for the box of shells, then forward again to the mortar, adjusting the range and direction by a degree or two. In spite of their mutiny he could not quite bring himself to drop one where Glew and Crick had now joined the two Sandinistas still able to fight the blaze.

He dropped the shell down the pipe, pushed his hands into his ears and felt a sudden wave of relief as the earth shuddered beneath his feet. It was the tone of Deeta's voice that did it: he knew he was no longer in command, that the responsibility had shifted to her.

Presently Montalbán was beside him, helping, making a two-man crew of it, and at almost the same moment a salvo of rockets shredded the air and rain like razors, screaming into the more distant parts of the plantation. Mick Strachan was on the job.

Winston sat under the broad, flat, succulent leaves of a plant that looked like a cross between a huge pineapple and a yucca, knees drawn up to his chin, waterproof cape round his shoulders, M16 by his side. He was about fifty metres from the bridgehead and hidden from the track and Bennett and Wintle too on the other side, but where he was he was comparatively dry and tolerably comfortable. And in spite of the ebb and flow of battle some two kilometres away, the crump of mortar, the rattle of small arms, he daydreamed and dozed and daydreamed, playing a game he liked to play when he was bored or couldn't get to sleep: remembering in the right order every girl or woman he had ever laid, with as much detail as he could recall.

The first was easy. You never forget the first. Both of them twelve, he lean and bony, she with puppy-fat and little breasts too big to be just fat with squidgy, dark-chocolate nipples, and, he soon discovered, a little toothbrush of wiry, black hair on the lips of her plum-coloured cunt. They had been in a changing cubicle in the Splash-Down, one of those places where kids go to slide down tubes of varying lengths and steepness to splash into small pools. It was her birthday party and she'd wanted it to be memorable because her dad, who had a second-hand guitar shop in Stockwell Road, had said it was the last he was paying for. The changing rooms were unisex but there were lots of cubicles all with bolts. Of course they hadn't done anything serious – just a very close look at each other, a tentative feel . . .

The first real one had been a redhead called Moira, an Irish girl of fourteen, who wanted to know if it was true what they said about black dicks . . .

Then the third, the first time with an older woman, almost twice his age. He'd knocked on her flat door: 'Clean your windows, ma'am, wash your floors?' And she'd shown him what it's really all about, how it works, and on the third attempt she went off like a bomb and he was hooked.

After that the order got a bit vague in his mind. The women gossiped, and the girls overheard them, and the news got round the neighbourhood from Lambeth to Stockwell, Battersea to Walworth, wherever young wives gathered – outside school waiting for the bus home, down the jobcentre – that there was a stud living at the back of Kennington Park Road somewhere who always rang your chimes, was clean, and respected your right not to get in the club. In all, it added up to a better deal than most got from their boyfriends or regular partners.

Winston just loved women, really loved them, all women so long as they had a bit of fun in them, and what really made him happy was giving them all a really great time . . .

He wasn't too sure about that Deeta though. Sexy yes,

and game for it, so all the lads said, but he suspected that deep, deep inside there was a space where fun should be.

All of which was why, when a woman dressed for battle and carrying an AK47 took up position between him and the track, covering the bridge, and then signalled to another on the other side who in turn signalled to a third he could not see, he was completely unable to do anything about it at all.

He knew he was in the shit now. Well in it. They'd certainly not pay him his second whack and if enough of them survived then what they'd do to him would make the punishment the Strachans had had look like playground teasing.

Still, Winston had faith in human nature. He got up as silently as he could – only his knee cracked, and she didn't hear it – and using all his jungle craft he slipped away into the sugar cane, knowing that he was in a warm climate and if he presented no threat he'd be looked after. He left the M16 behind, and as he emerged from the cane into an orchard he pulled a cherimoya from its bough, peeled back the faceted skin and bit into the soft, creamy flesh, let the sweet, vanilla-ish juice run down his chin, and felt a lightening of his heart. Custard-apples in Brixton Market were expensive, and disappointing. But straight from the tree . . .

Glew watched the fourth batch of rockets streak only metres above his head. Then he set off back to the bunker, crossed it, swung himself over the wall and marched across the cane stubble towards what had been Geoff's sangar under the trees and saplings. And he refused to duck when the next lot went over, telling himself not even Mick Strachan would take his head off that way. He damn near did though. Glew unholstered his Browning from his hip, and held it, double-handed but pointing down, until he was ten metres from the edge of the copse.

'Mick. Leave it.'

But Strachan lunged sideways for his newly cleaned SLR and Glew took him out with a double tap to the head and throat.

'You'll have to call in Bennett and the others. Take out those fucking renegades, and get that rocket thing working again.'

Parker looked up at her, put down the shell he was about to drop into the tube, reached for the headset, and opened up Bennett's wavelength.

'Gordon, we need you here now.'

'Sorry, Mr Parker. We're pinned down. Me and Wintle. At least three AKs on the other end of the bridge, well positioned. We don't stand a chance.'

'Smithy?'

'They must have bushwhacked him.'

Parker switched off, removed the headset, and repeated what Gordon had said.

Crouched down over the small rucksack she always carried, rain streaming out of her hair, Deeta pulled out a black box with fingerpad keyboard, similar to the GPS receiver she'd used before but smaller. She extended an aerial to about twenty centimetres, and dabbed buttons.

'What's that?'

'Come on!'

'Radio beacon? Simple yes-no signaller?'

'You got it.'

'Christ, we'd better move.'

Goodall knew he was on a hiding to nothing: no real cover, and poor visibility as the rain intensified and the wind sent leaves and other light debris swirling across the plain below him. Although it was still not eleven o'clock the darkness was like dusk. And here they came again, scouting now, not out of the jungle to the right, but further back, coming through the plantations. No way could the men out on Parker's right flank have seen them – they were almost behind them. He swung the gimpy round, scrabbled in the mud and debris from some crop that had been cut to get a decent support for the biped, but it was no good.

'Fucking Sylvester Stallone, then, I'll have to be.'

He stood, swayed beneath the weight of it all, set the gun for five-round bursts and fired one off from the hip. He followed the streak of tracer, at least a hundred metres short, then tried again, but this was no way to fire the fucker. Still, he'd given them a fright: they were falling back and Stevens, Henchard and Gurkha Bill had spotted them.

But the tracer had given away his position and he died cut to ribbons by a burst from an RPK four hundred metres to his left.

They came, it seemed, out of the eye of the storm. Three evil darts, markings taped or painted out, three Mirages straight up the north bank of the San Juan, out of the Caribbean. The enclosure blossomed beneath them into chains of billowing flame, red and orange, that reached thirty metres in seconds and belched out palls of black smoke that not even the rain and wind could flatten. Parker guessed they were from the Colombian carrier they had seen at Limón. As the heat rolled over them he looked up at Deeta.

She was exultant.

'I love the smell of napalm,' she cried. 'It's the smell of victory.'

Epilogue

The Sandinistas held a democratic debate which lasted fifteen hours. As anarchists, they could reach no decision until they had all agreed to it. Esther and Daniel wanted death. Most of the rest were more forgiving, especially when they knew that the one who had shot Juanito was himself dead. Eventually Esther gave way and Daniel followed soon after. They handed their prisoners over to officers of the elected Chamorro government who released or rather sold them to Associated Foods International. AFI repatriated them.

The Costa Rican Rural Guard confiscated all the unused weaponry and Dobson claimed, through intermediaries, the full two-fifty grand Finchley-Camden had placed in escrow, making over a hundred grand profit on the way.

Even though he saved a small amount on the second payments to the men, Finchley-Camden still had to sell Wrykin Heath to pay off his Lloyd's debt. He now lives over the shop in Baker Street with shiny-shoes Duncan. His wife has divorced him.

Was the mission successful? Difficult to say: but if the media doesn't report an amazing Third World breakthrough in maize production in the next year or so, then almost certainly the Colombian napalm achieved what the soldiers of fortune could not.

Mary Goodall got her jewellery and Jack Goodall his Beetle.

And Winston? He joined the Sandinistas and is shacked up with Pili. She's had one baby, is expecting the next, and is looking forward to the one after.

OTHER TITLES IN SERIES FROM 22 BOOKS

Available now at newsagents and booksellers
or use the order form opposite

All at £4.99 net

22 Books offers an exciting list of titles in these series. All the books are available from:

Little, Brown and Company (UK) Limited,
PO Box 11,
Falmouth,
Cornwall TR10 9EN.

Alternatively you may fax your order to the above address. Fax number: 0326 376423.

Payments can be made by cheque or postal order (payable to Little, Brown and Company) or by credit card (Visa/Access). Do not send cash or currency. UK customers and BFPO please allow £1.00 for postage and packing for the first book, plus 50p for the second book, plus 30p for each additional book up to a maximum charge of £3.00 (seven books or more). Overseas customers, including customers in Ireland, please allow £2.00 for the first book, plus £1.00 for the second book, plus 50p for each additional book.

NAME (BLOCK LETTERS PLEASE) ....

....

ADDRESS ....

....

....

☐ I enclose my remittance for £_____

☐ I wish to pay by Access/Visa

Card number

☐☐☐☐ ☐☐☐☐ ☐☐☐☐ ☐☐☐☐

Card expiry date

☐☐ ☐☐